LITTLE
WHITE
LIES

LITTLE WHITE LIES

A Novel

ELIZABETH COOKE

WRITING AS ELIZABETH McGREGOR

Copyright © 1996 by Elizabeth McGregor

Cover design by Kat JK Lee

ISBN: 978-1-5040-1945-3

Distributed in 2015 by Open Road Distribution
345 Hudson Street
New York, NY 10014
www.openroadmedia.com

LITTLE
WHITE
LIES

ONE

*H*E STOPPED ON THE THRESHOLD to touch something she could not see.

'What is it?' Beth called.

She was at the top of the stairs, looking down into the flagstone hall, a dark space pierced by an eight o'clock sun. It was the last week of May, and already warm.

David wasn't responding; he was simply looking at something in his hand, immobile. She wondered if her husband had heard her at all. She started down, raking her fingers through hair still wet from her shower.

'What is it?' she asked again. It crossed her mind that his concentration was fixed on some inner, alternative thought, and not her at all. It didn't surprise her, just fixed that dull ache of exclusion tighter.

He had a piece of paper in his hand. As she walked forward, she saw him screw it up and put it in his pocket.

'Is it a letter?' she asked.

'No,' he said. He held out his other hand.

In his palm lay a dead bird. Beth's reflex reaction was to step back from the glossy black body at once.

'Where was it?' she asked.

'Just here, in the porch.'

She edged past him and looked into the road outside. From the door of the Mill House, the lane curved slightly downwards towards the grey slate roofs of the houses at the village edge. The river lay like a white band through the sluice-gated field, and the world was an impossibly acid green down there: field, grass edge to the road, tree on the bend.

'Its neck is broken,' David said. He moved his fingers fractionally and the head dropped. Then he walked into the garden, carrying the small limp body to the shadow of the hedge.

Beth stood shuddering at the thought that he had picked it up and held it. Revulsion. 'You'll be late,' she said. It was eight fifteen; he was usually away before eight. Coming back, he had picked up his brief-case, and was passing it from one hand to the other.

'What are you waiting for?' she asked him. She glanced back into the house; if he were late, he would make her late too. She had an urge to close the door on him.

'Will you be all right?' he asked.

Already half-turned away, she stopped and stared back at him, surprised at the question. 'Why shouldn't I be?' She was at the kitchen door now, and threw away the last remark. 'Drive carefully.'

He didn't reply. In another second or two, she heard his footsteps along the little driveway, then out on the road where his car was parked.

A minute later, from the kitchen window with its view over the village, she saw his car moving very slowly over the bridge, between the field and the wood.

She ate breakfast with the plan of Oak Rise propped against the marmalade jar. Then, over coffee, the dishes cleared away to the sink, she laid it flat on the table, standing over it.

On tracing paper, she was to re-draw part of the landscape plan, and she wondered how much the builder's discovery would mean further revision. Alan Pritchard had phoned her on Saturday, telling her that, working alone with the excavator that morning, stripping the topsoil, he had found a grave.

The landscaping, like the building, was postponed.

'I'll tell you,' he had said over the phone, 'whatever it is, you can be sure that I'll get it.'

She had heard his wife, Helen, laughing and saying, 'Nonsense!' in the background.

'I'm *telling* you,' he had retorted. 'Dewpond, underground stream. What was it back along, at that garage?' Alan's accent became more pronounced when he was irritated. 'Old infill. Methane! Now this. Bloody grave, if you like!'

'Is it very old?' Beth had asked. Roman sites were sometimes uncovered around Stourminster; when the nearest light industrial unit had been built five years ago, they had found a cemetery too. 'Is it Roman?'

Alan had sighed deeply. 'It's old all right; you tell me. Course, I had to get on to the Police, Home Office. There's no flesh, just bones.'

He had told her she shouldn't bother to call in that morning, but she had insisted. 'Just to get an idea of rescheduling,' she'd said. But it was really her curiosity getting the upper hand.

An hour later she was loading her van, when she saw another car coming down the lane. Pulling the sacks of peat into the back, she was distracted by its slow progress—a white roof drifting soundlessly above the top of the hedge. It stopped before it got to the gate.

Beth stood up and watched, wiping her hands down the sides of her jeans.

I hope you're not coming here, she thought. I haven't got the time. She slammed the door of the van and went to check the house.

'Ossy?' she called. Long ago, they had christened their cat Chaos, after the mess it caused wherever it went. It was old now, though, and very overweight; a tabby with green eyes, habitually lying in the hedge or the shade of a tree. Sometimes, arriving at a job, she would find him curled on one of the sacks in the back of the van, regarding her with superior calm as she opened the doors.

There was no sign of him now in the house. She wondered vaguely if he had killed the bird and brought it to the step, as he might have done years ago. She edged the food and water dishes into the porch with her foot, glanced in the house to see that the boiler light was off, and pulled the door hard.

'Is it Mrs March?'

She turned. A policeman stood on the path.

'Sorry?'

'Mrs March? Is it Mrs . . .' He glanced at a piece of paper in his hand. 'Mrs Elizabeth March?'

'Yes.'

He stepped towards her. 'Can we have a word? Maybe inside?'

'Is it about the tree?'

'Pardon?'

'The tree.' There was a petition in the village to save the Queens Oak: a spindly, disease-ridden, dying specimen on the corner of the green. Someone last week had said they would chain themselves to the damned thing if she carried on and cut it down, as the Parish Council wanted.

'It's not, no.' The man was looking at her front door, and inclined his head gently towards it.

'Oh, all right,' she said. She got her keys out of her pocket, opened it, then turned round. 'What is it, then?'

He tried to step into the house with her.

Beth stopped dead, something catching in her throat, as if the air could neither get in nor out. He put one hand under her elbow, and she snatched it away. 'What *is* it?' she asked.

The world suddenly hitched to a dead stop—a frozen picture in which only the blackbirds, fighting in the hedge, could move, their wings beating against the green branches.

'I wonder if you can tell me,' he asked, 'if your husband still owns a car with this registration number?' And he held out the piece of paper.

She stared at it. She could never remember the van's registration, never mind David's. 'I don't know if that's the number,' she said. 'I know it's new. Last year. It's silver coloured.'

'And your husband's name . . . ?'

'David Alexander March.'

The wings were battling inside her head. The edges of the stairs, the corners of the flagstones, looked incredibly clear, as if a pen had been run over them to outline them.

'Was your husband driving his car this morning?'

'Yes, of course . . .'

He glanced towards the sitting room, with its straight-backed fire-side chairs and baker's-oven hearth. 'A car of this registration, of which your husband was the registered owner . . .' He cleared his throat. 'This morning, on the Yeovil road, at Stag's Fall . . .'

'When?' she said.

'At about half past eight.' She had been looking at the maps then. Looking at the maps. Finishing her breakfast. 'There was a head-on collision between this car and a lorry,' the policeman went on. 'I'm very sorry, Mrs March. The driver of the car was killed. He was identi-fied, about half an hour ago, at the site, by your doctor.'

'Today?' she asked. Ludicrous, ludicrous question.

She walked away.

She went out of the back door, wrenching the latch down. She walked down the slope of the lawn, down the three steps, on to the lit-tle piece of land that, last year, she'd rescued from a waist-high swamp of reeds and grass. It was a strip of turf now, garden-centre clean and neat, too neat perhaps, right at the water's edge—a stream that joined the river further down, straight and soundless, even when full, run-ning in a deep chalk bed.

She thought she might jump over. Just jump over the stream. It was only six feet wide here. She would go for a walk. Now. It was only a little stream . . .

'Mrs March?'

She was suddenly aware of the young lad—he couldn't be more than twenty-two, twenty-three—standing above her on the lawn.

She stared at him. 'What a godawful job for you,' she said.

He came down the steps. 'Is there anyone—a neighbour, a rela-tion . . .'

'David has a cousin, I think. Abroad.'

'A neighbour, then? A friend?'

Oliver and Julia.

She wished, strongly and suddenly, that Oliver Woods could come to see her. Not Julia—not her fussing, fragile and tense self-pity. Not today. Today she would rather it was Oliver. Cold as he was, he was calm.

Men like Oliver—the old school, the locked expression, the formality, the striped tie, the clenched hands locked behind the back—were made for such emergencies. The last to crack, she thought.

But he would be at work.

Julia would be at home.

'Mrs Woods at the Lodge. The next house down. It's . . .' She indicated the stone gates, a hundred yards down the lane.

'Will you come inside?' he said.

'No.'

'Just inside . . .'

'No.' Louder.

He raised both hands, a warding-off, calming-down gesture. 'You'll wait here?'

She sat down on the turf and looked at the water. It was a lovely morning: bright, warm, dry. Clear. Very clear, all around.

It was three miles from here to the main road—*the Yeovil road, the Yeovil road*—and the view showed every contour. She could pick out individual trees and their colours. *At the main road. Of this registration. Collision.* Inside the house, she heard the telephone in the hall begin to ring.

She slipped both hands under her thighs, flat on the ground, to stop them moving.

'I won't be long,' said the man at her back.

'All right,' she said.

She sat very still, listening to the sound of her own breath in her throat.

TWO

$\mathcal{T}$HE SWALLOWS WERE BACK.

They came every year to the stone-built shed at the back of the garden, under the two lilac trees that had grown tall. It was very hard to see the nest; it was high up and sheltered in the shadows.

Swallows in April. Swifts in May.

On a morning like this, you could stand on the grass and watch the birds incessantly threading the sky. Infinite patience.

Once, on holiday in Greece, they had gone to a hotel where the birds had built nests into the eaves. They spent all day tending their young in the dark hollows of straw and grey mud; beyond the circular hole, the fledglings complained of their imminent starvation, ever more demanding. The parents struggled to supply them, back and forth, back and forth. Shuttles on a loom.

Under the lilac, even the early morning air was heavy now. Dark purple blooms weighed down the leaves. It was difficult squeezing between the tree and the wall; more difficult still to see the nest.

In the bedroom that looked over the garden, the window was open but the curtains were closed.

She wouldn't wake now for hours.

THREE

$\mathscr{T}$HE MAPS WERE SPREAD on the bonnet of the car at Oak Rise, but neither of them were looking at them any more.

'How many?' Alan asked.

The representative from the County Archaelogical Department smiled at him. 'Many?' Alison Warley was very big: broad-hipped, round-faced, bookish; a Sitwell face, aristocratic and heavily boned; an Indian scarf tucked in the neck of her Guernsey sweater, dangling earrings. Their very movement, swaying back and forth against her neck, irritated Alan Pritchard intensely.

'Y'know. *Many*. Are there *many* of these buggers, or just the one?'

She laughed. 'I've no idea yet.'

Alan hitched his not inconsiderable bulk against the bonnet and crossed his arms. He was a short, broad, red-faced man; he looked like a well-wrung, fifty-year-old bear with a hand-knitted sweater stretched across his stomach. 'I'll tell you what I should have done,' he said. 'I should have come back myself on Sunday and shovelled the whole lot up, the whole site. That's what I should've done.'

'Well, thank heavens you didn't,' the woman remarked calmly. 'The loss of a site like this—'

'You listen to me,' he said.

Alison stepped back a little from him. He leant over the bonnet, pointing a finger. 'I'll tell you about loss. Money loss. I own this site, and I'm committed to working on it. You understand what I'm saying?' He knew people who'd found stuff like this and carried on, poured concrete over it. 'There wasn't anything here. No barrows, nothing. Council put a sewer through here twenty years ago, and *nothing*.'

'Yes, it does happen . . .' They looked back at the plot of land, eighty yards by sixty, on the crest of the Dorset downland hill. A warm early-summer wind blew across them.

Alan waved his hand over the maps. 'How long, then, for all this?'

She smiled. 'Very hard to say.'

He fisted both hands. 'Well, you *must* say.'

'I can't. Not just now.'

He turned on his heel and walked away from her. His shoulders had that ache, like blood pinched in a muscle, a cramp begging him to hit someone. 'For a nice man, you've got a bloody awful temper,' his wife Helen was fond of telling him.

He walked across the rise, looking to left and right. The police were supposed to be here, weren't they? He shouldn't have rung them; it was obvious now. *Christ.*

Ahead of him the enormous field stretched in a voluptuous roll. The valley was two miles wide at this point, dissected by three straight and narrow farm roads. It was a stunning place. The kind of place—exposed to the wind, high up, quiet, a chalky green downland—that he would have liked himself.

It ought to have been a good, profitable job, this forgotten tangle of blackberry and elder.

The bank would . . .

He suppressed a groan. Apeshit. That's how the bank would be. Softly, deadly apeshit. An excavation would take . . . *hard to say* . . .

He started to walk back to the car. Alison Warley had gone to the grave and was standing six feet from it, her index finger pressed to her lips. He looked down with her, closing one eye so that the nearest annoying earring, making its faint tinkling noise, would be out of his sight.

She looked over her shoulder at him. 'You'd better ring these people.' She gave him a printed card, the name of a company that specialised in archaelogical excavation. 'They do a lot of work for builders,' she said, 'when they're allowed to. When it hasn't all been covered up again.'

He took the card, grimacing. Below them, the bone of the arm in the grave showed as a neat, nut-brown line. At that moment, at the edge of the site, by the hedge and its swathe of bramble bushes, a police car turned in.

'Better late than never,' Alan said.

The car stopped, and he saw then that it was a Traffic Unit. A large man got out, pulling on his uniform cap.

'You've took your bloody time,' Alan said as George Mayall came close.

'Morning, Alan. Miss Warley.'

'Hello,' she murmured.

'Got a pile up.'

'You're one man and his dog, you lot,' Alan said sarcastically, keeping back a smile. 'One accident and you're stuck.'

George looked at Alan directly. 'You're needed.'

'Eh?'

'Mrs March.'

'Beth?' A cold hand momentarily pulled a thread in Alan's chest, a spike of hard wire over his heart. 'Never her, is it? In the van?' He'd known Beth March for six years. When she first came, with her cards and brochures, he'd silently given her six months. He couldn't have imagined one woman doing such a heavy job. But that was before he'd seen her behind the wheel of a JCB, or on her knees laying pavers, or wrestling with a delivery in the rain, her dark clothes soaked.

'No,' the policeman said. 'It's not Beth. It's her husband, David.'

'Oh . . . bloody hell,' Alan said, his face blanching. 'Bloody hell.'

'Yes. Bad thing.'

There was a momentary silence. The maps, held down by a single stone on the car's bonnet, ruffled in the wind, flipping a curl of paper backwards and forwards.

'They radioed there was no one about. She asked for you.'

Alan took his car keys from his pocket.

FOUR

$\mathcal{R}$OSIE,' SAID JULIA WOODS. 'Rosie.'

She was at the door of her daughter's room; her child lay in bed, even though it was late. Julia walked to the window and drew back the curtains.

Rosie stirred complainingly. She was six, but very small for her age, and dwarfed in the large double bed. She rolled from side to side.

'Rosie,' said Julia. 'Time to get up.'

'Why?' Rosie mumbled.

'We have to take you to the doctor.'

Rosie groaned, her eyes still shut. 'Oh, *why* . . . ?'

Smiling, Julia came to sit on the side of the bed. She smoothed her hand across Rosie's forehead and, at last, the little girl opened her eyes.

'Am I still hot?' she asked.

'No, darling. You're cool. Very cool. Do you still feel sick?'

'No.' Rosie searched her mother's face for a sign of approval. Rosie was fair, as fair as her mother, with very blonde, almost white-blonde hair, and thick fair lashes. She had pale skin and small neat features.

'How are you feeling?' Julia asked.

'Tired.' Rosie attempted a stretch. 'Isn't it school?' she asked suddenly, sitting up, her eyes rounded. She was a conscientious child, with a horror of being late, or wrong, or singled out in any way from the others in her class.

'We've got an appointment,' Julia said. 'Hurry now.'

Rosie swung her legs out of bed. 'I'm so tired.'

At the door of the bedroom, Julia stopped and looked back. 'That's what we must talk to the doctor about,' she murmured.

FIVE

OLIVER WOODS STOOD at the entrance to the cul-de-sac, his hand still on the door of the car. He always had the same feeling approaching Lilian Davis and her brother: a sensation of smothering. The front window of the huge decaying bungalow looked directly over at the lay-by where he now stood. He saw the curtains twitch. Lilian had already seen him.

She opened the door before he knocked.

'Oliver, dear,' she beamed, showing a set of yellowing teeth. 'Come in, come in.' Taking his elbow, she breathed gin on him, at nine in the morning. He noticed that she had put eyeshadow on, seemingly with a knife. The green muck was weighing down her eyelids.

'Well, you'll see it all now,' she told him, nodding towards the living room. 'You'll see what I have to contend with.'

She gave him a push. Oliver frowned, irritated, but walked forward, squeezing his tall, angular frame into the room. Arthur Davis was on a fireside chair, facing the far wall. He was rocking gently backwards and forwards, so that the chair made hitching movements on the rug.

'Look,' Lilian said.

She was alongside Oliver, pulling down the neck of her cardigan to show a wrinkled neck. 'Look what he did to me this time.'

There was a bruise, certainly. And the livid twin rakes of finger-nails in the flesh. Oliver registered the slant of them, down from the woman's right ear.

'He did that?' he asked.

She smiled, stretched up, and whispered in Oliver's ear. 'He's a dan-ger,' she said.

She nodded, as if this sealed the confidence between them. Lilian had once been an India wife, a Colonel's daughter; she had brought her trophies with her to her brother's home—the elephant's foot, the Javanese table, the tea at four, the gin-and-waters. Time had eradi-cated her charm and left her greedy snobbery. She had the breeding, she had often told Oliver, through those rotted teeth, while her brother had the money. 'Ridiculous,' she had said, on their very first meeting. 'Do you know what he would spend it on? Horses, dogs. . . .' She craved Arthur's fortune as assiduously as he kept it from her.

'You see, don't you?' she demanded, now. 'A woman shouldn't be forced to live with a man like that, should she?'

Oliver said nothing. Lilian's will was burning a hole in his hand, transmitting itself through the leather of the case. He wanted only to put it down somewhere and leave.

'I'll make a cup of tea,' Lilian said. She glanced at her brother. 'You see . . . you see . . .'

When she was gone, Oliver glanced around. He caught sight of himself in the mirror over the fireplace. Approaching sixty, he looked older. The thinnest fringe of wispy white hair hung at the base of his skull; liver-spotted skin marred his face, emphasising the weary look in his eyes. The expression he wore was bitter. Cold.

He moved to the side of the chair.

'Good morning, Arthur,' he said.

Lilian Davis's brother did not look up. He was watching his own hands pleating the hem of his sweater, winding it around his thumb and forefinger, letting it drop, taking it up again.

'Arthur,' Oliver said. 'Are you feeling well?'

There was no reply for long seconds. Then, the faintest nod of the head. In Arthur's lap, one hand made a trembling thumbs-up gesture.

Oliver went out to the kitchen, the will now in his hands. He put it down on the first available surface, grimacing behind Lilian's back at the state of the greasy cupboards and sink.

'He seems perfectly quiet to me,' he said.

Lilian put her hands on her hips. 'You think I do this to myself?' she demanded, tilting her head to one side to display the scratch. He did not reply. Seeing his expressionless face, she smiled. 'You understand,' she said, reassuring herself of the fact if he would not. 'We're in this together, aren't we?'

'You can always reply on my help,' he told her.

Before his illness, Arthur had run a local hardware company, a chain of profitable little shops. He sold out to a chainstore, but had never enjoyed the profits. Parkinson's had taken hold, and, as soon as the illness showed—as soon as it was possible that he might die from it, and she would be the closest living relative—Lilian was on her brother's back like a leech. But Arthur was unlikely to die as quickly as she had thought. Three years later, she was still wishing him dead, or—quicker still—committed.

'I ought to have some thanks,' she continued. Oliver recognised the familiar whine. The voice of the martyr, the wringing of the hands. 'What I suffer,' she said. 'No one knows. If he was in his right mind, if this was something else, arthritis, whatever, he would want me to sort out his money, you know. He would *want* it.'

Oliver had been over this ground before. Parkinson's was not dementia.

'What does Dr Archer say?'

Lilian waved her hand. 'Him! He's a bloody fool.'

Oliver considered her obliquely. Not such a fool if he's seen through you, he thought.

'None of you see the way he raves,' Lilian was saying, in a lecturing tone directed at the ceiling.

It was true. Oliver had never seen Arthur rave at all. In fact, the old man could still hold a conversation. Had done so on Oliver's last visit. They had talked about the cricket and the chances of the County that season. He remembered Arthur's frightened, choked monotone. One eye on the door for the sound of Lilian coming down the hallway. The trembling hands.

'Can you smell it?' Lilian said.

'I'm sorry?'

'The *smell*.' She made a disgusted face. 'The *incontinence*.'

Oliver turned. He pointed at the will. 'You read it over,' he murmured.

The will was nothing more than an excuse to get him round here, to sway his vote. Lilian had nothing of her own to leave. It was Arthur's will that was the point of issue between them. That and a Power Of Attorney.

Oliver looked along the hallway, and, quite suddenly, David March sprang into his mind.

The thought struck him like a blow. Realisation swept through him, a shadow racing across the sun. The same thought—that sickening, drowning feeling—that had cost him his sleep over the last fortnight.

They would never get out of it, he thought. *It was too late.* Panic danced for a second, turning his palms slick, drying his throat.

They were as damned as the man fifteen feet away from him now, locked in the living room chair. Locked into the same claustrophobic decline. Oliver suddenly, desperately, needed oxygen.

'I'll see myself out,' he said.

'But your tea . . .' Lilian protested.

'I must go.'

The air outside was blissfully fresh.

Lilian stood on the doorstep as he negotiated the path with its border of dying petunias. 'You will help me?' she called. 'Oliver? You will come back? Come on Friday. Oliver . . .'

Oliver did not reply. His mind was elsewhere.

There might be hope, he was thinking, as he put the key into the car's ignition. *After all, no one knows yet.*

SIX

_A_LAN GOT TO BETH'S HOUSE AT TEN O'CLOCK.

There was a young constable on the doorstep. George Mayall stopped to talk to him. Alan could see Beth standing on the top lawn, looking across the field beyond. She had her back to him and looked very small and square—defiant, almost, by the set of her shoulders.

He walked down to her. 'Beth?'

She glanced at him. He had expected to see a difference in her face: sadness, grief, tears. But there was nothing at all. She wore the usual slightly preoccupied look that she had when weighing up a garden, calculating in her head. Beth was nothing if not capable, but he was surprised to see any strength now.

'Alan,' she said. 'I'm sorry about this. I know you're busy.'

'Christ! That doesn't matter.'

'Is it archaelogical, then?'

'What?'

'The body. Is it recent, or what?'

'Beth . . . Look, why don't you come in?'

She smiled a little. 'They all want me to come inside,' she remarked. 'Even you. Why is that?'

19

He couldn't reply. He didn't know why.

She resumed looking at the field. 'I don't think it's him,' she said.

'Who?'

'David. I don't think it's David.'

He glanced over his shoulder, to the two men still standing by the gate. 'They wouldn't make a mistake,' he said. 'They check before they come out to anyone. George said Doctor Ellis certified . . . He was along five minutes later; he saw it was David's car.'

'But it wasn't David in it.'

He took her arm. At first she resisted a little—after all, he hadn't touched her before. Then, she suddenly followed. He walked to the bench at the back of the house, in the shade. 'Sit down,' he said.

She did so. 'It isn't him.'

'All right. Tell me why.'

She turned in the seat so that she was facing him. 'There was a suitcase in the car,' she said. 'And a passport in it.'

'David's passport?'

'Yes.'

'Where was he going?'

'You don't see, do you?' she said.

'See what? Was he going abroad?'

She laughed softly. When she spoke, it was with the same amused, careful voice. '*Someone* with David's passport. But not him.'

'Beth—'

'It couldn't be him, could it?' she said. 'He wouldn't have packed a case, got his passport, gone anywhere without telling me, would he?' She followed the line of the seam in her jeans with her index finger, biting her lip. 'I know things haven't been so good, but he wouldn't lie. He wouldn't just go. Not like that.'

'So you think—'

'That someone's stolen his passport.'

Alan tried not to gasp, or laugh. She was evidently totally serious. 'And the car?'

Beth sat back, crossing her legs at the ankle and looking down at them. 'I know it's far-fetched,' she said evenly, 'but it's the only explanation. I've got to go to the hospital and identify him. But it won't *be* him. I know that already.'

He pressed her hand. Getting up, he went back to the gate. George Mayall was about to get back in the car.

'George—'

'I know what you're going to tell me,' the other man replied. 'But it's certainly David. I saw him on to the ambulance myself.'

They all looked back into the garden. Beth had bent down from the bench and was, absent-mindedly it seemed, pulling little weeds from the border.

'The driver of the lorry said the car just veered straight into the centre and across in front of him. David was doing about eighty.'

'On Stag's Fall?'

'Yes.'

Alan turned to the constable. 'The passport—the case. She doesn't believe it's him. And doing eighty . . . that's not like David, either. He's a careful driver.'

George Mayall gripped Alan's arm. 'They get this way. They don't accept it, even sometimes when they've seen the body.' And he gave Alan's arm a pat, by way of reassurance. 'I've called Beth's doctor,' he added. 'It's shock, you see? Just the shock.'

'Where was David going?' Alan asked. 'Do we know?'

The constable bent down; Alan was shorter than him by five or six inches. 'More important, who was he going with?' he said.

Alan stared at him. He knew David only sketchily, but he would never have categorised him as a ladies man. Alan always saw him in his mind's eye with that habit of his, taking off his glasses and rubbing the bridge of his nose, measuring his words before he spoke. The first time he had met him he remembered being intrigued at the couple— such a live-wire woman married to such a quiet man.

'No one,' he said. 'No one.'

The constable straightened up, shrugging his shoulders. 'Suitcase, though?' he said. 'And passport?'

Beth was walking towards them.

Alan gazed at her, feeling overwhelmingly sorry, words choked in his throat. It was like looking at his own daughter. They were similar in height and build: five foot five, compact-looking, both with a cap of closely cropped, shining brown hair. He imagined breaking news like this to Sally, imagined her walking up the path of her own house with that slightly questioning expression. Beth was coming now with the same steady, sturdy gait as usual, arms swinging.

'God,' he murmured. 'Oh, God.'

SEVEN

$\mathcal{H}$ELEN PRITCHARD WAS JUST GOING OUT when the phone rang.

'Damn,' she muttered, considering it from the doorway. She snatched up the receiver. 'Hello?'

'Helen. It's Alan.'

'I'm just going out.'

'I know. Listen—'

'I thought you were Marjorie again about those ruddy church flowers.'

'Do I sound like Marjorie? Listen. Beth March . . .'

Helen glanced up at the clock. She had to be at the office by eleven, and was mentally making a shopping list in her mind. *Potatoes, parsley, eggs.* 'Who March?'

'Beth. The landscape gardener.'

'Of course.' She shook her head, smiling at her own forgetfulness. 'What about her?'

'Oliver Woods lives next to them. We can't get hold of his wife. You always say she's in and out of the office.'

'Yes, she is.'

'Do you know where she goes on Mondays?'

23

'No. Why?'

Down the line, Alan sighed. He lowered his voice. 'Look, I'm at Beth's house. David was killed in a road accident today. We want to get hold of Julia. When you get in the office, can you ask Oliver if he knows where she is?'

Helen momentarily closed her eyes. 'Yes.' She offered no other questions.

'Will you ring me back?' He gave Beth's number, which was already scrawled on the memo board above the phone. Helen didn't interrupt him; merely repeated the numbers for his benefit.

'I'm going now,' she said. 'Leave it to me.'

She put down the phone.

It was only a five-minute walk to Oliver's office from Helen's house. Turning on to the main road into the small County town, Helen had no compulsion to run. There was no emergency she could conceive of that would have forced her to break into a sprint. Nevertheless, her speed was brisk. She walked like a Sergeant Major—straight-backed, quickly, rigidly, her coat drawn around her with one hand, the other holding her straw shopping basket.

She looked unremarkable. A middle-aged, matronly woman, with an archetypal bluish perm, little make-up and flat shoes, she could have been a headmistress, a vicar's wife, a librarian of the old school. Except that, under her breath, as she walked, she was murmuring, in careful time to each step, *shit, shit, double shit* on Beth's behalf.

The offices were the last building at the top of the town, next to the roundabout. The building stood on its own, an unappealing single-storey modern block. A sixties box build, with grey walls and grim purple paint on the windows, seemingly abandoned in a concrete patch of land. A single brass nameplate was on the door: OLIVER WOODS, SOLICITOR.

Helen went in, glancing back at the traffic snailing at the roundabout, a lorry, hissing air brakes, trying to negotiate the tight turn.

Inside the building, there was a distinct smell of disinfectant.

Christina, the other part-time secretary, was already at her desk in Reception.

Helen lumped her bag on to a chair. 'He's here, I suppose.'

'He's got Mrs Thing with him.'

'Which thing?'

Christina grinned. 'The rich divorcing thing with the Pomeranian.'

Helen sighed. She stood, drumming her fingers on the counter. 'Has Julia been in?'

'No.'

'Damn.' She looked down the corridor, to Oliver's office at the far end. As she did so, his door abruptly opened.

Out came the lady with the little dog. It snuffled in her arms, hanging over her elbow and staring at Helen as she came level with it.

The owner was talking. 'If I showed you the letters . . .'

'Yes, bring them in.'

'It's monstrous. I mean—'

'Monstrous. Absolutely. It boils down to this, often.' Woods smiled. 'If we allow it.'

There was a brief silence while the client tried to decide if she had been rebuffed.

'Let Mrs Pritchard show you out.'

'No, no. I'm fine. Thank you.'

Helen stood to one side to let her pass. The Pomeranian bared its teeth.

Oliver Woods went back into his office. He walked to the window and stood looking out, removing a packet from his coat pocket, flipping it open and taking out a cigarette in one adept movement. He smoked concentratedly, like a man swallowing medicine, pulling shreds of tobacco from his lip.

Helen waited, then tapped on the open door.

'Come in,' he said without looking round.

'Have you had a call from Elizabeth March?' she asked.

Woods turned. Back to the light, his dropped shoulders and hunched appearance became obvious. He was a tall man, who wasted his height. He looked particularly unwell today, Helen thought, with his dullish skin and flu-like eyes. When he had first taken Helen on, five years ago, she had had an urge to mother him. He had killed it in two weeks flat.

Oliver Woods was not the type to be cosseted. He also did not grasp the concept of conversation. If she had tried to talk about last night's television, or a news item, or even the weather, he was capable of giving her a look of utmost irritation. It was only his professional talent and his air of upper-class superiority that kept him his clients.

But Helen had a grudging admiration for the way he had the nerve to cut people dead. She had once heard him call a pompous sod in a Barbour jacket just that—*you pompous fucking sod in a waxed jacket.* And this was a man for whom he handled the lease of a huge estate— a man who netted the firm thousands a year. Oliver Woods consistently said what should never be said, what politeness demanded was unspeakable.

She was still not sure if she liked or loathed him. Last Christmas he had point blank refused to have a drink with them—just her and Christina. He had waved his hand when she asked him, as if she had said something laughable, preposterous. And yet, on Christmas Eve, he'd handed her an envelope with a £500 Christmas bonus.

'Mrs March?' he asked now. 'No.'

Helen hesitated. She knew the Marches and the Woods were neighbours, and that Beth and David were Oliver's clients.

'Beth is trying to get hold of Julia. It's urgent.'

Oliver was shuffling files on his desk, splaying the pile she had put neatly there the night before. His body language expressed boredom.

'Would Julia be at home soon, do you think?'

'I really do not know,' he said. He glanced up. 'Is this of any interest to me?'

'David. David March is dead.'

Woods did nothing, said nothing, for perhaps fifteen seconds. Then he murmured, 'I see.'

'It was a road accident.'

Oliver offered nothing else. Helen felt herself begin to redden. *You might show some emotion,* she thought.

She tried again. 'Shall I get her on the line for you?'

Oliver looked back, over his shoulder. 'Julia has taken Rosie to the doctor,' he said. 'This latest lethargy.'

Finally. 'Right. I see. When will she be back?'

'I have no idea.'

'Was there an appointment time?'

'Ten.'

'Ten . . .' Helen looked at her watch.

Oliver said nothing. He finished the cigarette, and pressed it into an already full ashtray.

'I'll ring her, if that's all right,' Helen said.

Just as she was turning to go out, Oliver walked from behind the desk and handed her a card that he had taken from the pocket of his waistcoat. 'This is her mobile number,' he said. 'I gave her a mobile phone last week. Ring that.'

EIGHT

$\mathcal{M}$UMMY, Rosie called from the back seat of the car. 'Stop.'

Julia Woods glanced in the rear-view mirror. She was driving at fifty along the back farm road to the village. She hardly heard what her daughter was saying.

'Mum-*mee*.'

'What is it?'

'You mustn't *do* that.'

A junction was approaching; Julia changed gear, and then realised what Rosie was talking about. She was going too fast. The car slewed slightly to one side, and clipped the uncut verge.

'All right. We're going slow. See? Very slow.' She glanced at Rosie's pale, anxious face in the mirror. It was terrible to say that she disliked anything about her own child, but it was true that she hated that screwed-up, critical expression that reminded her so much of Oliver.

'Where are we going?' Rosie asked.

'Home.'

'Not school?'

Julia looked down at her hands on the steering wheel. The harder she fought to keep them still, the more they trembled. She glanced into the mirror, and saw a face where the lines of preoccupation were already visible. Twin frown lines between the eyes; deep score marks at the side of her mouth. She smiled relentlessly, but the lines didn't denote humour. They screamed anxiety. 'No school yet,' she murmured. 'You have to go home and change.'

Julia watched the needle of the speedometer as they came into the village. She crawled along now, staring at the familiar landmarks. She had never hated the place so much as she did this morning.

She loathed the neat little shelter by the hall, with its tiled red roof and noticeboard and litter basket; she hated the curve where the grass was cut yellow, and the wire fence at the side of the river, and the house at the edge of the road, with its stone lintel and inscribed black date. Each one was an accusation. Her throat closed tight. In the back seat, Rosie flopped sideways, sighing, bringing her feet up almost to her chest, and plugging her thumb into her mouth.

'Mummy, I'm car-sick,' she murmured.

Julia signalled left to turn into the drive of her own home. The Lodge belied its name; instead of being a period building, it was a large and ugly forties house, soulless-looking, set at the head of a curving gravelled drive. Bay windows held panes of leaded glass with yellow stained panels. At the gatepost, a rhododendron hung forward. Oliver had planted it himself last year. She was going, she thought, *today,* to come out with a hacksaw and cut it down. *Cut it down to the root.*

'Look,' Rosie cried, hauling herself upright again. 'It's Ossy.'

Julia looked up the lane. Beth's cat, Chaos, was standing in the centre of the road, his tail swishing from side to side.

Something caught her attention beyond him. Beth's van was in the drive of Beth and David's house; Beth herself was standing at its side, talking to a man. Suddenly both of them looked back at Julia. Rosie was knocking on the window, waving.

She had no option but to stop; the man was walking fast towards her, his hand held up. Rosie wound her own window down and starting calling the cat. 'Chaos . . . Oss . . . Here then, here . . .'

'Mrs Woods?'

She stopped the engine and opened the door. 'Rosie, don't do that. Ossy doesn't like it. He doesn't want to play.'

'He does, he does . . .'

'Mrs Woods, I'm Alan Pritchard. Have you—' his eyes strayed to Rosie—'got a moment?'

'Well, I . . .'

'It's Mrs March.'

Julia looked past him. Beth had vanished.

He leaned down, his voice falling to a whisper. 'There's been an accident. Mr March has been killed. She's been trying to get in touch with you. We've been ringing all round. And a lady from your husband's office . . .'

Julia had put her hand to her mouth. 'I forgot my phone,' she said. 'I didn't take it.'

Rosie was opening her door. 'Oss . . .' The girl got out and ran up the road, holding out her arms to the cat.

'Oh, Christ,' Julia whispered. '*Christ, Christ.*' She got out, calling Rosie's name, saw her turn in at Beth's gate.

'Will you come?' Alan Pritchard asked.

'I can't, no,' she said.

The man simply looked at her. 'You've got to help me out here,' he said. 'Please.'

She stood up, slipped a little as she closed the door then followed him.

When they got to the house, the front door was open, and they could hear both Rosie and Beth in the kitchen. As they came down the hall, they could see that Beth was calmly making tea, her hand on the kettle, waiting for it to boil, her face turned towards the child. She was smiling.

'And what else?' she asked.

Rosie held up her hand, ticking off each finger. 'No swimming and no fast running. No gymnastics.'

'Ah, what a shame. You like that.'

'Yes, and I nearly got my badge. It's not fair. And it was ages and ages. We waited ages.'

The kettle snapped off; Beth began to pour.

Julia stood at the kitchen door, her hand on the latch. She held it tightly, until it became actually painful. She felt as though her feet had been stuck into concrete; in the small of her back, Alan Pritchard's hand was insistently pushing her.

Beth came across.

'I don't know what to say to you,' Julia said.

Beth gave her a look that equalled her own embarrassment. Their slight friendship had not prepared either of them for this scene. In the past, at occasional village events, at even rarer coffee mornings, they had talked easily despite their differences: Beth, capable and busy; Julia, tall and pale. Their roles were not reversed now.

Beth came and held Julia by both arms, fingers pressing inwards, recognising the other woman's incapacity to move. Julia saw, then, what was coming: that Beth would be placating *her*, making *her* tea, soothing *her*. The prospect was grotesque. She took first one hand and then the other from her own arms, and held Beth's hands. 'I'm sorry,' she said. 'Sit down. I'll do the drinks. Sit down, Beth.'

When she put the cups down on the table, Alan Pritchard made a face at her over Beth's head. *You see what I mean?* his expression said. Beth was behaving as if nothing very unusual had happened.

'Listen . . . If you want to, you can go,' Julia said to him. 'I'll stay here.'

With Alan gone and Rosie in the garden, the two women looked at each other.

'I've got this urge to run away,' Beth said. 'I want to get in the van. I just want to get away.'

Julia said nothing. Instead, she put her hands over her own face. She pressed her fingers hard against her eyes in an effort to stop the tears. 'Oh, I don't know what I can say to you,' she murmured.

Beth looked sideways, at the rim of green that could be seen above the worktop through the window. She was fighting with the inappropriateness of everything, the need to travel in another direction, other than the one in which she was being pulled. She wanted to think about something else; she wanted to *be* somewhere else. She couldn't hold a conversation with Julia; none of the topics, the convenient lines along which they had travelled before, were any good.

'This is all . . . so stupid,' she whispered.

Opposite her, Julia looked up, her eyes fixed on the movement of Beth's mouth.

NINE

$\mathcal{O}$LIVER WOODS WAITED at the counter of the pharmacy. Although staring straight ahead at the shelves, he was not thinking of the medication at all; he was still thinking of David March, and the last time that he had seen him.

The woman came out from behind the dispensing-room door. 'Is this a repeat prescription?' she asked.

'I believe so.'

She smiled, taking a bag and wrapping the bottle. 'Lovely weather.'

'Yes. Very nice.' Oliver's expression darkened unconsciously. There would not be long; perhaps only a matter of days. He saw his own hand plunge straight into the fire, from which, like a magician materialising substance out of thin air and flame, he would be expected to make things clean and calm.

But here in the fire were other pictures: the house, and his own daughter's small enquiring face looking up into his; Julia, with that taut and irritating tremble that replaced a smile.

And then there was Beth.

'Five pounds twenty-five.'

He paid the money. Another image: his accounts, rows of numbers translated to heavy coin. He used to be able to flip those heavy half-crowns between his thumb and finger. They didn't make those thick coins any more. They made small fingernail-sized discs that slipped through your grasp. It all drained away.

Like sand. And ashes.

He turned, the package in his hand.

The street was crowded, the sun very warm. It was almost midday. He turned left, and the sun lay in a bar across his shoulders, throwing his shadow ahead of him, foreshortened and squat.

He had the urge to run, instead of seeing the nightmare out.

Bloody lucky David.

He waited at the crossing, looking at the cars trying to beat the amber. His feet itched to step forwards into the path of the traffic.

Bloody lucky.

TEN

$\mathcal{I}$T BEGAN TO RAIN THAT NIGHT.

Softly at first, just as it was getting dark, the rain touched the glass of the windows as gently as trailing hands. Then, across the river valley, Beth saw the clouds coming, black roller-coasters, chasing the remnants of light from the sky.

She stood at the French windows, watching the drops bouncing on the slabs of the patio outside; a chair, the same chair she had sat in that morning with Alan Pritchard, slipped in a gust of wind. She ought to go and get it in, she thought; it was only a light wooden one. Instead, she watched as the frame tipped and fell. Water began to hammer. She heard it rattling like a drum on the Velux window on the stairs.

The house itself had fallen eerily quiet.

She had gone with Julia to the hospital at half past one. The same young policeman was there to meet them. She had told him that there was no need to come.

'It doesn't matter,' he'd said.

They'd had to meet a man from the Coroner's Office. He was waiting at the Casualty Reception. A tall, broad man with white hair. He looked rather glamorous, as though he had stepped from the set of

35

Dynasty, resplendent in a blue suit with a blue silk tie and dazzling white shirt. He had the faultless, smooth manner of some sort of guide. *The guide to a stately home,* Beth had thought, following him to the lifts.

While they had waited, in the stream of outpatients—mothers with pushchairs, elderly couples, the flow of unsure humanity—someone along the corridor was yelling a name—*Daniel! Daniel!*—and a baby was screaming.

The world hadn't lost its unnatural clarity. The flagstones that had leapt, three-dimensional, when she had looked at them in the morning, had retained their living outline all day. And in the polished hospital corridor everything had gleamed with the same sense of virtual reality. She expected, at any moment, to see the face of her glamorous escort seethe and writhe and pop out like a hologram, to find that he was nothing more than a projected image. The lift buttons were an impossibly livid red, and the floor was almost *too* flat. Shiny and smooth and flat. Their feet, as she kept her eyes sealed to the floor, looked huge, a domed travesty against the floor's shape.

Julia had held her hand.

That was strange too. Not unpleasant, but not comforting. The fingers in her own had trembled while the lift floated—freefall to hell—downwards. The *Dynasty* man had pressed *Sub-Basement*. It was macabre and ridiculous, to descend underground like that. A cliché, a fault in design, she had thought.

The doors had opened, and they emerged into another long corridor. The tall man led the way—*on your right is the Jacobean dining hall, damaged by fire in 1562 and restored . . .* No, she had to stop that. She had to keep level. Like the floor. Like the floor . . .

She had glanced at Julia. Her friend immediately returned her look, sensing the turn of her head. Julia had gone home before coming here, and changed her clothes. Instead of the bright pink jacket and checked skirt of the morning—new, Beth remembered thinking—Julia had put on a navy coat. Seeing her coming back, Beth had said, 'There isn't any need,' then paused. 'Is there?' She had looked down at her own dirty, scuffed, gardening clothes.

'No,' Julia had said. 'Just as I was getting Rosie into the car she spilled ink on me. She was carrying her fountain pen and trying to change the cartridge, and she squeezed it . . .' She had given Beth a tremulous smile. Rosie had been installed with a friend for the afternoon. 'That's all,' she said.

Standing beside Julia and the stranger and the policeman in the neat dark uniform, Beth had had an irritating conviction that she was out of place. They had come to observe some ritual for which one had to be properly dressed, it seemed; like a wedding or a christening. Like a job interview, where one was required to be smart without being loud.

She had begun brushing her trousers, pinching away flecks of dirt. As she walked, she had tried wetting her thumb and rubbing at a grass stain on the front of the trouser leg.

Julia had squeezed her hand.

Beth had made a helpless face. 'Have you ever done this before?' she had asked. They were turning a corner.

'Rebecca,' Julia said.

'Yes . . . oh, yes. I'm sorry. Of course . . .'

Rebecca was Rosie's younger sister. She had died, aged two, two years ago.

Julia had smiled. 'One gets so much love from all sides,' she'd said.

There was no time to question the remark. They were being shown into a small room, brightly and fluorescently lit. Five or six lounger chairs surrounded a coffee table. There was a bunch of flowers in a vase. No magazines, but a box of tissues. Beth had looked at them wryly.

She was longing to tell the man that whoever was inside, waiting for her on the table, it was not David. She felt nervous only because she would be required to look at some complete stranger.

All morning she had turned the problem over in her mind, thinking that David must have been trying to help someone out. She had rationalised that he had given his passport to someone who perhaps was going across the Channel for the day on business, and had found, at the last minute, that their own passport had run out. Foolish, probably. But possible.

As for the car . . . She tried not to think of the car. She had pushed it into a neat pocket in one side of her head, and it had lodged there obediently, in collusion with her. The explanation for someone using David's car would come to her too, given time. She was quite sure of that.

David would come home tonight.

The man had opened the door and Beth had stepped inside. Julia had followed, saying, 'I want to be with her,' to the men behind; then, turning back momentarily, added, 'I know her, you see. I do know her.'

It was a small chapel. The policeman had explained that, as David had been identified by his own GP at the scene, this was by way of a memorial room rather than one for identification. It was just like a private church, with rows of wooden seats, except, where the altar should be, a body was laid on a table, covered with a sheet, with only the head and neck visible.

Beth had walked up to it. Julia followed a yard or two behind.

Beth had stopped within two yards, frowning. A cry of relief was frozen in her throat. Seeing the discoloration of the neck and around the hairline, she had, in her shortsightedness, taken this to be a man of much darker colouring than David. She had narrowed her eyes.

But the darkening was something brought about by death: blood settling at the edges of his face, in the lobes of his ears, and around the base of his throat.

David's face had been unmarked, though infinitely more relaxed than David in life. He had looked almost boyish, without the drawn-down lines of worry and tension that time had unwittingly scored in his face. She had realised, staring at him, that his habitual expression in life, especially lately, had been a frown of unease, and a smile where only one side of his mouth was pinched upwards.

Julia had come up behind her. Beth hadn't known until that moment that she had been swaying. She wanted to take a grip of something solid, because she felt—just for those few peculiar and appalling seconds—that she was floating upwards.

Julia was weeping. Behind them, the door was open a crack. Beth had turned, side-stepped Julia, and strode towards it. Outside, the policeman and the man had been talking; they jolted to silence in surprise.

'Where are his glasses?' Beth had asked.

The policeman had blinked rapidly. 'I . . .'

'His glasses. His clothes. Where are his clothes?'

'I can get them for you,' he had said.

'He wouldn't like to be dressed in that thing. He's very smart. He likes to look nice. He would like to have his own clothes on,' she had said, her voice rising.

'Right. Right. I expect the medical staff . . . well, the undertaker will see to that, I'm sure.'

'Who is dealing with it?' asked the man from the Coroner's office.

Beth had stared at him.

He had actually said *it*. Dealing with *it*.

'I mean the funeral,' the man added.

Julia spoke, behind Beth. 'We'll let you know,' she said. 'In an hour or two. It'll probably be Hurrolds.'

'Yes, yes . . . that's fine. We—er, we liaise with them quite a lot.'

Beth had wrenched open the outer door.

Finding herself back in the corridor, she had walked swiftly back the way she had come. She had almost broken into a run, such was her desperate need to get out.

But, just as she came to the corner, a group of people blocked her path. There were about twenty of them, all young. There were three or four at the front who were, it seemed, in the middle of a joke. A girl was pulling the front of her white coat, complaining that it didn't fit her. There was an air of palpable nervousness; they were coming to a halt at an unmarked door further up from the chapel.

It had struck Beth at once: that they were medical students. They were going into the mortuary.

She had pushed past them, got to the stairs, and slammed open the fire door. Taking the steps two or three at a time, she had found herself at ground level. There was a window open there, and shrubs outside pressing up to the glass. She took several long gasps of air.

In no more than twenty seconds, her little following group came up behind her. She had heard Julia's heeled shoes on the floor, tapping like irritating hammers, invading the quiet.

The man in the blue suit had laid a hand on her shoulder. She had turned to him.

'Oh, dear Beth,' Julia had said. She put an arm around Beth's shoulders, tried to hug her.

'Those people, back there,' Beth had said.

'Who?' Julia asked.

Beth had tried to shrug her off. She was talking to the Coroner's man.

'The students?' he asked.

'Yes.' She had gulped down more air, trying to steady her voice. 'Can you please ask them,' she had whispered, 'please . . . not to touch my husband.'

Beth glanced around herself now. The small table light in the corner was on, spilling a circle of light. Outside, the rain had lessened.

She walked to the centre of the living room. David's suitcase lay on the couch. She had bought it for him last Christmas. She reached down to touch the familiar green binding. There was no real damage to the case: just one side had been pushed in; the corners were broken. She hesitated a second, wringing her hands. Then, she carefully unzipped it.

David's clothes lay as neatly as he had packed them: *too much*, she thought immediately. She ran her hand over the contents. All the things he had taken! Shoes, shirts, sweaters . . . all packed tight.

She shook her head, rifling through the clothes. He had packed to impress, for . . . She pressed her index finger between her brows, shaking her head all the while. She let out a small and helpless sound. He had packed for a long time, for something new, everything new . . . She touched the case of his spare glasses.

For a new life.

There was even the contact lenses he so rarely wore, in a special transparent pack from the optician. She held it up to the light. There was a white label, with a date stamp. Only two days ago.

She let the clothes fall from her hands.

She dared not look at the envelope that the police had handed her along with the case and the briefcase. Almost apologetically, they had explained that these were objects found inside the car, which had probably fallen from the parcel shelf or the wide dashboard.

Alongside the case was David's briefcase. This, unlike the suitcase, had taken a battering. It had been alongside him on the seat, not in the boot. A deep gash had ruined the top, and the pale lining was showing. Breathing heavier now, Beth turned it on its side and stared at the combination lock. David had chosen the numbers. She ran her thumb over the reels. She had no idea what the opening combination might be.

She squatted down, and tried the obvious. Her birthday, eight; his birthday, fifteen. And the year of his birth, fifty-one. Nothing . . . nothing.

'God damn you,' she whispered.

She sat back and looked at it, and it struck her that it was stupid to try to save the case by opening the lock. It was useless now—good for nothing. She sprang to her feet.

Out in the garage, she walked along the row of neatly cleaned and oiled garden tools, eventually taking down a small hacksaw. Weighing it in her hands, she brought it back inside.

She began to cut through the top. It was very difficult, even for her—and she thought of herself as being very strong. She couldn't do her work otherwise. But this was no tree; it wasn't a brick to be cut or shaped. It was part of David, as much a part of him as his own skin, his own hands.

She felt as though she was murdering him.

When she could at last get to the papers inside her heart was beating hard, and there was a poisonous taste in her mouth. She reached in and grabbed, closing her eyes. She pulled until everything was out, letting it all fall to the carpet. Only when she was quite sure that there was nothing left inside did she turn to look.

There was the financial section of Sunday's newspaper. A batch of letters, invoices, and notes—all with the letterhead of a firm she did not know, some carpentry firm north of here. Perhaps to do with the accounts he had been working on. There was a handkerchief, folded neatly, and a cheque-book, and a computer notepad, and David's wallet with his credit cards inside.

She shook her head, regarding the fanned and shuffled contents. The handkerchief was the worst; she reached out and pulled a file across it, as you would cover the face of a corpse.

Finally, she turned to the envelope.

It was foolscap size, and thick. She opened it, biting her lip, and looked inside. There was a small tape, of the kind that might fit a dictation machine, a padded envelope with nothing in it, and a blue pamphlet much like an airline ticket. She retrieved this last item with thumb and fingernail. But it was not an airline ticket; it was a ferry ticket. For a sailing that morning, at eleven thirty.

Beth sat on her heels, reading it three or four times. The booking was in David's name. Only *his* name.

And it was a single, not a return.

She looked up, staring at the room around her. Only last night, David had sat on this couch, easing his feet out of his slippers as he read the evening newspaper. They had watched the news on television. He was doing a crossword. They had barely spoken half a dozen words all night. She could see that same newspaper now, tucked on to the bottom shelf of the table alongside the light; she could even see David's lettering, the figuring of the crossword anagrams. He had only filled in three clues, she saw. And yet he had been sitting there for over an hour.

This was a small, high-ceilinged room, pleasantly untidy. Various cushions littered the chairs and sofa; a deep wine-coloured rug lay before the open fireplace. Magazines and letters and rough sketches of hers were spread over the oak table in the corner.

She passed her hands over her face. All the time he had been sitting here, throughout the recent weeks and months, something momentous had been going on in his life. Probably occupying most of his thoughts. And yet she had not known a single thing about it. She had never had the least suspicion, never guessed.

Her fingers, straying over the contents of the case, rested briefly on the computer notepad. She turned to it listlessly, opening the diary file. David had loved technological toys. She preferred her own battered black desk diary, with its innumerable scrawled additions and alterations to the days, the dog-eared margins. The book seemed alive to her, where the Psion was dead. She gazed at its little grey face.

David's previous busy month scrolled up on the screen; she noticed Oliver's name once or twice. There were careful notations of other meetings. A visit to the VAT offices. The car servicing. The renewal of insurance policies. Even a calculation of the car's mileage.

Then, as the present month came through, she saw with surprise that the days became blank, the entries unfilled. From two weeks ago, there was nothing, even though he had been going to work as usual.

She looked at the ferry ticket still in her hand, and the breath was squeezed tight in her chest. She experienced a fleeting moment of suffocation.

Then she closed her eyes, and flung the notepad to one side. Gasping, she began to tear the blue ticket into as many pieces as she could, the fragments fluttering around her like confetti.

She began, despite—or perhaps because of—her earlier dead calm, to cry, the drops splashing on to her hands.

And she kept thinking about the last moments that she had seen him that morning; of him standing on the step, with the dead bird. Lifting its loose neck with the tip of his finger.

ELEVEN

$\mathcal{O}$LIVER WOODS' CAR PULLED INTO THE DRIVE AT SEVEN.

The rain was beating down, and Julia, looking from the darkness of the front room, saw him frowning for a second before he got out.

He did not hurry, however. He walked to the door, and she, running along the hall, managed to get there just a fraction before he had to ring the bell.

Opening the door to him, she didn't speak. Nor was she spoken to. Instead, she stood by while he took off his coat. Taking it from him, she shook it a little, hanging it in the cloakroom. With his eyes on her, she spread a piece of newspaper on the floor under the coat. She straightened up.

'Did you see me?' she asked. 'I did it right.'

'Where is Rosie?' he asked.

'At Michaela's.'

'Is she coming home?'

'Not until tomorrow.' She saw him open his mouth to speak, but beat him to it. 'I didn't ask them,' she said. 'They offered. Just an hour ago. They rang me up and offered.'

He thought better of whatever it was that he was going to say. She followed him along the hall. Turning in at the living room, he walked to the fire.

It was a pleasant room, well proportioned, with a large bay window. A fire burned brightly in the grate. Oliver leaned with both hands against the mantelpiece.

There was a collection of Belleek on the broad marble sill: stranded and woven porcelain baskets with a yellowish lustre, whose feminine delicacy might have pointed to Julia's choice, but which was, in fact, his own. The baskets, with their shiny glaze, their complicated frozen petals and leaves, were a nightmare to keep clean. They had to be washed, rather than polished, weekly. Every week Julia agonised over handling them, certain that she would break one. For this reason more than any other, she worried over the elaborate masterpieces with their deathly colour. She was perpetually tempted to smash them to pieces.

Oliver finished his inspection. He turned, and stood with both hands in his pockets, gazing at his wife.

'I went with her to the hospital,' Julia said.

'Well,' he said calmly. 'What have you to tell me?'

She met his gaze. 'We had to go down to a little chapel—'

He waved his hand impatiently. 'I don't mean that,' he said. 'Let's not drag this out. To prolong this would be insufferable, don't you think?'

'Yes,' she said.

'We would want to come to some profitable conclusion.'

'Yes.'

'You see?'

'Yes, Oliver.'

'Good. What have you to tell me?'

She looked away from him. Not by turning her face or head; that would have been unthinkable. But she glanced along the mantelpiece behind his shoulders, at the figurines that he laid so much store by. 'I didn't know,' she murmured.

He pursed his lips. There was a silence of perhaps thirty or forty seconds. An interminable time.

'You knew nothing at all about this trip?'

'No, Oliver.'

'Nothing *at all*?'

'No.'

'He said nothing to you—*nothing at all*—about his going abroad?'

'Was he going out of the country?' she said.

He smiled then. 'You mean to tell me that you didn't discuss the fact at all?' he asked. It was almost the voice of a counsellor or a friend.

'But I don't *see* him to talk to, Oliver. Why don't you ask Beth?' she said.

Oliver shook his head, clicking his tongue against his teeth. At last he sat down, straightening the crease in his trousers with pinched finger and thumb. 'Oh, Julia,' he intoned softly. 'You do disappoint me. I can't tell you how much you disappoint me.'

She thought he was not going to say anything else; he picked up the evening paper from the table beside him, and began leafing through it. She took a step back, saw no reaction, and turned. She went to the cabinet and poured him his drink. Three fingers of Scotch. No ice. No water.

'Where was he going?' Oliver asked.

She turned back to him, the Scotch wavering in the glass. She forced herself to hold it straight, and went over to him, holding it out in front of her. 'Here you are,' she said.

But he didn't look at the glass; only at her.

'I was with Rosie,' she said. 'I took Rosie to the doctor.' She tried to change the subject. 'The doctor said how well I've done. He said I had been wonderful, Oliver. "I have yet to see a more patient mother," he said.'

Oliver continued to stare at her. Her expression flickered; her voice lowered. 'You can see what antibiotic they gave me,' she said. 'I wrote the name down.'

He rewarded her with absolute silence; his gaze wandered to the drink, and back again at her. He gave a great sigh; the sigh of a forbearing parent faced with perpetual rebellion.

He put down the paper. 'That reminds me,' he said. He reached into his pocket and took out the small brown bottle he had got from the chemist. He held it out to her.

'Thank you,' she said, taking it. She flashed him a smile of increased confidence. 'He never told me anything,' she said. 'I swear.'

He stared at her. 'I spoke to the police. They say that he had a packed case. His passport. Ferry tickets.'

'I took Rosie,' she whispered.

He stood up abruptly, reached out, grabbed her arm, and wrenched it upwards, drawing her in towards him. He smelled strongly of his cigarettes. Instead of turning her face away, she raised it to him. He saw something come to life in her; it was almost pleasure. He dropped her arm in disgust and walked away.

He went back to the couch, sat down, and took up the paper again. He opened it and snapped the pages once or twice to straighten them.

'I'm telling you the truth this time,' she said.

He did not respond to the note of rising insistence in her voice.

'Look at me,' she said. 'Listen . . .'

But he had already shut her out, closed his door in her face.

TWELVE

$\mathcal{B}$ ETH WAS NOT AWARE OF HAVING DOZED, but jolting upright in the chair now she realised that she must have slept, maybe for more than an hour.

She opened her eyes into darkness; only after a moment did the lines of the living room become clear. And, without being able to distinguish the floor in the shadows, she felt as if she were floating in the armchair.

She sat forward, pressing her feet hard to the floor. The vertigo was still there. She had been dreaming of lying in water, only her face in the air, her body drifting inexorably downwards into the cold depths. She had woken just at the point that her weight would drag her under, and could still feel the liquid lapping at the corners of her mouth and eyes. She could still hear the ticking, tapping sound.

'Oh God,' she whispered.

The last time that she had been in utter darkness like this had been with her mother. The dark, and the bird at the window.

She was fifteen when her mother had died in a state hospital. She had kept a vigil over the last two nights. There was no father for company: he had died when she was small. Her mother had been strong-willed, like her, absolutely refusing to believe in her illness. At the end she had refused—even with her rock-like repugnance of the cancer, and the nursing, and the ward—to let go and die. She had lain in the bed, propped up to a sitting position, too furious to lie down, cursing anyone who came near her. She still tried to work, her locker piled with reference books and the yellow legal pads she liked to write in, and her precious Mont Blanc pen. She had taught chemistry at a local polytechnic and had been in the middle of writing a school reference book, a simplified guide to basic science. She didn't want to let that go, either.

Beth remembered the large-featured face on the stacked pillows, scored by the sulphur streetlight outside. Her mother had expressive eyes. A high forehead and a wide-lipped mouth, and long-fingered hands: all of them signals of her never-still, never-silent life. In the darkness of the last night, her hands moved repeatedly across the bedding, her fingers fluttered towards the cabinet.

It was summer, and dawn had come at four in the morning. Beth had sat, watching the wretchedly slow hours drag past on the clock, with her chin propped in one hand, the other occasionally stroking her mother's forearm. The daylight was just a white line on the horizon at first; then the sky paled, and she began to see the frames of the window, the line of the lawn beneath the window, the leaves of the beech tree. There was a ten-minute limbo, when everything lacked colour: the beds in the ward, the flowers on the lockers, the shrubs in the gardens below.

And it was at that moment that a sparrow flew to the window and landed on the ledge outside. Beth had seen its yellowish feet, little scaly strands. It looked in at her. And then it began beating its wings against the glass.

The nurse said afterwards that they often had trouble with the birds. The windows were set deep in concrete bays and were hard to clean, and insects collected in the ledges, and the birds would come and scrabble at the glass. It was a perfectly reasonable explanation. But it didn't help. There was something terrible about the small bird and the sound of its feet and wings, its insistent scratching in the half-light. And it was just at that moment that her mother had died, suddenly arching her back, her eyes cramped shut.

Shocked, Beth had stepped back, a cry for help stuck in her throat. In the incongruity, the other-worldliness of that moment, she had turned her head and her gaze had fastened on the rows of brightening roses in the grounds below. Between the appearance of the line on the horizon and the arrival of the bird, all the garden had changed. The colours had a sudden vocal brilliance. She had never forgotten their luminescent brightness. Even now, that particular shade of coral could stop her, if she passed it in a garden, or at a florist's window. Its mute significance struck her like a blow.

Beth sprang up now, recognising the drowning sensation from the dream. She went to the small table and switched on the light. Immediately, her breathing slowed. She touched the table, for comfort and orientation.

She was here, at home. Not with her mother.

Strange. She had not thought of that night for a long time. It was not that she had suppressed it, exactly; it had sunk, gradually, into a mass of other memories. If she had been asked, for instance, what she remembered about her mother's illness, she might have quoted the loneliness of being an only child, coping at an early age with a parent's death, that early need for total self-reliance. She would remember all that red tape, and her move from Derbyshire to Bristol, to live an awkward two years with an aunt before she left for college. She might have remembered the funeral. But not that last hour alone, in the dark.

Her first instinct was to tell David; then came the realisation that she would never be able to tell him.

She glanced at the clock. It was half past three in the morning. It would be light, that first releasing rim of white on the horizon, in just an hour. She could wait until then, she thought, and then try to sleep.

The ticking noise was still there; she put her head on one side, trying to locate it. It was not the clock. As she listened, it stopped. She turned her head, looking all round herself.

'What *is* that?' she murmured.

She went to the window and drew back one curtain. The garden was pitch dark—there were no streetlights here. As far as she could make out, there was no movement outside, no animal near the gate.

Yet, as she turned away, the noise started again: a sweeping, scratching sound.

She went out into the hall, and understood, only then, that it was coming from the kitchen. She had closed the door. She switched on the hall light and went to the kitchen door.

Opened it.

In the first second or so, the room looked perfectly all right. Then she noticed the specks on the floor. White specks. Then the table. The top of the kitchen table was a mess: sugar lay in a trail, the bowl turned over. Pieces of paper from the memo board stuck on the ridged top of the radiator, torn from their usual place on the wall above.

The bird had seen her first.

It was on the draining board, its wings trailing at its sides. It was only small: a swallow, breathtaking to be seen up close, with its precise black-and-white colouring. It was trembling violently, and, as she let out a gasp, it fluttered back to the window, where it had obviously been trying to get out.

Beth's heart began slamming in her throat—huge, disproportionate blows, closing off the oxygen. It was only a bird. Only a bird. A very frightened bird . . .

She glanced, automatically, at the cat flap. Chaos wasn't in the kitchen, but she had no doubt that this was again the cat's doing. The bird beat its wings frantically. It threw itself at the glass and, just for a split second, Beth could see two birds—the one in the room and the one in the reflection—beating the barrier of the window pane.

She had told people about the bird against her mother's window. Someone had said that birds meant death. 'Birds are an omen,' they had told her. 'That's what it was . . . the bird before she died. Birds know. The spirit passes into the bird, and leaves . . .'

She had been just sixteen when she was told that. She knew what her mother would have said: 'Crap.' Just like that. 'Utter crap.' And it was, she knew. People just died. They vanished. They didn't rise up and pass into the nearest living creature; they didn't walk the night. They didn't come back. They just ceased to live, and it was over, like a day is over.

And yet, the bird at the glass, the eye locked blankly on to hers . . .

She tried to walk a step or two forward, but she was shaking. 'It's only a bird,' she said softly.

She couldn't imagine how a swallow could get into the house. It wasn't as if they were a real garden bird, the kind that came and sat on the back of one of the chairs, like the robins did on her own lawn. They weren't like the jackdaws, a family of which haunted the twin chimneys of the rectory. A cat could covet garden birds like that, and sometimes catch them; but not swallows. Swallows and swifts were different. They flew at height. They never came to take scraps; they never came close enough.

The bird came to a staggering halt on the sill. Heart hammering, Beth reached past it and opened the window.

'Go out,' she said. 'Here it is . . . the outside. Go out.'

But she couldn't stand it. She couldn't look at its palpable terror. She ran back, switching off the light, and slammed the door behind her.

She went up the hall, her fist at her shoulder, easing the stitch of pain there. At the outer door she stopped, resting her forehead on the black oak, running her hand over the iron bolt.

It didn't mean anything. Not bad luck. Or anything . . .

The need to get out of the house picked at her, like a hand through the wood door, snatching at her clothes, her flesh. She knew it was panic, even hysteria. So easy to let that scratching need to scream take over.

The need to scream, to vanish, to run.

Beth leaned against the wood with her whole body weight, as if that alone could silence the scraping. She slid down the door, pressing her fingertips to the edge where it met the wall, pushing the grain in a mime of sealing the stone to the wood.

On the floor, she wrapped her arms around her knees. 'It'll be light in a minute,' she told herself, hearing the flagrant lie and yet repeating it. 'It'll be light.'

And, after all, a bird couldn't bring bad luck.

She closed her eyes, holding her legs tightly. The hallway still rolled.

THIRTEEN

*I*T WAS AT SEVEN O'CLOCK THE FOLLOWING MORNING that an ancient Citroen pulled into the Oak Rise site.

The day was still, the sky clear with the promise of perfect weather. The majority of this small village lay below the hill, and there was little noise now on the chalk ridge above it.

A man got out of the car and stood for a moment gazing at the spectacular view. Then he opened the car door, and at once a terrier— a flash of liver and white—rushed out, circled the ground madly for a few seconds, then promptly disappeared over the rise.

'Come here, you bastard,' the man called, in an easy voice that held no hope at all that the dog would obey him.

Rhys Owen was about thirty, with shoulder-length dark hair. He had owned a firm of archaeological excavators in partnership for the last eight years. He looked around slowly and carefully, resisting the rush to the grave site, taking in the contour and texture of the ground.

Rhys liked the dead. In fact, he much preferred them to the living. After all, the living talked and wandered about. The living got in the way and offered advice. They invariably complained about money and time. It was only the dead who lay obediently still, frozen in their last arrangement of limbs, weapons and clothes. Offering silent and obliging testimony, oblivious to the passage of the years.

He took a battered blue-and-ochre tin from his pocket. Rhys allowed himself four hand-rolled cigarettes a day. Smoking was a fault he was almost proud of, not least because he liked to see the horror on the face of non-smokers. Especially those who *used* to smoke.

A half-mile away across the down, one of the straight farm roads dissected two vast fields of early grain, a light brown line running through two neat green pages, like the inner spine of an open book. He focused on the field alongside, narrowing his eyes momentarily.

In this early light, at this particular angle, he could pick out a faintly darker line in the grass. There was definitely something under the slope that looked like three-quarters of a massive curve, perhaps eighty feet across. Not pronounced enough for a barrow or a ring ditch.

Noticing such irregularities was a kind of addiction, more pronounced than the token smoke; noticing the ridges in landscape when he ought to be watching his driving, for instance. Visualising other streets under modern ones. Reducing faces to bone. Looking for roads in empty fields. He saw ghosts everywhere.

In fact, he considered it one of the prime perks of the job.

Looking back, he was jolted from his line of thought by movement below the field, in the lane. He picked up a pair of binoculars, wiping the lens free of the dust and dog hairs.

Locating the moving shape, he realised that it was a woman, walking swiftly down the road just below the site of the ring-marked field. She was doing a hell of a pace. He swept his sight up and down the road for a dog—early risers were usually dog owners getting in the walkies before work—but there was no animal with this woman.

She was small and slight; he couldn't make out any other details. He watched her stride down the empty lane, between the low hedges, for more than a minute.

And then she stopped.

A little closer now, he could see that she was wearing a brown jacket with something red tied at her neck. She had halted at a gate, and was leaning on it, so still that you could have been forgiven for thinking that she had turned to stone. He waited for her to carry on.

She did not. Eventually his eyes tired, and he took the glasses away. The speck of red at her throat was just visible, if you knew where to look. And still it hadn't moved.

He put the glasses back in the car and plunged his hands into his pockets. The airmail letter was still there. He thought it stung his hand as he gently curled his fingers around it. She would expect a reply this time; even the paper was reproaching him.

His dog, Aesculapius, came back, trotting with an air of authority through the chalk. Seeing Rhys, it began its curious little dance of greeting, hopping on three legs as it approached him.

By eight thirty, Alan Pritchard had arrived. Alison Warley turned up soon afterwards and introduced herself to Rhys. The day before, Rhys had been granted a Home Office licence thanks to Alison's phone calls.

'Listen,' Alan said. 'I'm going to do an estimate in Yeovil.'

Rhys smiled; he had a lot of sympathy for builders held up by his work. And he was always grateful to men like Alan who actually stopped building in deference to a find.

'What time are you home?' he asked.

Alan considered. 'Six.'

'Can I call round?'

'If you like.' Alan handed Rhys his card.

'Tell you how much, how long.'

Alan gave a grimace. 'Thousands and weeks.'

'No . . . look, I know a couple of volunteers. We can always round up very competent excavation teams. But it depends on the numbers of burials. Maybe £500 per skeleton.'

'Jesus wept,' Alan muttered.

Rhys put a hand on his shoulder. 'Two days a grave.'

'Bloody Nora . . .' Alan replied. 'Let's hope there isn't fifty of the buggers, then. See you at six.'

'Thanks.'

Rhys went over to the grave, where Alison was kneeling in rapt concentration. As he came up to her, she pointed with a dental pick to a slightly raised outline in the chalk. Beneath the rounded edge to the skull was a circular indentation.

'There's something under here,' she said. 'There look . . .'

To the naked eye, there was little more than a brownish shadow in the light soil. 'This is shallow. Fifteen centimetres. Head at the west. Early eighth.' The Saxons had come late to this part of Dorset; pagan burials, with grave goods, had usually been late seventh, early eighth century.

Alison got up, brushing down her clothes.

'Right,' Rhys said. 'Let's get going.'

It was half past eleven when Rhys saw the walker again. He was standing and easing his back, looking towards the road, wondering vaguely about lunch and trying to remember whether he'd seen a pub in the village when he came through. The woman walked from the direction of the village this time; he recognised the red scarf at once.

How long have you been walking? he thought.

He expected her, after a cursory glance, to carry on. But to his surprise, she turned in purposefully at the entrance and walked towards him. At twenty yards, Aesculapius rocketed towards her, barking. She smiled slightly but carried on, the terrier yelping at her feet, prancing for attention.

She stopped and gazed at the graves.

They had uncovered a second, and were in the process of revealing a third. It looked like a full community; Alan Pritchard was not going to be pleased.

'Can I help?' Rhys asked.

She looked at him. For a second it seemed that she was almost surprised to see him; as if, in the few moments that it had taken her to walk from the gate to the car, she had forgotten his existence.

Her face was pale. It was a face of perfect and regular features that, as a sum total, made for a pleasant expression rather than any great beauty. The eyes were deep brown, lines marking the edges. Her hair was cropped short, and she had a little lipstick on. Her clothes were neat and unremarkable, pressed with a knife-edge seam in the jeans. She looked as though she might have taken particular care with it all.

But there was nothing about her that was right. He couldn't put his finger on it; it was a fleeting impression. Something in her face showed that she was making an effort.

And that she was very tired.

'I thought of *Ceanothus*,' she said.

'I'm sorry?'

The dog was making little leaping movements. She reached down and patted his head. '*Ceanothus thyrsiflorus*; it hangs down. It covers bare brick,' she said.

He didn't know what to say. He held out his hand to the dog. 'Aesculapius . . .'

She raised her eyebrows. 'What an awful mouthful. Why do you call him that?'

He shrugged. 'We were in Wiltshire once, and this villa—'

'But why that, I mean? The Greek god of healing. He ought to be Spike, or Rex. Shouldn't you?' she asked the terrier. 'Shouldn't you? Rex or something, a little dog like you.'

'Roman. Aesculapius was Roman. And he's Ace for short.'

She watched the dog trot back to him. 'No,' she murmured. She looked over at the graves again. 'I just thought of something that would . . . cover the brick . . .' And she turned away.

He wondered whether to follow her; if she would get home. Until she had spoken, she had looked perfectly OK. And even then she made a kind of sense. He thought of saying, *an evergreen would be very nice*. He knew perfectly well what *Ceanothus* was, and he liked to be polite. It was the policy of appeasement he used on most women.

But you never knew. She might turn funny; she might start shouting. She was obviously unbalanced.

The woman was now at the lane entrance. She looked down at the road and made a gesture with her shoulders—a shrug in reverse, drooping, as if winded.

He almost stepped forward, after her.

But she began, at that same instant, to walk very quickly, and he thought better of it.

FOURTEEN

$\mathcal{B}$ETH'S APPOINTMENT WITH OLIVER WOODS was at four o'clock on Tuesday afternoon.

She arrived late. Helen Pritchard was in Reception when she came in, and immediately walked forward, her arms extended. Beth looked away, almost closing her eyes as she turned her head from Helen's offered embrace.

'I was so sorry to hear your news,' Helen said. She thought at once that Beth, standing there so rigidly, clutching two plastic carrier bags, was at the edge, on the brink. She was so unnervingly still.

'Shall I take your shopping?' Helen asked gently. 'Shall I just put it behind the desk?'

Beth allowed the bags to be slowly taken from her. There was an awkward second of untangling the handles from Beth's wrist. As the older woman returned, Beth suddenly apologised, looking Helen directly in the face.

Helen wanted to hold her, but dared not offer again. 'It's all right. Come in. He's waiting for you.'

Oliver, too, came out to greet Beth with both arms held out in front of him. This time Beth leaned forward a little to receive his dry kiss on her face. As she drew back, she placed a hand on his arm. 'Oh Oliver,' she said. 'I'm so glad to see you.'

Oliver patted Beth's hand. 'My dear girl,' he said. Then, looking up, he told Helen, 'Some tea, please.'

Helen gave him a look, meant to be of warning, as she went out of the door. But he was not looking in her direction. He was bent over Beth, one hand on the desk and the other on the back of her chair.

'How are you?' he was asking as the door closed.

Beth shook her head almost imperceptibly. 'I'm all right.'

'I have been trying to ring you.'

'I've been walking all morning,' she replied. She glanced up at him. 'I couldn't sleep. I got home at . . . two o'clock, I think . . . and Mr . . .' She waved her fingers at her temples, a gesture of trying to remember. 'I always want to call him Harold. But it isn't Harold.'

'Hurrold?'

'Yes. Mr Hurrold was there. I'd forgotten.'

'I'm sure he understood.'

'Yes,' she said. She folded her hands in her lap deliberately. Slowly. 'He was very . . . very *kind*. I expect that's what they have to be all the time. Very *kind*.'

Oliver said nothing for a moment. Then, 'And did you manage to sort everything out as you wanted?'

'Yes,' she murmured.

Mr Hurrold had had an unhurried air about him. He had been dressed in a dark suit, and carried a briefcase. He resembled nothing so much as an insurance man, the kind that Beth's mother used to have calling every Friday evening to collect her premium.

Beth had brought him into the house and they had sat in the living room. She had realised that the heating was not on, that the room was cold, and that she ought to offer him tea—but she couldn't rouse herself to stand up. She had had to force herself to listen to what he was saying.

He held a calendar open on his knees, and had evidently asked her a question.

'I'm sorry,' she said. 'What?'

'Is there any preference for a day?'

'Day?'

'For the service.'

'No . . . no.'

'Perhaps Friday?'

'Yes. That's all right.'

'You'll have Mr March's family to contact. Will they all be able to make it by then?'

David had one cousin, working in Saudi. They had not been close, and she knew that the man travelled all over the world. She had only met him perhaps four or five times in the last ten years, and then he had never stayed for more than a couple of hours. Nevertheless, she had rung him last night, got an answerphone, and left a message to contact her. He had not done so yet.

'I think so.'

'Right, right . . .'

Hurrold had been very soothing. She had to give him that. Soothing without being sugary.

'Now, I wonder if we might talk about the type of thing you want . . .'

It was incredible. She had felt like grabbing his jacket and screaming, 'But I don't *want* it! How could I *want* it?'

Hurrold opened a catalogue, placing it carefully on the coffee table between them.

'On the phone you mentioned oak,' he said.

She stared at him. 'Oak?'

He had smiled. 'When you telephoned . . .'

She frowned. 'I didn't ring.'

He lifted another notebook on to his knee, underscoring his own handwriting with his fingertip. 'This morning?' he said. 'At nine o'clock? That was you?'

'I didn't ring you,' she insisted.

They paused, looking at each other. Hurrold obviously made a decision to let it pass. Beth, for her part, did not have the energy to pursue it.

Instead, he had showed her the different kinds of coffins, and they discussed the cars. Talking about cars was the worst of all—worse than the caskets and handles and linings. Beth had a twist of panic and hatred in her gut when she thought about the thing—this *car*, this *bloody, bloody car*—that had delivered David to his death. First thing that morning, at five o'clock, just as it was getting light, she had wanted to go to the police and ask them about David's car. She had wanted to see it—then, at that very moment. To touch it, or to kick it, or weep over it. Or to tear it to pieces with her bare hands.

Mr Hurrold and she had sat side by side on the couch to get the wording right on the announcement for the paper. She had pored over each letter, as perplexed as a child learning to read. They had lost their meaning, all the curves and lines. Even the usual words, the small words—*dear, on, the*—looked wrong. The alphabet had dissolved in her head to a series of jumbled shapes. She might as well have been reading Cyrillic script.

He had left after an hour, shaking her hand at the door. It was the first time that anyone had touched her that day. It was a nice hand—dry, warm, gentle—and yet it had thoroughly revolted her. The touch of another skin, a foreign skin. It was obscene to have touched this stranger, to have pressed her fingers in his, to have touched his palm. It had felt as intimate as adultery.

That was why she had not wanted Helen touching her when she had arrived here.

As if on cue with the thought of Helen, the tea was brought to Beth and Oliver. Helen said nothing, merely leaving the tray and going softly out of the room. Beth fixed her gaze outside Oliver's window, on the roofs of offices across the street. Slightly to the right was a hotel, the lights above whose name had come on prematurely. More writhing letters.

'Are you feeling well?' Oliver asked.

She glanced at him. 'Not really.'

'Is there anything I can get for you?'

'No, Oliver.'

He sipped his tea, then took a buff folder from a drawer in his desk. 'I know this is an appalling time for you,' he said quietly. 'But I think that you ought to be aware of your position.'

Both her and David's wills were deposited with Oliver. He had handled their house purchase ten years beforehand; it was how they first got to know him. Beth had a peculiar affection for Oliver. She liked his eccentricity. She was drawn, in a mesmerised fashion, to his ability to be absolutely cold-blooded, and not to feign politeness. She would find herself smiling at his rudeness, because it was so outrageous. If there was one thing she could not bear, it was the kind of two-faced smarm of the professional man. She knew where she stood with Oliver, trusted him completely. And pitied him his wife.

'My position?' she asked.

'Yes . . . the house, and so on.'

She knew there was no immediate cause for concern. The house was mortgaged, with an endowment policy. There was a small shares fund, left to David by his father, which provided a modest extra income every year; that, too, would now pass to her. She had not given money a second thought in the last thirty-six hours. David was meticulous in such things. Too careful, if anything.

Oliver opened the folder. 'As you know, the equity on the house is reasonably low: thirty-two thousand pounds, based on the last valuation.'

She watched him. His head was lowered, and his finger ran along the page. He did not look up. 'However, with the further charge and the surrender of the fund—'

'Pardon?' she asked.

He glanced up. 'The fund. David realised the fund three weeks ago.'

'He . . .' She stared, then began, faintly, to laugh. 'No.'

Oliver frowned. He took a letter from the file, passing it across to her. It was from David. In the baldest of terms, and without offering any explanation, he had asked Oliver to record that the shares in his father's fund had been sold. He asked Oliver to amend his will accordingly.

'I think there was a need for cash,' Oliver murmured.

'Cash?' she repeated.

He saw her expression. 'Would you like me to find out how much he raised?'

She sat back. It didn't matter how much. What mattered was why David had done it. Why he needed money. Why he had never told her a word about it. She raised a hand to her forehead, feeling very hot suddenly. And then it suddenly registered what Oliver had said to her.

'A further charge?'

Oliver nodded. 'But you knew about that, of course. You signed the form.' And, across the leather-top desk, he slipped a sheet of paper.

There, on the bottom, was her own name. She raised the paper close to her face. It was very like her handwriting. But it was definitely not her signature. She had never seen the form until now.

She started to read it from the top, got through two paragraphs, and then stopped. She looked back at Oliver. 'I have never seen this before,' she told him. 'I didn't sign this.'

Oliver raised his eyebrows, leaned forward, his elbows on his desk. 'That is a very serious matter,' he said. 'The charge raised another eighteen thousand pounds on the house.'

'Oh, Christ,' she murmured.

Oliver took the paper back and considered it, running his index finger across his temple and above his eyes.

Beth took a deep breath in an effort to calm herself, to slow her breathing down. 'David came to you with this form, with this . . .' She tried to think of a technical word, a word that held no hysteria. '. . . this proposal,' she said.

'Yes . . .'

'And he . . . did he . . . say *why* he wanted this extra money?'

Oliver nodded; he put his hand to his mouth briefly. 'For the extension on the house.'

'The . . . extension. I see. And which extension is that?'

Oliver began to shake his head a little. 'The conservatory and the brick paving; the workshop for you—'

'Yes, yes.' She said it to stop him talking. The continued noise of his voice was too much to handle.

David had never mentioned any extension. She had never asked for—or wanted, or needed—a workshop of any kind. They already had a small, albeit shabby old conservatory tacked on to the west wall of the house. There had never been any discussion about building work. And yet David had forged her signature on an application for a second mortgage charge to finance it.

Momentarily, the room tipped. She held tight to the arm of the chair, waiting for the sudden vertigo to stop. 'Don't you have to have a builder's estimate?' she asked. 'I mean, this is totally ridiculous. You can't do this behind anyone's back, can you? Surely? And don't you have to get a valuation before work starts, and one when it's finished?'

'That's right. That's the valuation I was telling you about.' Oliver was leafing through the folder again. He produced two photocopies: one of a valuation dated four weeks previously, one of a builder's estimate.

It was for £18,000. And it was from Alan Pritchard.

'David had arranged for this work to be done, and secured the loan, and . . .' She stared back out at the street. 'We had a bank statement last week,' she said, suddenly remembering. 'Our joint account. There was no money like this in it.' She turned her gaze on Oliver. 'Where did he put the money?'

'I'm afraid I don't—'

'Can you call in Helen?'

'Pardon?'

'Please, can you just call in *Helen*.' She had trouble keeping her voice under control. She was struggling with an instinct to get up and run from the room, almost identical to the feeling she had had on the morning of David's death, to begin running and never stop. Outpacing the truth that was thundering behind her, trying to catch her.

Oliver had pressed the office intercom. In another few seconds, Helen opened the door.

Beth was on her feet immediately. 'Helen, do you know about Alan giving an estimate? For work on our house?'

Helen's glance went from Beth to Oliver, and back again. 'Yes,' she said.

'What was it for?'

'A conservatory. One of those big ones, with heating. With . . .' She saw Beth's distraught expression. 'What's the matter?' she asked.

'What did David say to him? Did he say why he wanted it?'

Helen frowned. 'For you.'

'For me.' Beth reached for her chair, found it, and sat down. 'Why hadn't Alan started work? Oliver says that he got the money three or four weeks ago. Why hadn't Alan started?'

'Alan said that David told him to hold fire for a while. That he would ring and say when he could begin,' Helen said. 'When Alan found the grave on Oak Rise last weekend, he was hoping that David would let him go ahead now, with your house, while he was held up.'

Beth had been listening intently. Helen stopped; no one moved. Everything around them seemed to be unnaturally still.

'It's a joke,' Beth said.

'What is?'

'A joke,' Beth repeated.

'The extension?'

'It's just . . . just all completely mad . . .'

'What is?' Helen repeated.

There was a moment of silence. Then, Oliver said, 'Thank you, Helen. Just give us a minute, would you?'

Helen looked down at Beth before walking grudgingly away, turning to look back again at the other woman before she closed the door.

'Beth,' Oliver said. 'Beth.'

'I'm listening.'

He waited a second, got up, and went to the large book cabinet set against the far wall. From this, he took a bottle of brandy, poured some into Beth's barely touched tea, and gave it to her, closing her fingers around the porcelain rim. 'Drink it.'

She did so; drained the cup. Her face, white a few seconds before, began to flush slowly.

'This isn't good,' Oliver said.

She laughed, an exhalation of breath. But didn't speak.

'Would you like me to look into it all?' he asked.

She didn't look up. 'I never saw anyone come to do a valuation,' she muttered, thinking aloud. 'He must have arranged it—met them—while I was out.'

She stood up, smoothing a hand over her hair, over her eyes. Her fingers remained pressed to her cheeks for a second, then her arms dropped by her sides. 'David wanted a lot of money,' she said. 'Nearly twenty thousand—and then the shares. Maybe another five—twenty-five thousand pounds. And where is it? All this money—where *is* it?'

Oliver had come round the side of the desk and was standing very close to her. She thought he had said something, quickly, almost fervently, under his breath. But when he began to speak to her his tone was completely calm and even.

Your financial position will still be quite secure,' he said. 'You own the house outright; your endowment policy will pay the remaining sum due, and more besides.'

His remark seemed barely to have registered with Beth. 'He raised all this money,' she said softly. 'Because he was leaving. He was going abroad. He was leaving, with this money . . .' She stared at Oliver. 'That's right, isn't it?'

'I'm very sorry,' he said.

'He never said anything about this to you?'

'Not a word.'

'He *meant* it,' she whispered. 'He *planned* it. For the last six weeks or so. For the last month.'

'Yes . . .'

She closed her eyes. 'My God, he must have hated me,' she whispered. Her eyelids fluttered open, to stare at Oliver directly. 'I knew things were . . . worse, but . . . not like this,' she said.

Oliver's hand descended on to her shoulder, a weight that seemed to press her into the floor. She bowed her head under its pressure.

'All right. Let me look into it,' he said. 'Let me see what I can do.'

She sighed and got up, smiling very faintly. 'Thank you for being so kind,' she said.

'Not at all,' he murmured. 'I only want what's best for you. I want you to remember that.'

Before she went out, she turned again to him. 'Do you think . . . he was leaving *with* anyone?'

He paused for a fraction of a second before replying. 'I really couldn't say,' he told her.

* * *

When Beth got home, she carried the bags into the kitchen. The early summer evening cast a lovely light into the room: ochre mixed with the sharp green of the season. It was almost subterranean; the shifting colour of underwater light in pools. In another fifteen minutes, she thought, looking around herself, it would be gone.

Disorientation momentarily gripped her.

For a few seconds, she thought that something in the room had already changed. That someone, perhaps, had been there while she was out, disturbing the room in subtle, indefinable ways. The placing of the cups, the breadboard, the rack of knives, looked wrong.

She looked away from them, frowning.

She stood by the table, her hand on its wooden top, with the bags bunched beside her. She tried to reassure herself of being *here,* being alive and solid in this room. Told herself that nothing was altered or changed. She tried to think of herself from above, from outside, as other people thought of her—her height and colouring, her name, her work. The whole identity that belonged to her.

Somewhere in the village, people would be saying *that poor woman at the top of the lane.* They would speculate about the accident. They would be wondering what they could say to her. In the next parish, the vicar would be writing her name in his notebook. *I must go and see Mrs March tomorrow . . .*

And yet she wasn't here at all.

She had gone somewhere that had no rules or boundaries. She was at the fringe of reality, where fears of what might happen mingle with fact. She was unreachable; not *the woman at the top of the lane* at all, no one with so physical a presence. She had become a kind of visual trick, an illusion. Others could see her, but it was only a reflection, an image cast on the places where she used to be.

She turned to look at the bags.

Slowly, she emptied them out. She didn't know what she had been thinking of as she had walked along the street of shops towards Oliver's offices; she had gone automatically, out of habit, into the food hall of the department store and bought these things.

She ran her hands over the packets, and picked one up. It was a ready meal: chicken in a white wine sauce. It was a treat. Something she used to buy. Something David liked. They would joke about her pillaging this store and coming home with these parcels, these sinful opt-outs from cooking.

Treats . . . pleasures.

She shook the pile; other bundles fell across the table. Bread and preserves and soft cheese and fruit. The grapes that David preferred. Seeded. Red.

Putting them in the basket in the store, she had thought that she was doing exactly what she was supposed to do. That it was a positive step, that she was right to award herself something she liked. For comfort. For help. The grapes in a wire basket. And the chicken and the wine and the chocolate. It was what you were required to do, to fend off the feeling of drowning. You were supposed to assert the routines that kept you afloat; cling to them like wreckage. She had read about that a hundred times. Agony advice. Keep kicking, keep swimming.

These little familiar acts of buying and carrying and cooking and walking were designed to help. They would defend against the world; they would ward off the tide that threatened to engulf you. They would work magic, when all else had failed. They were stronger than prayers. All the ordinary customs: the key in the ignition of the car; in the door; the putting away; the lighting of a fire; the glance at the kitchen clock.

She was not hungry at all. She doubted that she ever would be again.

She bent down, lifted what she could in her arms, walked to the far side of the room, and threw everything that she had bought into the rubbish bin.

FIFTEEN

*R*OSIE LAY ON HER SIDE and looked at her room.

Everything was arranged very carefully here; each shelf, each box was meticulously ordered. All her toys had names. Even the desk and the cushion and her pillow had names. It was important to know. She wrote them in a notebook and kept it with her, anxious all the while that she had missed something. While the plastic animals and the stuffed bears and the books kept to their regimented lines, the world stayed upright.

Lost, it would begin to slip.

She knew that she had trouble remembering. Everyone said so, even her teacher, even her friends in class. Even Amy, who was her best friend.

And they were right; even while they spoke, she felt them drift and blur, felt her grasp slacken. Felt she would rather—if only for a second—lie down and sleep.

Downstairs, she could hear her parents' voices. Daddy's voice was deep and slow; Mummy's arched very high and light, fluttering like wings. She liked to hear them speak. It was much better than the silences.

She heard her mother now, coming to the foot of the stairs. It was almost dark; the clock on her bedside table said 20.48.

'Rosie?' Julia called. 'Rosie?'

She was too tired to reply, her head wedged on the pillow, staring at the open window. In the darkening sky, the swallows curved and swooped, crossing her angle of view. She would like to be out there, in the night sky. She would like to be very very small, and climb on their backs. And never come back to the clinging and sticky warmth of the bed that wrapped her so tight. But she knew that the birds were forbidden. Even to *look* at them was forbidden.

'Rosie . . . ?'

'She's asleep,' Oliver muttered. 'Leave her alone.'

'She's *ill*,' Julia replied, her voice as taut as a tightened instrument string. 'I'll just go up and check on her.'

Oliver's voice dropped. 'Leave her. Stop pestering her.'

'I must just see.'

'*I'll* see. Later.'

'No . .'

'You fuss too much. You smother her.'

'Someone should. Do you?'

'She is my daughter as well as yours.'

'You don't understand her.'

'Julia! Come back here. Julia . . . !'

Rosie heard her mother's step, the relentless patter of anxiety, coming towards her, up the long flight of stairs.

She pressed her eyes tight shut.

SIXTEEN

*H*ELEN PRITCHARD COULDN'T GET TO SLEEP THAT NIGHT.

At last, after lying looking into the dark for more than an hour, she got up. The house was cold; it was a quarter past midnight. She filled the kettle and spooned Ovaltine into a mug. At the bottom of the small garden, their house was overlooked by others in the forties-style row behind them. There were no lights at any of the windows.

She perched herself on a stool. It would help if she knew exactly what it was that was nagging at the corner of her mind. She kept going back to Beth March's visit that afternoon. The sense of unease was somehow connected to Oliver. Every time, however, that she began to consider the man, Beth's white face crowded out the picture.

When she had come home, meaning to talk to Alan about it, she'd found that a man called Rhys Owen was already speaking to him in the living room. The building plans for Oak Rise were spread over the coffee table, and the second she put her foot over the threshold Alan asked her for a cup of tea. She'd almost retorted that she was sick of making the stuff. Nevertheless, she took some in to them.

Alan had had a look she recognised only too well; with his arms crossed, he was watching the younger man drawing a light pencil line across the foundation plans. Alan's expression was supremely cynical and rebuffed, like a boy waiting outside the headmaster's office.

He'd taken his tea from her. 'We're a major site, you'll be pleased to know,' he'd said.

'Oh?' She had handed the second cup to Rhys Owen. He responded with a smile that was almost rakish: Clark Gable under a Nineties layer of long hair.

Men these days, she had thought, taking in the choker of beads at his throat, the gypsy-style knotted handkerchief, the dirty green gilet and jacket.

He drank the tea at a pace that would have scalded her throat. 'Marvellous,' he said. 'Brilliant. Thanks very much.'

She had been forced to smile, despite her first impression of him.

'I'm ruining your husband's life,' Rhys had said. 'We've got at least eight graves and a darker area here . . .' He touched the map. 'We have some grave goods. It's a . . .' He had glanced at Alan. 'Well, it *is* a major find. Sorry.'

Alan had put an arm around Helen's shoulder.

'What's up?' Alan was standing now in the doorway, tying the cord of his dressing gown.

The kettle snapped off. 'Do you want a drink?' Helen asked.

'Go on, then. If you're making it.'

She poured the water on top of the warmed milk. They sat down at the kitchen table, opposite one another.

'David March's estimate,' she said.

He put down his cup and made a mime of tearing up a piece of paper. 'I can forget that. Lucky I got this other thing in Yeovil to do, or I'd be laying men off.'

'It was a surprise?' she asked. 'For Beth?'

'So he said.'

'And you weren't to tell her about it?'

'No.'

'But what about when you came on site? She'd know about it then.'

Alan shrugged. 'David said that he'd tell me a date. Sometime after February.'

'And you weren't to say *anything* to Beth?'

He put his head on one side. 'What's all this about?'

She sighed. 'There's some problem over the money. I don't think they can find the money in the bank account. Beth didn't know you'd been involved.'

Alan finished his drink. 'These things are always a mess at first,' he told her. 'They'll unravel it. Sudden death . . . People's affairs are often in a state. Is she Oliver's client?'

'They both are. Were.'

Alan stood up, cleared her cup as well as his own to the draining board, and patted her shoulder. 'Come on up. You'll be dog tired tomorrow.'

'All right,' she said.

She spent a moment rinsing the cups, then dried her hands on a tea towel. Alan had reached the top of the stairs and she stood for a second at the bottom, listening to his footsteps.

She suddenly recalled Oliver pacing backwards and forwards after Beth March had left. Working in Reception, she had glanced back to his office, where the door was ajar.

After a couple of minutes, he'd rung through to her. 'Can you get me Burleigh and Country,' he had said.

She'd put through the call to Beth's building society. He was on for about five minutes. After that, he had left early, telling her that he was going home, stopping at her desk only to confirm the first few appointments in the morning.

He'd been his usual self, then: overbearing, brusque. She tried hard to recall every detail of those few minutes: some detail was scratching at the corner of her mind. She had heard the phone slammed down when the call was finished. She had heard Oliver say, in a tone of muttered exasperation, 'Ringing me.'

She paused now, at the foot of the stairs, an expression of amazement coming to her face.

It wasn't *ringing me* at all. Why would he complain at the building society *ringing* him, when it was the other way around?

She bit her lip, frowning.

Oliver hadn't said 'Ringing me', at all, she realised.

Oliver had said, '*Ruin* me.'

SEVENTEEN

$\mathcal{B}$ETH HAD AN APPOINTMENT on wednesday morning at the building society.

At the branch in the busy high street, she was shown into the manager's office. A woman rose to meet her, petite and dark. 'Angela Naylor,' she said, warmly shaking Beth's hand. 'Do sit down. Can I get you anything? Tea, coffee?'

'No thank you,' Beth replied. She was drowning in a sea of the stuff already; she felt that her system was probably ninety per cent caffeine.

'I'm so very sorry to hear of Mr March's death,' the manager said.

'You knew?'

'Yes. Mr Woods telephoned us.'

'I've come to talk about the second charge on the mortgage.'

'Yes. Just a moment, please.' Angela Naylor called up Beth and David's account on the computer.

Beth leaned forward. 'Mr Woods told you about the forgery?' she asked.

Angela Naylor swiveled her seat back to face her. 'Pardon?'

'My signature on the form, the application.' Beth tried to breathe deeply, slowly. She didn't want to come across as the hysterical wife.

'It was forged. I didn't sign it—I had never seen it until Mr Woods showed me a copy on Tuesday.'

Angela Naylor said nothing for a moment. Seeing her perplexed expression, Beth's heart dropped. 'He didn't tell you,' she said.

'I'm afraid not. No.' The woman was frowning. She glanced back at the screen. 'From this branch, mortgages are handled through our centre in St Albans,' she said, as if thinking aloud. 'They will have the original documents.' Her fingers tapped rapidly on the desk, an unconscious aid to thought. 'But there's nothing on record to show that there was anything untoward at the time of signature. And there wouldn't be, of course . . . No funds would be granted if there was any hint of discrepancy.'

Beth sat back, her eyes ranging over the desk, neatly arranged, in front of her. 'I can't understand why Oliver didn't tell you,' she said. The first faint tendrils of disquiet touched her at the mention of Oliver's name. 'He told me that he would see to it all. Look into it.'

'Hold on a second.' Angela Naylor opened her desk drawer, bringing out a small notepad computer, much the same as David's. 'Let me just call up my notes for yesterday.'

Beth looked away. There were a few seconds of silence.

'Mr Woods told me about your husband's death yesterday afternoon,' Angela said. 'I remember. Yes . . . we've told the insurance company that holds your endowment.'

'The endowment doesn't bother me right now,' Beth said. 'It's not the first part of the mortgage that's concerning me. It's this extra charge. It *isn't* my signature,' she repeated.

'Let's go through this step by step.' Angela Naylor gave her a brief, non-committal smile. 'You say that your husband has negotiated a second charge without your knowledge . . .'

'Yes. Oliver Woods showed me a copy of the form.'

'And what was your solicitor's reaction to your claim?'

'He simply told me that he would look into it. That it was a very serious matter.'

'It is.' Angela Naylor seemed to be assessing Beth; her attention was fixed on her acutely. 'But did he say in what circumstances he received the form? Was it signed in his presence?'

'I'm sorry . . . why? What difference does that make?'

'A solicitor,' Angela replied, 'is meant to have both parties in front of him when they sign. So that he can truthfully say that both are aware of the transaction. That's the whole point of the witness.'

Beth thought back to her interview with Oliver. 'He said that the charge had raised another eighteen thousand . . . that David had come to him with the form.' She raised her hand to her face, and with two straight fingers pressed the midway point between her eyes, concentrating. 'No,' she corrected herself, '*I* said that. I said, "David came to you with this form . . ."'

'And what did Mr Woods say?'

'He just confirmed it. He said that my position probably wasn't as bad as it seemed. That the endowment would probably cover more than the equity. But that isn't the point.' She looked at Angela Naylor, cold certainty pouring into her mind that Oliver had not been quite honest with her. 'Is it?'

'Not quite,' Angela agreed. 'The real point is that Mr Woods should have made sure that the signature was genuinely yours. He really shouldn't have witnessed without you actually being in the office.' She leaned back, crossing her hands on her lap, intertwining the fingers. 'However, it does occasionally happen, if we're being realistic,' she continued. 'Though strictly it isn't legal.'

Beth was trying to take it all in. 'He must have done that,' she said. 'David must have told him that I was happy about it.' Her eyes filled with tears abruptly; she lowered her head and put her hand to her mouth before continuing. 'A white lie,' she murmured. 'A little white lie. *My God.* That I had signed at home.'

'Perhaps. But . . .' The manager smiled hesitantly. 'Forgive me. But why should your husband say that?'

Beth did not smile in return. 'David was leaving the country when he was killed,' she replied softly. 'I knew nothing about it. Just as I knew nothing about him cashing in his trust fund or taking out this extra loan.'

'Oh . . . I see.' Angela Naylor's raised eyebrows threatened to climb into her hairline. 'Do you mean, then, that you don't have access to the advance?'

'Pardon?'

'You don't know where the money is that we advanced to Mr March for the house extension?'

'No,' Beth told her. 'I haven't a clue. And there's no work been done on the house. I don't think David ever intended there to be.'

Angela Naylor's finger strayed back to the computer. She tapped the keyboard for a while, then turned the screen back to Beth, so that she could see.

'This is a current statement of your joint account,' she said. The bottom figure hovered dangerously close to being overdrawn.

'The money isn't there,' Beth said. 'I've already checked. It never went in there.' She drew her chair closer to the desk, so that she could lean on it. She felt as if her flesh was turning to water; she could have happily laid her head on the fake-leather trim and slept, she was so tired. 'That's the reason I came to see you,' she said. 'I want to know if David had another account. I want to know where the money is.'

'I see.' The manager considered this a moment. 'Is the will in probate?'

Beth took a deep breath. 'No. Mr Woods is the executor.'

The two women faced each other, both turning over the problem of Oliver Woods in their minds.

After a few seconds, Angela Naylor unexpectedly placed her hand firmly over Beth's. 'At the risk of sounding like someone else you know,' she said. 'May I look into this for you?'

EIGHTEEN

$\mathscr{O}$H MY,' SAID ALISON WARLEY. 'This is interesting. *Very* interesting.'

She and Rhys were at the site of the first two uncovered graves on Oak Rise. The first grave, that Alan Pritchard had found, was a male. The second, female. They lay side by side in the chalk, the team uncovering them inch by slow inch.

Thirteen hundred years before, the couple had been laid in the ground on their backs, arms crossed over the pelvis, legs slightly flexed. The Saxons were tall; the man in the grave was six foot one, the woman barely an inch shorter. A knife had already been recovered from close to the man's head; but this was not what Alison found so interesting at the moment. What was fascinating her was the back of the skull, revealed by scraping and brushing just five minutes before.

'Hell,' said Alison. 'Unbelievable.'

The back of the head showed an enormous fracture, the cranial plates shattered. The two top vertebrae closest to the skull were fragmented, but lodged in the next was a large piece of shaped flint, with traces of brown linear marks at one end. The soil next to it bore the mark of faint scrolling, a shadow of curled thread. The shaft of an axe had been broken off close to the hilt, and the man had been put in the ground with the flint and the top of the wooden stake, with its corded leather binding, still protruding from the back of his neck.

'Look here,' Alison said to Rhys.

She was pointing to the arm crossed over the man's stomach. That, too, showed signs of force, broken at the elbow.

He crouched down in front of the first find, inspecting the revealed axe flint, his face an inch from the soil. 'And what about the Princess?' He had nicknamed her after finding her burial goods. The murdered man's companion had been tall and broad-shouldered, probably in her thirties. She had worn a necklace of three glass beads, a circular silver pendant with a glass setting, and two punched silver discs that might have fastened cloth around her shoulders.

'No signs of violence,' Alison told him. 'She's a lovely lot of bones, she really is. Look at those teeth. I want to do a dental decay analysis on this find, and osteoarthritis. And squatting facets.'

Rhys looked up at her. 'You say the loveliest things.' He pointed at his own position. 'Bet you've got 'em too. Show us your ankle facets, Alison.'

He stood up, grinning. 'Related, our two nice Amazons?'

'They are of an age,' she replied.

Rhys ran a hand through his hair. 'I wonder who killed him,' he murmured, thinking aloud. 'I wonder if *she* did.' Seeing Alison's expression, he went on. 'If this was a territorial battle, there would most likely be other male burials with similar injuries. Right? Wrong. The third grave is a male adolescent and the fourth a child, and the fifth another female—and this is not, except for the Princess, a royal inhumation. This man wasn't a king. She's at least the wife of a tribal leader, if not royal line herself. Who's this git she's next to, then? Less than half a metre between them. What's she doing planted next to this commoner? What was the relationship?'

Alison frowned. 'If there had been disgrace, it's most likely they wouldn't have rated a formal burial like this,' she said.

He crossed his arms, sighing. 'There's your mystery, then. They never even got the axe out of the poor bloke's head.'

He stared away, across the fields.

'So,' he said to himself. 'It's true, then. What they always say.'
Alison paused, glancing up at him.
'What?' she asked.
He smiled. 'The crime rates in these little villages is frightening.'

NINETEEN

$\mathcal{T}$HURSDAY EVENING, BETH WENT TO CHURCH.

It was not something she particularly wanted to do, but the vicar had—in that soothingly quiet way of his that stuck so hard in her throat—told her that it might *orientate* her for the service on the Friday. Perhaps he was also hoping that it would comfort her. She really had no idea. She obliged, at six thirty that evening, out of wry curiosity. She had not set foot in the place for over a year.

It was a plain, low building, hedged with yews, and leading directly out on to the water meadows beyond. A mixture of sandstone and slate and flint, it was solid-looking in the last of the sun.

She opened the door and stepped into the cold of the aisle. She walked towards the altar and stopped by the choir stalls. The vicar had removed both altar rail and pews, but by a miracle the choir stalls had been preserved. She sat down wearily in the nearest.

There were flowers, neatly arranged, by the pulpit; early miniature white dahlias, looking very pale and fragile. Her eyes strayed to the stained-glass window.

There, in cobalt blue and ice white splendour, was Christ as the Shepherd of His Sheep, the figure looking rather glamorous in a swathe of white linen and a mass of pre-Raphaelite hair, and the sheep appearing rigid, in a country setting that mimicked the view beyond the church door. Christ in the English countryside, she thought.

She looked down to the space in front of the altar; there were two black trestles there, spaced about five feet apart. For a second, she was mystified as to their purpose; then she realised, with a flood of feeling, that this was to take David's coffin in the morning.

She stood up and walked to them, deliberately stepping between them and looking from side to side. Glancing down at the floor, she saw fresh scratches on the stone, and realised that one of the supports had been moved—dragged, or kicked, to its unaligned position. She pulled it back into place, wondering vaguely at Hurrold's carelessness. Left like that, they would never have supported the coffin properly.

But the slippery surface of the painted wood chilled her blood, and she straightened, and moved away. It was like breaking a magic circle; touching the dead.

Beth had felt nothing but anger in the last two days, since she had seen Oliver. Silent disbelief had metamorphosised into rage.

In the morning, in this place, she was burying a man she didn't know; someone she had imagined herself close to, but who had become a total stranger. She had thought David to be a dispassionate, controlled man; now, that image was as thin and breakable as glass.

She had convinced herself that he must have been leaving her for someone else. There seemed to be no point in ignoring the obvious any longer. In the last couple of years, they had drifted into that parallel state of companionship that had more silence than sound. Sometimes, if he had spoken, she had set her face, trying not to show her impatience. His very even tone, the long pauses between his words, had come to irritate her to an irrational and exaggerated degree—something that she knew was not right. Yet it had not seemed worth destroying this comfortable ship in which they languished together. For what? For months of change in order to lead a very similar life. She had occasionally wondered what she might do if she met someone. If David met someone. And she had dismissed it as so unlikely . . .

The irony of that struck her now, and she pulled an agonised face in the shadows of the church.

She had gone through his things a second time, and the sense that he was preparing himself for someone else's company had seemed, on another inspection, to hit her between the eyes. She had gone through his wardrobes too, and found most of his oldest clothes, that he always wore in the evenings and at weekends, abandoned. Like sloughing off an old skin.

Last night, in the early hours of the morning, she had given up trying to sleep, got out of bed, and got dressed.

Alone and dry-eyed, she had cleared everything that had belonged to David into the study: the attic room on the converted third floor of the house. It had originally been the grain storeroom, and had windows that opened on to a small balcony. She had envied David this room, but now she couldn't wait to lock the door on it and all it contained.

The removal had taken her over two hours. She had even removed copies of credit-card slips that he had signed from the memo board in the kitchen; she had taken his magazines from the bedside table. She went through the house eradicating him, and following behind with a bucket of hot water and cleaning fluid and a sponge, trying to take even the smell of him away.

It was the sense of rejection that hurt the most. The feeling of exclusion. She felt so humiliated at having been lied to. He must, for all his dryness, have found it funny—even if only marginally funny—from time to time, for her to be so utterly in the dark. He must have smiled occasionally to himself at the ease of his deception. At her blindness.

She turned on her heel now, and walked swiftly to the church door.

God knew how she would go through with this in the morning. The vicar had asked her what hymns and readings David liked, and she hadn't known. She couldn't even venture an opinion. Her confidence that she could choose on his behalf was completely destroyed. They had settled on the most banal things: the twenty-first Psalm, and 'Abide with Me', and the Bible reading about *many mansions*.

'That will be all right,' she had told the vicar. 'Just have that . . . it'll do. It'll be OK.'

He must have been astounded at her lack of visible grief, at her carelessness. But she had been longing for him to leave as soon as possible; she had wanted to stop discussing the whole bloody subject. In fact, she had almost bundled the man out of her house.

The undertaker had had to ring her to remind her about the flowers. The florist who was organising the funeral with him had remarked that there seemed to be no bouquet from her. He had asked, in that businesslike voice of his, if he could place an order on her behalf. But she—who supposedly had such green fingers—couldn't think of a single bloom that she liked.

'Shall I say roses?' he had urged. 'Roses are very appropriate, I find.'

'All right,' she had said.

'And the colour?'

'Anything.'

'Perhaps . . . white? Or red?'

'I don't know. Red. Have red.'

They probably all thought she was heartless. Or mad. Or both.

She hadn't even anything to wear. No dark dress or suit. She hadn't searched through her own clothes, but she knew it without looking. She lived in jeans and overwashed shirts. She stopped now, her hand on the latch of the heavy wooden door, and pressed her head against the cold metal, half smiling, half grimacing.

'I ought to go and buy something,' she murmured.

She imagined herself going into Marks & Spencer when it opened in the morning. Taking down a black jacket and skirt that she would never wear again; writing the cheque.

Christ God, if only tomorrow were over, she thought.

If only it were a month, a year from now.

As she closed the church door, she looked up the narrow village street. Along the top of the low churchyard wall came an intermittent flash of a skipping child. Beth watched; at the gate, the child stopped and bent down.

'Hello, Rosie.'

Rosie glanced up, a grin suddenly on her face.

Beth walked up the path. 'What are you doing?'

'Hiding.'

Beth took her hand. 'And why is that?'

Rosie pulled a face. 'She's been talking ages and ages.'

Beth looked to her left. Julia was about a hundred yards away. She was standing by the open window of a house whose wall was right on the lane edge. Beth knew that it belonged to an elderly couple, Frank and Elly Mayhew. She often called on them to keep the garden tidy, since Frank, in his retirement, had fallen prey to arthritis. She liked them; although Elly was an inveterate talker who tended to repeat the last word in your own sentence in an unconscious mimicking fashion.

As she and Rosie got close to the cottage, whatever conversation had been going on with such intensity dried up; the two women looked at her as if expecting her to do something irrational, wild or dangerous.

'I don't like waiting,' Rosie said to Beth. 'When we were in the car. We just looked at the water. It was hours. I was looking for the different birds. But we just came back again.'

'Birds?' asked Beth, amused, looking down into her upturned face.

'There are lots; they can live on the sea. Andrew in our class says. I wanted to see them.'

Beth squeezed the small hand. 'Well, another day.' She was not paying attention; she was watching the faces of the two women as she got closer to them. As she reached the open window, Elly said nothing at all; Julia merely bit the edge of her lip. A bright lime scarf was wound around her throat; she was wearing a thick, sandy-coloured foundation and eye-shadow, and a violent pink lipstick. But it looked like caricature; she was still a deathly colour.

'You look awful,' Beth said. 'Are you OK?' She leaned forward to kiss Julia's cheek.

Julia put her arms around her. 'Forgive me,' she whispered into Beth's hair.

'For what?'

'For not coming to see you.'

Beth shook her head. 'I want to be on my own,' she replied. 'I've been in the garden working.'

'I've seen you. From the top windows.'

'There's enough people around. The vicar. Alan. He came with someone from the site.'

'Why?'

'They were on their way somewhere. He called in to bring me some flowers from Helen. And a cake. I just find myself being very rude.' She grimaced guiltily. 'Even to Alan.'

The van had arrived yesterday lunchtime, as she dug the bed she was tending for a crop of sweet peas. She had gone out to meet it, wiping her hands on her trousers.

'What are you doing?' Alan had asked.

She shrugged. 'The garden.'

'You ought to rest,' he had said.

She had given him a grim smile. 'I'd go mad,' she told him. 'I can breathe outside.'

She had noticed a man sitting in the cab, and recognised him as the same person that she had spoken to at Oak Rise. He had raised a hand, leaning forward to look at her, and given an expression just short of a smile.

Beth now raised a hand to her eyes. 'I wish everyone would stop,' she said. 'I wish that this . . . *thing* would . . . It's so unreal. Bizarre.' She dropped her hand, tracing the lines in her palm with an index finger.

Rosie was hopping around them both, kicking up first one heel and then the other, slapping each hand against the soles of her feet. 'Look,' she said. 'This is dancing. It's German. You've got to do this . . . watch me. Watch.'

Elly had disappeared from the window, but now came out from the side of the house. She was wearing an apron, with a tea towel tucked rakishly into the waistband. Her hair was tightly permed and bright yellow, and, beneath it, her face was working overtime on a series of distortions. Beth saw, with a pang, that she was trying not to cry.

'Oh, I'm that upset for you,' she said.

'It's all right, Elly.'

She clasped Beth's hand between her own. 'Poor Mr March. We haven't talked of nothing else. What an event.'

Beth smiled half-heartedly. Elly categorised everything in the village as an event: the jumble sales, the fête, the coffee mornings, the occasional accident, the newspaper boy not delivering the evening paper, a cat digging up their daffodil bulbs. All *events*.

Beth tried not to watch Elly's hands tying and retying the tea towel. Orange and brown sixties' swirls on a yellow background.

'I must go,' Julia said abruptly, taking Rosie from Beth's side. 'I'll . . . I'm sorry, I must see Rosie to bed. To tea. I'm sorry. I'll see you in the morning, Beth.'

Beth caught her arm as she was turning. 'Julia, you haven't got anything I could borrow?' she asked, desperately embarrassed. 'To wear? I haven't got anything dark. I haven't even got a skirt.'

'Skirt. Oh dear,' Elly said, sympathetically.

For a moment, Beth thought that Julia hadn't heard her properly. The other woman's eyes ranged over her.

'Mummy,' urged Rosie, bored. 'Come on.'

'Tomorrow,' Beth repeated. 'It doesn't have to fit. I can leave the zipper down a bit, or pin it.' Julia was taller and thinner than she was.

'Mummy . . .'

Julia glanced from her friend to her child; she allowed herself to be dragged a pace or two backwards by Rosie. Mother and child stumbled for a moment on the road, Rosie's feet scrabbling on the asphalt, her body leaning impatiently at a forty-five degree angle.

'I'll come round,' Julia said.

'Thanks.'

Elly was pulling Beth's arm, trying to guide her towards her own front door.

'I'm sorry,' Julia repeated. 'Rosie's been poorly again today, and you can see how agitated she is . . .'

'It's all right,' Beth said. 'You go. I'll see you in the morning.'

Elly began to stroke Beth's sleeve, murmuring, 'Morning, morning.'

The last glimpse that she had of Julia was of her lifting Rosie into her arms, turning her face in to her daughter's shoulder.

TWENTY

*I*T WAS, HOWEVER, Helen Pritchard and not Julia who knocked on Beth's door on the morning of the funeral.

She stood on the doorstep for two or three minutes, listening to an unbroken silence, and then glanced at her watch. It was a quarter to nine, and the service was at ten thirty.

Inside the stone porch, on one of the ledges, was a small brown paper package with Beth's name printed across it. It had obviously been hand delivered, and was taped tightly. Helen looked at it for a moment, then lifted it. It felt like cloth; something light. She put it down again, puzzled.

After another few moments, she edged towards the window to the right of the door. It was a large sash window and the curtains were open. She cupped her hand against the glass and looked in.

She could see blankets on the couch and, curled comfortably in their obviously still warm centre, was Chaos. The large tabby cat was watching her with eyes like two green points of light, its tail twitching. A book lay open and face-down on the side table, next to an empty glass. The table lamp was still on, an ineffectual pool in the light of day.

Helen tapped lightly on the window. There was no response. She looked back at the doorstep, where she had put the two bags she'd been carrying.

'Hell,' she murmured. 'What's she doing?'

For a second, she fought down a little frisson of panic; it occurred to her that Beth might be lying unconscious—or worse—somewhere in the house, that she had been unable to face the coming day and had taken the quickest course away from it. Then she shook her head slightly, to rid herself of the idea.

She walked past the door and took the narrow path up the left hand side of the house. She reached the brick patio, and crossed it to the kitchen door. To her surprise, she saw Beth at once, standing at the sink, leaning forward on to it. The door itself was slightly open.

'Beth,' she called. 'Beth?' She went in.

Beth didn't turn her head. Helen saw that the younger woman was a frighteningly greyish colour, her knuckles white where she was gripping the edge of the work surface, her eyes fixed.

'Beth! What is it?'

Beth's eyes flickered. One hand came up and fluttered over her chest.

'Beth, sit down . . .'

Helen stood at her side, listening to the gasps for breath. Beth's skin was clammy, her hands cold.

'Is there a pain?'

'No, I . . .'

'Tightness?'

'No, no . . .' Two twin spots of colour unnaturally pricked Beth's face, just below each eye.

'Beth, come along and sit down. Just this chair. Just here.'

At last, Beth did as she was told. Helen pulled a chair next to her, and massaged her hands between her own. 'I'll call your doctor.'

'No. I'll be OK.'

The colour was coming back more strongly now. To Helen's dismay, she could smell whisky on the other woman's breath, sour and stale. Beth's hair was tousled, her clothes crumpled. Helen wondered how much Beth had drunk during the night and how much sleep she finally got. Dismay washed over her as she thought of Beth alone in the house, drinking, and trying to read. Sleeping downstairs. The light on all night. Those bloody awful empty three o'clock and four o'clock hours.

'What happened?' Helen asked.

Beth began to smile faintly; a little reflex tic of embarrassment. 'I don't really know,' she said. 'I came into the kitchen, and I was looking out . . .' She placed her hand flat on her chest, just below the depression at the base of her throat. 'It felt exactly as though my heart *stopped*,' she said. 'The weirdest, the strangest thing . . . just *stopped*. My head felt . . . my ears were ringing, like air compression, you know? In an aircraft? I heard you knock on the door . . . and then—' She banged her hand against herself. 'It came back. *Bang-bang-bang-bang*. Like that. Like being hit in the chest.'

Helen had continued stroking Beth's other hand. 'Palpitations,' she said. 'Stress.'

'That's what it is? My *God*. That's what people are having when they talk about heart flutters? *Christ*.'

'I'm sure that's exactly what it is. It's hardly surprising.'

'I've never had a thing like it. Never.'

'Let me call your GP.'

Beth caught her hand tightly as Helen got up. 'Don't do that,' she said. 'It's all right now. It feels perfectly all right. Really.'

'But—'

'Please don't bring people in here.'

Helen heard the fear in Beth's voice; she leaned down and pressed her own face to Beth's in an expression of sympathy. 'Then let me make you breakfast.'

'I couldn't,' Beth said. She leaned her arm on the table and rested her head, covering her eyes with her hand. 'I'll be sick, Helen.'

'Rubbish. Toast and weak tea, absolute minimum,' Helen told her. She looked around for the kettle, cups and saucers. 'And while I'm doing it, you'll go right upstairs and shower. I'll call you when it's ready.'

'I'll just get a wash.'

Helen took her to the door of the room by her hand, a mother leading a child. 'Shower, and wash your hair,' she said. 'Put on your face. And find some nice perfume. And brush your teeth. And get *dressed*.'

Beth gave her the merest ghost of a smile.

She took the first step of the stairs.

The funeral cars drew up outside the house at twenty-five past ten.

There were four additional people in Beth's house by then: Helen and Alan, Julia and Oliver. While Beth had been dressing, Helen had tidied the room, whisking away the blankets, opening the windows so that it was flooded with fresh air. She had cut a bunch of roses from the garden, a shade of deep reddish apricot, that now blazed on the table in front of the open sash window. She had laid a tray with a white cloth, and sherry, and fingers of Madeira cake. She had polished the tables, the sills and the frames of the paintings. When Beth came down she stood for a moment in the doorway, looking around her.

Julia had arrived with Oliver at ten. Beth went to open the door, wearing the dark blue skirt that had been in the package on the doorstep. Helen had ironed it, but it hung far too low, almost at Beth's ankles. 'It doesn't matter,' Beth had said, as Helen fussed to smooth it down.

She had put a white cotton sweater over the skirt, and found a navy and white scarf. She felt hugely detached, almost comical: a clown in someone else's clothes. She had found a pair of black patent shoes that she dimly recalled had been bought for a Christmas dinner two years ago and never worn since. They gleamed oddly on her feet, with their rigid black fabric bows across the toes. She had felt all morning increasingly stupid and tired, the victim of some pointless practical joke.

Julia had kissed her as she came in; Oliver too. He smelled of drink—what, she couldn't be sure—and she recoiled a little before remembering that she probably smelled the same. Whisky half obscured by soap. She looked into his pale blue, almost colourless eyes and wondered, for a split second, if *he* had lied to her, like David. He had smiled at her, and the feeling drained through and out of her. She had to trust *someone*. Have a rock in this raging sea.

'Come in,' she had said.

Helen was standing with the tray. They each took a glass and drank silently. Beth sat down in the armchair.

'At least it's dry,' Oliver had said.

No one commented.

'Nothing more depressing than rain on a day like this,' he added.

The doorbell rang again.

It was Alan, looking as uncomfortable as Beth in a dark suit that was far too small for him. He walked over to Beth and squeezed her hard rather than kissing her.

'Isn't that what they call a quart into a pint pot?' she had asked.

He'd laughed. 'Gallon,' he had said, twitching the waistband of the trousers with a guilty look.

There was an excruciating moment of silence.

Looking at Julia, Beth had thought she looked painstakingly lovely. She had obviously been to the hairdressers; her suit was expensive, her nail lacquer and lipstick matched. She had been very careful, Beth thought. It was nice of her. Oliver, at her side, looked ill by comparison.

Helen saw the funeral cars first.

She stepped back from the window, saying, 'They're here.'

Everyone stood up; Beth saw Mr Hurrold come through the gate, propping it open with a stone from the flower border. Beyond, the black car made a purring sound, like a large black cat, sleek coat shining in the sun. There were her red roses, in a voluptuous spray of gypsophila and evergreen. Beth smiled at the faces around her. 'It seems ridiculous,' she said. 'It's only a hundred yards to the church. Can't we walk?'

Everyone looked at each other.

Oliver stepped forward. 'I'll sit with you in the car,' he said. Then he corrected himself. 'We'll both sit with you.'

The vicar was waiting by the lych-gate of the church as the cars pulled up. Beth and Julia and Oliver got out, and watched as the pall bearers took David's coffin on their shoulders. There was an agonising moment as one of them struggled to balance; the roses on the coffin dipped.

'Take my arm,' Oliver said.

Beth looked at him, grateful.

They followed the vicar into the dark porchway, and through the door itself. On the threshold, Beth stopped, amazed to see that the small church was almost full. The villagers turned their sympathetic faces.

She recognised people whose gardens she had worked on, linking their faces to borders and colours, to walls, to scents, to shapes. She saw that someone had been in decorating the church with a mass of flowers, a contrast to the evening before, a compliment to her own work, a link of understanding.

'Oh, thank you,' she whispered.

The choir was the Choral Society from Stourminster; Beth turned her head to look at them. They were singing the *Sanctus* from Fauré's Requiem, one of the few classical pieces that Beth knew, because David often played it. Someone must have told them, although it had not been Beth. She wondered who would have known him well enough to have picked this piece. The only time he really played it was on the tape deck when he was driving.

Walking to the front, she ached inwardly at this seemingly irrelevant fact; a piece of knowledge, uniquely David, that was no use any more.

Julia leaned forward and whispered in her ear as she approached the first pew. 'Elly asked them to come,' she said, meaning the choir.

Beth recognised a few of their faces; she wondered if she were supposed to smile. She sat down, alone, with Julia and Oliver taking their places behind.

She thought suddenly of Rosie, wondering if she were at school. Rosie with her hand in the glass biscuit barrel, balancing a cup of tea warily on her lap while Beth had spoken to Julia on Monday. Rosie's blonde head last night by the church.

The vicar got to his feet.

'The first hymn . . .'

She and David had been to a funeral only last year. It was someone that David had been to college with, someone who had died of a heart attack in his early forties. The funeral had been at the fringes of the New Forest, in a lovely village, in the same church where the couple had been married. Tragic and terrible. His wife, and three daughters barely in their teens next to her.

She closed the hymn book and sat down.

The vicar was on his feet; he looked at her with a faint smile of encouragement.

'It is always shocking when someone of David's age . . .'

The rose bouquet was not quite straight on the coffin. Her fingers itched to get up and put it right.

'. . . is taken from us so suddenly . . .'

She looked at the choir. The woman nearest to her was gazing at her with large, thyroid-looking eyes of watering blue. Beth knew her, but couldn't place her. She had an image of the woman being behind a counter, and giving Beth something. She began to run through the places it might be: the doctor's, the bank, the library . . .

'There is always the question in our minds . . .'

Beth closed her eyes. A knot was gathering in her chest, tying itself tightly. She began to breathe through her mouth, and, as she parted her lips, abruptly the image of David's car, flipping sideways, with one wing crushed, the glass shattering from the windscreen, marched wholesale into her mind.

Rosie had asked her if David had died.

She had told her, *Yes, David* . . .

With that, the thought of Rosie connected with David's death, a shock passed through her. She sat up, opening her eyes, the knot over her heart suddenly strangling her, the blood thundering at once in her throat.

Oh God. GOD . . .

All the things he had put on the dashboard. The passport and the ticket, for the ferry at Poole. Those things flying in concert with the rolling and crashing of the car. The ticket for a ferry that left the quay and threaded past the islanded coastline. She and David had taken Rosie to Brownsea once, to see the birds. Choppy brown-blue sea. The ferry . . .

'*We just looked at the water. It was hours . . . we just came back again.*'

When?

Monday.

She tried to think of what Rosie had said in the kitchen on Monday, in those few seconds before Julia came in. Rosie had run through the hall, calling Beth's name, smiling, and, at the sink, had reached up to the glass biscuit jar—the glass jar, and Beth filling the kettle, looking at her over her shoulder, numbed and disbelieving, convinced she was about to find it had been some mistake, some error, half listening, half turning the hours over in her head, the image of the shattered car, and Rosie said . . .

Rosie said . . .

'It was ages and ages. We waited ages.'

And yesterday, near Elly's house.

'We just looked at the water . . . we just came back again.'

They looked at the water. Somewhere that Rosie thought Beth recognised. The sea at Poole, by the ferry.

'It was hours . . . but we just came back again.'

On Monday. Waited on the dock, for a long time.

For a car that never came.

David's car.

Beth got to her feet.

The church aisle was receding and free-floating; the faces from the choir mere specks of white. Only the lopsided roses loomed huge, broadening obscenely as her gaze dragged over them. She saw the vicar put out one hand, palm down. Beth turned and looked at Julia.

The other woman had her head down, her arm crossed over her stomach.

We waited.

Forgive me.

Julia on Monday. Ashen, in the doorway of the kitchen. Julia, wearing a brand new outfit for a routine hospital visit. Julia, weeping in the mortuary chapel. Julia, unable to visit since the day of David's death—unable, even, to face her that morning. Julia, crying openly now. So desperate and dependent, so unhappy at home. And the one who had known about the *Sanctus* Requiem . . . because she had heard David playing it, alongside him in the car . . .

Yesterday . . . *forgive me.*

Julia looked up. Oliver leaned forward, one arm on the back of Beth's abandoned pew, opening his mouth to say something. At the back of the church several people rose; one stepped out into the aisle. Voices murmured in surprise. The vicar had stopped speaking and she heard him walk forward, his shoes tapping against the uncovered stone.

'It was you,' Beth said.

Julia's hand dropped from her body.

'My God, it *was* you,' Beth repeated.

Yesterday.

Forgive me.

Beth looked at Oliver, and saw exactly the same dreadful expression as Julia's; nothing like guilt, more like fear.

'All this,' Beth said.

She meant that all this—the accident, the money—all this had been for Julia. And then, the other meaning hit her. All this *today*, the funeral, was not for her at all, but for Julia. Julia was the bereaved here, the lover, the loved. *Dearly beloved husband of . . .*

She was not the wife at all. She was in the wrong place, playing the wrong part. This was nothing to do with her at all.

'Mrs March . . .' the vicar said.

'Beth.' Oliver's voice. Almost a command.

She put down her hymn book on the edge of the pew.

By the time she came out of the church and into the sunlight, she was running.

TWENTY-ONE

*R*HYS OWEN WAS KNEELING at the farthest corner of Alan Pritchard's field. He had been working on this area for the last three hours, and a persistent sharp pain in the centre of his back was begging him to stop. It was almost eleven o'clock.

Sighing, he leaned back on his heels.

The geophysics survey had shown a darker area here, close to the hawthorn hedge. When the topsoil had been taken off, they could see that it was a deeper burial than the others, set apart from the row. Whereas the others were set into the chalk very shallowly—one was only four inches below the surface—this was nearly a foot lower. And it was not due to the distribution of the soil level, or the beginning of the slope of the hill. It had actually been dug deep.

Rhys sat back with a grunting sigh, scratching his head. 'Curiouser and curiouser,' he said to himself.

The remains were of a male. The body had been bundled into the ground, into a space that was more of a pit than a grave. There had been no ceremonial laying-out here. The legs were drawn up to the chest and the body was on its side, the arms curled peculiarly, the hands turned inwards. Of the upper leg—the left—the knee had been brought up almost level with the hip, the thigh lying at right-angles, and the foot was turned like the hands, twisted to one side.

This man had been literally crammed into the ground.

There were no grave goods. No wood lining, no stone pillow, no flint mounds at head or feet; nothing that might have held grave markers, or been the basis of a ritual barrow or mound. No one had wanted to know where he was. He was outcast in death from his community, with his face turned away from the rising sun that held the promise of the afterlife. He faced the ignominious cold eternity of the north.

The body was almost completely revealed now. The teeth were worn down; there were signs of osteoarthritis in the shoulders. He was a man who had survived the peak rates of death of his time, the accidents and battles of youth, and come through into old age unscathed. He ought to have been respected and honoured. He ought to have been lying next to the Princess.

Rhys smiled to himself. If he weren't very careful, he could construct a veritable Peyton Place from this site: elders lobbed over the cemetery wall while young studs were buried in state next to their monarchs. He whistled contentedly between his teeth.

Getting up from his crouching position at the side of the grave was not an easy process. His back momentarily locked and groaned; his forearms ached.

The rest of the crew were taking their break in the various vans and cars parked near the entrance; walking fast, Rhys waved at them as he passed. Aesculapius was curled on the driver's seat of the Citroën, watching him with one ear pricked expectantly.

'All right,' he said, slapping his leg.

The dog was out of the open door of the car in two seconds, leaping around him with yaps of delirious delight, only pausing to take nips out of the bottom of his nearer trouser leg. 'Get off,' he said. 'These are decent cords.' He picked up a stone and threw it towards the road. 'Get down there.'

He walked out into the lane and stopped, looking up and down. He had no real wish to go into the village, pretty as it was. He was afraid of getting into some long-winded conversation with one of the villagers who seemed to be forever hovering in wait, furthering the pruning on already savagely cut-back roses or trimming invisible leaves off hedges.

He shook his head slightly and turned right, towards the empty lanes and fields. The terrier was nosing in the hedge about fifty yards ahead of him. There was a verge on both sides of the lane about three feet wide, and a ditch under each hedgerow. Aesculapius was in one of these, only identifiable by his wagging white stump of a tail.

Abruptly, there was a roaring sound at Rhys's back. He stopped and turned, knowing at once that it was a car, but intrigued at the speed. Only as it came over the crest of the hill and began pelting down in his direction, however, did he fully realise the wild rate that it was doing.

'Ace!' he shouted. 'Aesculapius!'

The terrier's head appeared; he came out from the ditch and trotted into the road.

Rhys began to run.

The van must be doing over sixty, he thought. On a little road like this. He reached into his pocket as he went, trying to find the piece of thin rope that occasionally served as a lead.

'Stay!' he called.

The dog usually obeyed, but it was standing close to the verge now, watching him, trying to determine if this were a game. Aesculapius had no road sense at all; he spent most of time on farmland, or else firmly shut in the van at Rhys's side. Where Rhys lived was a courtyard of houses, with no traffic passing in front of the door.

He heard the van brake—a momentary squeal of tyres—and glanced back: it was almost on them. He glimpsed a female face behind the windscreen. Then the brakes went on again.

Aesculapius had run into the centre of the road. Looking back to the dog, Rhys cursed loudly. The van braked again and swung left to avoid the terrier, bouncing up on to the verge, through the waist-high fringe of cow parsley with its spreading white crowns. At the last moment before hitting the ditch, the driver corrected and straightened. The dog ran backwards, then, frightened, to its left. Straight into the altering line of the van.

Rhys couldn't see the impact. He saw the van stop, heard a bump.

The front wheels dug into the ground and the woman's head snapped forward, her hands flying up for a second, off the wheel and in front of her face. Then the engine cut out.

'Ace . . . Ace . . .'

Rhys ran forward. He only looked once at the driver, then stepped in front of the van's bonnet. Aesculapius was in the left-hand ditch, on his side, motionless.

He heard the van's door open.

'Christ! You've bloody well killed him,' he said. He knelt down by the dog, feeling its body. The terrier lay loose and warm in the untouched grass, its body on a slope at the ditch's side. But it was still breathing.

Rhys looked up at the woman, who had come round the side of the bonnet to stand behind him. 'What the hell kind of speed were you doing?' he demanded. The woman's face was completely white, her eyes red-rimmed. She was visibly shaking.

He stood up, torn between her and the terrier, between a feeling of fury at her carelessness and pity at the expression on her face.

'Have you got a mobile?' he asked.

'A—what?'

'Mobile. *Mobile phone.*'

'Oh.' She looked around her, as if she expected to find it lying somewhere on the ground. 'No. I haven't.'

'A blanket? A rug?'

'I—'

'In the van. Have you got a rug in the van?'

She stared at him as if she were trying to decipher a foreign language. 'I've got some sacking,' she said.

'Right. I'm taking him to the vet. If you get me the sacking, I'll wrap him in it.'

'Yes,' she said. But she didn't move.

Exasperated, he wrenched open the driver's door of the van, looked in the back and found the pile of sacking almost immediately. He saw that there were shrubs in there, small ones, that had probably been in their black plastic tubs until a minute ago. Now, the back of the van was littered with soil.

'Look,' he said, kneeling down by the dog and talking to the driver over his shoulder, 'can you take me into Stourminster?'

She nodded.

'You know Ware Walk, the vet on the corner? By the pedestrian crossing?'

She gave him a totally blank look. He had Aesculapius in his arms, a lightweight, slack bundle; her eyes were fixed on the dog's head.

'Fucking hell,' Rhys muttered. Then, louder, he said, 'Look. You hold him. I'll drive. Give me your keys.'

She spread her hands, helpless.

'Right,' he said. 'Sit in the passenger side.' He was pushing her with his hip, towards the left hand side of the van. 'Open the door,' he told her. 'Right. Sit in. Come *on*. Now . . . seat belt. Now hold him.'

She obeyed him mutely, opening her arms so that he could put the dog on her lap, and then rapidly covering the animal with her hands, like a mother tightly grasping a baby, massaging him.

'Don't squeeze him. Just lightly. Lightly,' he said.

He raced around the other side. The keys were still in the ignition. He started the van, and the engine rolled, complaining. The wheel seemed to be stuck. 'Jesus H. Christ,' he fumed.

'The reverse gear doesn't work very well,' the woman whispered beside him.

He tried again, and managed to get it to reverse off the banked verge. It hit the uneven tarmac with a rusty-sounding thud; he shoved it into first and jammed his foot on the accelerator.

The road was a single track, running parallel with the main road far below, along the ridge of the hills. To the left was a glorious view of the valley, the cars on the bypass threading like coloured beads along a grey string. It was a sight that distracted drivers at the best of times. Even now, doing the maximum he dared around the series of semi-blind bends, Rhys automatically glanced over. When he did so, he saw to his horror that the woman was crying.

'Look,' he said. 'Don't do that. There's no need for it.' *You're not the injured party here*, he wanted to add.

They reached Stourminster in another ten minutes. Rhys swung the van into the car park of the veterinary centre, and leapt out; through the glass doors, he could see the reception area, and a nurse talking to a man by the counter.

He ran around the passenger side of the van, opened the door, and took the dog carefully from the woman's lap.

Running to the offices, he did not realise that she was not following him.

It was an hour later when Rhys finally emerged from the veterinary surgery. He saw that the van had gone, raised his eyebrows cynically, and walked past the empty parking space to the road. Here, he crossed over, dodging traffic, and stepping over the low chain barrier to the footpath beyond.

It led to the rear of the row of shops in Stourminster's main street. Walking up through the narrow alleyway that connected Ware Walk to the centre, he found what he was looking for: a small café with a blackboard menu outside.

He pushed open the door and went to a table in the corner next to the window, sitting down with a gusting sigh of weariness.

'What can I get you?' asked the waitress.

'What is there?'

'Soup? Fish?'

He fiddled with the hand-written menu.

She leaned over and pointed. 'There's a nice meat pie, or we've got a curry . . .'

'Curry,' he said. 'And a drink, please. Hot chocolate.'

She smiled, taking away the list. She was a motherly-looking woman of about fifty. 'Are you cold? That lot'll warm you up,' she said.

'Yes,' he told her, realising that he was. It had gone through to the bone in the last hour, without him registering it.

'Won't be long,' she said.

Rhys fished a sachet of demerara sugar from the bowl, opened it, and poured it into a dessert spoon from the place setting in front of him. He ate it in one go, crunching it, unconscious of the sideways looks of neighbouring customers.

The vet had sedated Aesculapius, and the dog had been X-rayed. He had seen the terrier only last month, for the annual booster shots;

like Rhys, he was a fan of terriers, preferring their bloody-minded enthusiasm to the doe-eyed devotion of other breeds.

'You can breathe now,' he'd told Rhys as they looked together at the X-rays. 'He's broken the hind leg—see, there?' He had pointed with his pencil. 'Shock, bruising . . . and the break. All treatable. In fact, the shock's the worst.' He had turned to the dog, lying on the surgery table, wriggling weakly under the nurse's hands, claws skittering along the melamine, and pulled back the dog's upper lip. 'See the gums? Going white. We'll run a drip to him to correct it.'

'Thank God,' Rhys had said, with feeling. He had run his finger along Aesculapius's snout, and been licked in reward by a small dry tongue. 'I can't do without the little bugger.'

The vet had smiled. 'We'll keep him in for a day or two. Set the leg tomorrow. You can come in tonight, if you like.'

Rhys had shaken his hand gratefully. 'Thanks, I will.'

Sitting now with his hands around a mug of hot chocolate, Rhys stared out at the alleyway and the people going along it.

Shoppers passed each other loaded with bags. He watched a woman negotiating a pushchair past two pensioners, her face pinched with impatience, her mouth down-turning as they said something to her. She had caught the older man on the back of his heels.

The mother's face, pale and sullen, reminded him of the woman in the van. He knew her from somewhere, and was trying to think where. The *speed* she'd come off that hill . . .

The food arrived; he sat back, and put down his cup. 'Oh shit,' he murmured.

The waitress raised her eyebrows. 'Pardon?'

He was staring down at his plate.

'What's the matter?' she asked. 'It's what you ordered.'

He glanced up at her and blinked. She stood with one hand on her hip. He began to wave his hands apologetically. 'No, no . . . it's not the meal. It's fine. Fine, really. Great.'

She paused another moment, then evidently decided not to pursue it. She walked to the hatchway to the kitchen, leaned on it, and looked back at Rhys.

He was still staring blankly down. Eventually, he picked up the cutlery, stabbed the nearest piece of meat with the fork, and rested his forehead on the back of the other hand, the knife waving in mid-air.

'Shit, oh shit,' he repeated to himself.

In all the worry over the dog, the familiarity of the driver had been wiped from his mind. But it had come back now, with resounding force.

It was the woman that Alan Pritchard knew. The woman whose house they had called at earlier that week.

Beth March, the woman whose husband had been killed on Monday.

TWENTY-TWO

*J*ULIA CAME TO BETH'S DOOR at nine o'clock that evening.

The house was in darkness; she paused in the stone porchway, staring at the handle of the bell for a long time until she realised that the door was, in fact, ajar.

She stepped forward and pushed it. 'Beth?' she called.

The name fell into complete silence. Hesitating, Julia glanced back to the drive. The van was parked there; from her bedroom window that afternoon, she'd seen Beth return, walking swiftly inside with her head bowed.

'Beth . . .'

Chaos came out from the kitchen, walking through the shadows with superior grace, his tail perfectly straight and upright. To watch him was to understand where the word 'catwalk' came from: that swinging, precise, arrogant step.

Julia crouched down, holding out her hand. 'Come here,' she whispered. 'Come and talk to me.'

The cat stopped. It sat down on the flagstones, then lay down, turning over on to its back, looking at her upside-down. She inched forward and touched it with the tips of her fingers, running them up its stomach and resting them on its neck. She felt the thready, fast pulse, pressing the flat of her fingertips harder against the fur.

'Where is she?' she asked.

She stood and went into the living room. There was no fire, no signs of occupation. The roses from the morning were curving over in symmetrical arches, the result of being in the sun all day. The tray with the sherry glasses was still on the table.

She went through to the kitchen, saw the same emptiness, glanced at the dark garden, and came back into the hall. She paused for a while at the foot of the stairs, her tongue resting uncertainly on her bottom lip, her hand on the banister, eyes roaming over the steps ahead of her. Then, she walked up.

Beth was in the spare bedroom, in the dark, lying on the bed. She was still wearing the clothes that she had worn that morning, and was apparently asleep, one arm hanging over the side of the bed.

Julia edged in, a step at a time. As she got nearer, she could see that the other woman's face was puffy, swollen from crying; her right arm was spread out to her side, touching the wall. It looked as if she had collapsed here. Her head was at the foot end of the bed.

And Julia couldn't hear her breathing.

She put her own hand to her mouth, creeping to within an inch of Beth's outstretched, hanging hand.

'Beth?' she said. 'Beth?'

Suddenly the hand reached out and grabbed her by the wrist. It was such a shock to Julia that she shouted, pulled back, and half dragged Beth with her.

In a second, she was looking down at Beth's face in the gloom, a face upside-down as the cat's had been; the hand had fastened on her like a vice, the nails digging into her skin. She found herself bending over to release its pressure, bringing Beth's face into hard focus—a series of harshly drawn lines, a Dürer drawing, a Munch painting in the twilight.

Then Beth wrenched her forwards. Julia lost her balance and tipped over, landing on her knees beside the bed. Beth let go of her wrist and scrambled to her feet, getting behind Julia and hauling her under each arm. Disorientated, Julia could not make out what the other woman was trying to do; then she realised that Beth was attempting to pull her from the room and out on to the landing.

She was so much taller than Beth that it was almost funny; cartoonish and crude, like a little square tug pulling an ocean liner, like Hermia pulling Helena through a midsummer night. She stood and tried to turn around, but Beth seized her arm at wrist and shoulder and heaved her forward. There was momentary, fleeting surprise at Beth's strength; then Julia found herself looking down into the black gulf of the stairwell, the pressure unrelenting on her arm.

'Beth!' she cried. 'Beth . . . please, please . . .'

For the first time, Beth spoke. 'Get out of my house,' she said in a hoarse whisper. 'Get out. Get the fucking hell *out*.'

Julia tried to turn so that she was fully facing her. 'I want to talk to you,' she said.

Beth pushed. Julia slipped down the first three steps, a cry of surprise and fear escaping her, until she managed to get her footing. Despite its suddenness, the push had not been very hard. She looked up; Beth was now above her, three or four inches higher than she was.

'I must talk to you,' she repeated.

Beth's breath snagged, and for an instant Julia thought that she had begun to nod slightly, then she realised that sheer force of emotion was pushing Beth's head up, as if she were trying to nudge an invisible spot in the air with the tip of her chin. She was shaking violently.

'Please, come downstairs,' Julia said. 'I know how you feel. I know you don't want me here. But I've *got* to talk to you, Beth. I must explain.'

She could hear the cat now, oblivious to the scene being enacted above it, purring as it rubbed against the banister and the bottom steps.

Beth seemed to make a tremendous effort to put one hand to her forehead. 'I don't care what you want,' she murmured. 'It seems to me that you've had what you wanted for a long time.' The hand settled on her own neck.

'It wasn't planned,' Julia said. 'It wasn't something either of us enjoyed.'

'Oh really?'

'I mean, we didn't enjoy deceiving you.'

'Well. That's nice.'

'David always cared about you.'

'I can imagine.'

'Beth . . .'

Beth began to laugh harshly. 'Yes, I can really imagine you discussing my feelings.'

Julia was smiling. 'I never meant it to happen. I asked David to help me over money. To advise me how I could get hold of money, to leave Oliver.'

Beth stared at her. 'You were leaving him?' she repeated.

'I was trying to think of a way,' Julia said. 'David always paid such attention; he always listened.'

Beth ran a hand over her forehead. 'I'm not interested.' She stepped forward, and Julia retreated, backwards, down the steps. Closer to the bottom, she turned and descended quickly. Beth came after her. Instead of turning to the door, Julia headed for the living room. She reached the nearest couch and sat down in it heavily, and, after a moment of apparently trying to control herself, abruptly began to cry.

'Oh, for God's sake,' Beth said. 'Go home.'

'I'm so sorry.' Julia fumbled about for a handkerchief and, finding one in the pocket of her jacket, wiped her eyes. 'I loved him too,' she murmured.

Beth watched her silently. She felt sickened, dead.

'We were going to Spain,' Julia whispered. She glanced up at Beth, who was still standing by the door. 'It wasn't me,' she continued. 'I wasn't the reason for going. That's not what forced the issue. It was the money.'

'You took my money,' Beth said. 'Thousands of pounds.'

Julia stopped crying, handkerchief midway to her mouth. 'What?'

'The second charge on the mortgage. Going to Spain with my money and leaving *me* to make the repayments every month. *And* the trust fund.'

Julia shook her head. 'You didn't love him,' she said. 'You haven't mentioned him once. He told me about you, and I never really believed it. He said it was just—like an arrangement, that all the love had gone out of it—'

'What?'

'You. Being married. He said—'

'He said *that!*'

Julia's mouth turned down, like a child that had been slapped. 'And he was right,' she said. 'You haven't shed a tear for him, poor David . . .'

Beth paused. She had never been so angry in her life, and the force of it frightened her. 'I think you had better go,' she said.

But Julia was still talking. 'He was so worried about money, and all you can think of is your own . . .'

'Ours,' Beth corrected. 'Mine and David's. He took a second charge on the mortgage; I knew nothing about it. He *stole* it from me.' Light dawned gradually on her face. 'So that he could give it to you.'

Julia said nothing. She was looking down into her lap, and in the shadows Beth couldn't make out the expression on her face.

'I'm right, aren't I?' Beth said. 'The two of you forged that application, to finance this venture to Spain.' She choked on the last few syllables, still more out of rage than grief. The enormity of the betrayal by her husband was staggering.

Julia at last looked up. Her voice was small, and very calm. 'I don't know what you're talking about,' she said. 'All I know is this thing with Oliver. They've been throwing cash at it for months, and it's just got worse and worse. The investment fund . . .'

Beth's mouth dropped open, working soundlessly over Julia's sentence. 'What fund?'

'Oliver's deal.'

'*What* deal?'

'Why . . . this shipping thing.'

'David . . . and Oliver?'

'David found the discrepancies on Oliver's accounts, and somehow Oliver got him to invest his own money, because he said that it only needed a few more thousand . . .'

Beth waved her hands as if to brush away Julia's meandering tone. 'How much?' she demanded.

Julia stared at her. 'I don't know.'

It was more than Beth could stand. She strode away, hitting her hands against her thighs, then putting both balled fists to her eyes. 'Jesus,' she whispered. She turned. 'You're trying to tell me that you were leaving the country with David, and you didn't have a penny? And this—' She searched the air, helplessly, for a way to describe it. 'This *deal* had sucked up David's trust fund, and the rest? And I never heard a word about it!'

Julia shrugged. It was a very controlled, even careless gesture.

Beth looked down at her with contempt, then turned away, walking into the kitchen. At the sink she ran the cold tap and leaned down, splashing her face with icy water. Then, with the drops still running down her neck and arms, she filled a glass and drank it down.

Behind her, Julia came into the room. She switched on the light, and stood wiping her face with the handkerchief. Then she dropped her hands. Looking ahead into the window, Beth could see her reflection and her own; two statues in a white-walled box.

'Tell me something,' Beth said.

'What?'

'Did Oliver know about you and David?'

'Yes.'

Breath drained from Beth's body; she felt the blood pulsing hard in her head.

'How long has it been going on?'

'A year.'

'And Oliver knew all that time?'

'No. He found out about four months ago.'

'How?'

'How what?'

'How did he find out?'

Julia stared at Beth's turned back. In the glass, Beth saw her reach for a chair and lower herself slowly into it. 'He came home early one afternoon.'

Beth turned to face her. 'In bed?'

'Yes. Almost.'

'Your bed?'

'Yes.'

Beth swallowed hard. 'What did he say?'

'Nothing, really.'

'*Nothing?*'

Julia looked up at her. 'Nothing. He said nothing about it. He'd known, I think, that we were seeing each other, but he'd never questioned me about it.' Her eyes slipped from Beth, and an expression of satisfaction came to her face.

'What did he say when David died?'

'He asked if I had been leaving with him.'

'And you told him—'

'No. I told him nothing. I said I knew nothing about it.' Her mouth trembled violently and she put a hand to it.

'But you come and tell me,' Beth said. 'Thank you very much.'

Julia's mouth sagged down in almost a parody of grief, a child's expression. 'Oliver doesn't care about anyone but himself,' she said.

Silence descended. The two women were immobile on opposite sides of the room, Beth staring down at the top of Julia's head.

'Oliver,' Beth said, at last. 'Oliver signed the form.'

'What form?'

'The bloody mortgage form! The form for the second charge. *Oliver* signed it, to get money out of David. Because of *you*. The affair. That's the hold he had over him.'

Julia frowned. 'I don't understand,' she said.

Beth hadn't heard her. She let out a small, strangled noise, a primitive sound. 'Him too,' she said. 'All of you. Doing this to me.'

Julia sprang to her feet. 'Is that all you ever talk about?' she yelled. 'Money? You're just like him. *You* ought to live with him; you are just like each other. *People* matter! People like me—that's what matters!'

Beth immediately looked around the kitchen. She wanted something heavy. Sense rolled out of her head—sense, reason, restraint. All she wanted to do was obliterate the sanctimonious self-pitying expression on Julia's mouth.

'*I* loved him,' Julia said, beating her fist against her breast. '*I* loved him. *Me*. You didn't! And *he* loved *me*!'

She was within reach.

Beth, hand fisted, hit Julia on the side of her face. Once she had touched her, it released a spring of fury; she waded into the other woman, slapping and punching and pushing her.

Julia did nothing to resist. She fell backwards, her hands over the top of her head, trying to protect herself. She bumped into the table, and crouched down, as though she was going to crawl under it. Beth caught her hand on the wood, and the dazzling white-hard sensation of the wood slamming into her own hand, jarring the bones in her knuckles, stopped her as if she'd walked into a force field.

Julia was by now actually on the floor, curled into a ball, whimpering like a dog.

Beth stepped back. She was gasping for breath; she knew, in that instant, that she was quite capable of actually killing someone. Another minute or so and perhaps she *would* have killed Julia with her bare hands. Once begun, the temptation to go on was overwhelming and curiously satisfying. She would have liked to know the sensation at the end of the act; liked to have stood over Julia's body.

Seeing this image in her own head, she looked at her hands. 'Oh God,' she said.

Julia didn't move for another few seconds, then she got up. She was not bleeding; the blows had been too wild, too inept for that. Her attitude was almost casual, as if she'd been waiting for the violence. Then she began to look at her hands and arms, run her fingers over her face. 'Oh, what you've done to me,' she said.

'I'm sorry,' Beth said. Bile rose in her throat; sickness at the apology. 'I shouldn't have done that. I'm very sorry.'

Julia looked at her unblinkingly. Then, she asked in a level voice, 'When did you sleep with David?'

'What?' It was the last question that Beth had been expecting.

'David. When did you last sleep with him?'

Beth was too surprised to protest. She held her hands in to her chest, cradling them against herself. 'I don't remember.'

Julia nodded. 'No, you wouldn't,' she said. She took a step closer, to within a foot of Beth. She began to smile. 'I slept with him on Sunday,' she said. '*Sunday.*'

Beth gaped at her. Julia stroked the side of her face, where she had first been hit; she felt carefully around her mouth and eyes.

There was nothing to say. Nothing Beth *could* say. She couldn't remember when she and David had last made love, but it was some time ago. She couldn't say that she had desired him—really *desired* him, or anyone—for a long time. It had died at some indistinguishable time in the past. They never quarrelled about it, or mentioned it, but the lovemaking faded. Sex had become intermittent, unimportant. She had supposed, if she ever considered it at all, that most marriages faded like this, out of tiredness or familiarity.

She stepped back, steadying herself against the work surface behind her. She felt as if Julia had looked at her naked flesh. Seen inside her. Of the two, she was the more disgraced now: revealed, in an instant, as a cold, selfish bitch denying her husband what he was forced to look for elsewhere.

'It wasn't like that,' she murmured.

Julia, in turn, sat down, still fixing her with the same unwavering look. She was well aware, it seemed, of having scored a point, touched a nerve. 'You didn't love him at all,' she said.

'Yes . . . I did.'

'No. You just lived with him. You got along. You had a quiet life. But that's not love.'

'It is. You're talking about being *in* love; loving is something different.'

'You didn't love David,' Julia repeated. 'And he didn't love you.' She leaned forward, her index finger resting on the base of her throat. 'Me,' she whispered. 'You see? Me.'

Beth turned away. Tears sprang to her eyes and she let them run, not bothering to raise her hands to her face.

Very slowly, Julia got to her feet. She stood and watched Beth for a while, then, without another word, she walked to the door of the kitchen, along the hall, and out of the house.

TWENTY-THREE

*I*T WAS VERY DARK IN THE GARDEN.

The cat sat in the lee of the wall, deep in the weeds that fringed the bushes. The earth was still warm here, and the cat was slumped on its side, lazily waiting.

'Chaos,' said a voice. 'Chaos . . .'

It had seen the figure long before hearing it, but showed no signs of caring. It gave the imperious look that only a cat could command, its eyes reflecting as twin circles of yellow in the dark.

'What have I got, Chaos?'

Its gaze rested on the outstretched hand. At last, a flicker of interest showed. The cat stretched, then bunched, drawing its back legs in to its body.

'Very nice, eh, Chaos? Nice. Look.'

The cat got to its feet. Through the dank-smelling dock and dande-lions, it walked at a low-slung sway, watching without blinking, drawn to the shape that hovered less than six feet away.

At the very edge of the border, where the lawn ended in its spray of withering, unwatered pansies, the cat stopped.

The bird was motionless, but that didn't mean that it was dead.

Chaos eyed it hopefully, ready for the semaphore of fear, the upward struggle.

The hand leaned closer.

'Come on, nice cat,' came the seductive whisper. Low-throated, calm. 'What've I got for you, eh? Look.' And the hand tipped the dead bird over, rolling it on to the ground.

'What is it, Chaos?' came the murmur. 'Don't you want it? It's for you. For . . .' The body inched forward behind the outstretched fingers.

'For a very, *very* . . . good . . . cat . . .'

TWENTY-FOUR

*R*HYS REACHED THE FOOTBRIDGE IN RECORD TIME.

He stopped there, looking at his watch and trying to work out how long it had taken him this morning. Fourteen minutes; that wasn't bad. Fourteen minutes from his house to the midway point of his exercise run meant that he was almost two minutes fitter than this time last month.

Getting his breath a little, he grinned, and leaned his back against the stone. Early morning sun warmed his face. He set hurdles like this all the time—not that he was anything like an athlete, but because he liked to beat himself. He did it habitually; beating himself at the time it took to shower, or write a report, or play computer golf on his 486 in the attic. It went like this: if he started the day with a six below par on Cypress Creek, it was a good omen. Something would go smoothly today. Evens, he'd coast. But above par, and he was doomed, out in the rough.

The running was a chore he endured twice a week. He hated exercise, and pounding the path alongside the river bored him, just as weights or swimming bored him; but he did them as an antidote to the prolonged hours of bending that was turning his back into a torture zone.

He looked at the water that was swarming and chugging through a series of low weirs. Brighter light was now was catching the currents; across the way, allotment gardens lay in alternate green and brown bands. A man was patiently putting up bean sticks; a dog was barking in one of the houses on the other side.

He thought at once of Ace in his little wire box at the vet's, and of the accusing look the dog had managed to give him yesterday evening despite the medication after the operation. The dog's expression was eloquent: *You utter sod,* it had said. *What sort of game d'you call this?* Rhys had poked his fingers through the mesh. 'Coming out soon,' he'd promised. The terrier had thumped its tail once—a meagre, polite concession—then closed its eyes.

Rhys eased himself off the bridge and walked. The path skirted the bottom edge of town, and an assortment of buildings crowded the land on the right hand side: small warehouses, decaying piles of timber, a couple of long-closed shops, a unit of car repairers. He began to jog. He had an appointment with Alison Warley at ten at the museum, and had promised, as a favour, to pick up her films from a photographic laboratory before then.

He emerged at the bottom of the long High Street, checked the road, and jogged across it. He was near home now, at the end of his circular route.

He started up a street of an even more curious mixture; Georgian houses, an antiques warehouse, a Salvation Army chapel, a chiropractor's clinic, and the Prehistory Museum, where a life-size red stone tyrannosaurus was parked behind the railings, its head back and teeth bared, permanently squaring up to a hawthorn hedge. He'd first seen this street on a dark night in November, as he circled the area trying to find the house listed on an estate agent's letter. The sight of the dinosaur looming out of the rain had given him a jolt.

But the red giant had turned out to be a good omen; he got the loan he'd been applying for to start the business. And the town, much smaller than the city where he'd grown up, was this curious mixture everywhere. A tyrannosaurus past hand-in-hand with a pedestrian precinct and car park future; paving stones masking Neolithic man.

Even sitting waiting in the bank, he'd noticed that there was a plaque on the wall behind the cashiers, saying that it marked one of the original Roman gateways. Squinting, he'd seen that there was a glass booth about three feet square, showing a section of neatened-up Roman wall, lit with an amber light, incongruous behind the per cent posters and VDUs. He'd warmed to the place at once and, taking the tyrannosaurus as a metamorphic thumbs-up, he'd ordered business cards and bought the house he'd looked at the previous rainy night.

Twelve years ago. Straight out of college. One of those leaps in the dark, where you land by accident right on your feet. He wiped his forehead with the back of his sleeve now, puffing as he approached the last hundred-yard incline. The clinic and the museum and the chapel drifted past. He drifted too, lulled by tiredness into disjointed thoughts.

The body shoved into the last grave occurred to him; the old man, with his aching back and shoulders. Rhys badly wanted to see Alison's pictures; wanted to know what proportion of the find the museum would take. Wanted to know where the outcast old man would be put next, his hands bent under at the wrist, his feet turned inwards and crushed down by soil into a configuration of agony . . .

Then, Rhys saw Beth March.

She was thirty yards away, locking her van. Without really thinking, he waved his arm, and shouted.

'Hey—hey!'

She had begun to look into her purse for some money for the parking meter.

'Hello!' he shouted again, crossing the street.

She glanced up. He saw with a shock that she was absolutely white in the face, her eyes shadowed. She fumbled with the money and dropped it.

He was up to her now, and bent down to help. 'That's all right—let me,' he said. He found the coins and stood up, holding them out to her. 'Was that all of it?' he asked, looking again round his feet. 'Forty pence?'

'Yes.' She put it in the meter. He saw that her hands were shaking, and the coins slipped once or twice around the mouth of the slot. 'Thank you.' She turned to him, pushing back her hair.

'My dog's all right,' he said.

A smile dawned on her like magic. 'Is he?' she asked.

'A broken leg.'

'Oh—I'm glad. *Really* glad.' And she meant it too, he saw. In fact, she meant it so much that her eyes filled suddenly with tears. 'I thought I'd killed him,' she said.

She leaned suddenly on the roof of the van.

'It's just his leg,' he repeated.

She put both hands on the van now, fists clenched; she was breathing like an asthmatic.

He was seized with panic. 'Don't you have a—thing for taking air in—you put in your mouth . . .'

She smiled. As she did so, her face assumed a more terrible colour than the awful white; it turned grey, blue at the very corners of her mouth.

'Oh Christ,' he said.

'I'm OK. This happened yesterday too.'

'Can you breathe?'

'I'm not asthmatic.' She changed position, pressed one hand on her chest. 'It's all right.'

He searched her face, convinced she was about to collapse. 'You look like shit to me,' he said.

'Thank you.'

'You do.' He gripped her by one arm. 'Open the car and sit in it.'

'No. I'm going to walk.'

'You're sure?'

'Perfectly. I'm fine.' She looked down, pointedly, at his hand on her. *You are not*, he thought. 'Where are you going?'

'My building society.'

'Which one?'

'On Ryemall.'

'You can't walk up there. It's a long hill.'

'I've got an appointment at nine.'

'They can wait. Come here.' He took her proprietorially by the elbow and guided her forward.

'No. Look—where are we going?'

'To sit.'

She made a murmur that was hardly a protest.

His house was two minutes away, off Ware Walk. A yellow door in a Victorian terrace, with a concrete patch for a front garden, nine yards square. The door opened into a dark hall, and then out into a room of surprising light, and a yet more surprising garden.

Beth walked to the patio doors, her eye immediately drawn to the two Tai Haku cherries, and the apple tree right at the back, with a wood bench beneath it.

'Sit down,' he said.

'I'm better.'

'You'll make *me* feel better if you sit down.'

'Can I go outside?'

He unlocked the doors and pushed them back. 'Be my guest. Please.'

She walked down the stone path and sat down under the tree. Its leaves were bright green and smooth, with dead blossom knuckled in the heart of each bud, and the first nub of the fruit showing. She looked up through the branches, momentarily closing her eyes, surprised at herself for coming here, when she ought to be somewhere else.

'Is it Burleigh and Country?' Rhys was standing in front of her with the Yellow Pages open at B. 'It's the only one listed at Ryemall.'

'Yes,' she told him.

'Right.' He went back inside. Through the open doors she heard his voice, and the single ring of the phone receiver being replaced.

In another minute he came out again, with a tray, and a folding picnic table under one arm. She helped him straighten it, and he put the tray on top.

'I fixed your appointment for twelve. She's OK about it. Now the . . . coffee and cake . . . biscuits . . .'

She smiled. 'Healthy.'

He poured the coffee. 'Carbohydrates. I don't think, seeing as you're dead on your feet, that you're in any position to comment,' he said.

He handed her a plate and some of the food, and she tried to eat.

After not having had any quantity of food for five days, the concoction tasted thick and sweet; too sweet. She found herself having a hard time chewing and swallowing. No saliva. She had dried up inside.

'Alan told me,' Rhys said. 'I rang him last night—about something else—and I said about Ace . . . He told me about the funeral.'

She replaced her cup. 'What, exactly?'

'That you'd left the funeral.'

'Did he say why?'

'No.'

She leaned forward, resting her elbows on her knees. 'I don't suppose they told him. Or anyone,' she observed.

'Why don't you tell me?' Rhys said.

She looked at him. 'Why should I?'

'Why shouldn't you?'

'I mean, why should *you* want to hear it?'

'Sometimes it helps.'

She started to laugh, a totally humourless, acid sound. 'I doubt that you could help.'

'You never know. Let me try.'

'What are you? Saint somebody?'

He said nothing. She put both hands to her face. 'I'm sorry,' she murmured.

He gave her plate back to her. 'Eat something else.'

'I can't. I can't swallow things.'

'Try the chocolate shortcake.'

She took a piece politely, looked at it, looked at the plate, the tray, and at him. Then, she began to cry.

She held the plate tightly, the biscuit swerving around on its slippery china surface. Rhys's gaze flitted from her face to the plate. Wrenching sounds came out of her; it sounded like someone being hit repeatedly, fresh whip strokes on every note.

He sat mesmerised for a second then leapt up, grabbed the plate, put it down, and pulled her to her feet, passing his arms around her.

She shook in his grasp; she was very thin. The noise rose for a while—*Someone will think I'm killing her*, crossed his mind—and then subsided rapidly. She pressed her face into his shoulder, her hands hanging at her side. He felt at his hip for a pocket with a handkerchief or a tissue, then realised that he was still in his track suit. He eased her away from him when the cries had quietened a little more.

'Stay here,' he said.

He came running back with a toilet roll. 'Sorry,' he said. 'It's all there is.'

She tore off a piece and wiped her eyes, then sat down again.

'Tell me,' he said.

'I can't. I can't even start it.'

'On Monday.'

She gazed up and past him. 'David died on Monday. On Tuesday, I found out he owed money. A lot of our money was missing. Wednesday . . .'

'Go on.'

'I can't remember.'

'OK. Friday, then. Tell me about yesterday.'

She sighed and took another piece of the paper from the roll, blowing her nose. 'My husband was leaving the country with my friend. He owed a lot of money. I think my solicitor is probably defrauding me. My friend is my solicitor's wife.' She dropped the used paper on to the tray.

'Holy shit.'

'You like that word, don't you?'

'Is there another?'

She smiled thinly. 'Probably not.'

He stared at her, trying to digest what she had said. 'What else happened yesterday?'

'I found out about David and Julia . . . the friend.'

'Quite a nice little friend. When?'

'At the funeral.'

'Oh Christ.' He got up again and put his arms around her, out of simple, automatic compassion; the kind of compassion he would have felt for a crying child, even for a stranger on the street. She stiffened— the embrace was very awkward, with him half kneeling, his face pressed hard against hers—and he drew back.

'I can't sleep, I can't eat,' she said.

'I'm not bloody surprised.'

'I can't look at the bed. I stay downstairs all night.'

He considered her, his eyes ranging over her. 'What are you going to do?' he asked.

'Go out of my mind. That seems about right.'

'After that?'

For the first time, she actually genuinely laughed. 'After my breakdown? I haven't checked the diary.'

'You should.' He got up and pulled his chair close to hers, then sat down, taking her hand in his. 'This solicitor first. Fire him and get another. The building society—'

'That's why I was going up there; they rang last night and said I really needed proof, something to back up this claim that my signature on the form was a forgery.' She withdrew her hands. 'David got thousands from them, and forged my name. Or someone did.'

'The solicitor?'

'I can't prove anything. How could I? It's my word against his.' She paused. 'I thought he was my friend,' she said, each word punctuated by a long pause.

'Handwriting. A handwriting expert could say it was a forgery.'

She shook her head. 'I don't know. It's very like mine.'

'The building society said that?'

'They're trying to be fair. They are *trying*.'

'Sounds like it,' he said sarcastically. 'What about this friend?'

'She wants me to understand. David loved her, she loved him, et cetera.'

'I hope you told her to fuck off.'

Beth sighed—grinding, slow. 'I don't know her. I don't know David. And I don't know *what to do,* if I should do anything.'

'What do you mean?'

She spread her hands helplessly. 'What's the point, really? David is dead and Julia might as well be. I'll just get another solicitor and move away. Sell the house, leave the village.'

'Why should you?'

She put her hand to her wet face and wiped away further tears. 'I don't cry,' she said. 'I didn't cry when my mother died. I don't cry at films. I'm not the kind of person that ever cries.' She shook her head. 'I can't stand the kind of woman that does,' she said.

'You have a good excuse,' Rhys said. 'Might as well do it properly.'

She stood up, began to walk, and stumbled slightly, catching her foot against a plant that sprayed over the stones. He said nothing, but he took her arm, ignoring her reflex shrinking from his touch, and took her inside.

Here, the room was speckled with sunlight. He led her to the couch and pressed on her shoulders, forcing her to sit. 'I'm going to get a shower and change, then I'm going into town. I've got an errand. I'll come with you to Ryemall,' he said.

She didn't look at him. After watching her for another moment, he went out.

Beth pulled her legs up on to the couch. It was very soft, spread with cushions cut from some kind of thick plush carpet-like material. She leaned her head against the yielding arm, her gaze wandering around the walls and bookcases.

She hadn't noticed its details when she first came through; now, they leapt out at her. It was a feminine room of the kitsch, over-homely variety. Where the fireplace should have been was a small hearth with a pot of dried flowers, an ornamental brass kettle on a trivet, a set of brass fire irons—the kind that would never be used. On the shelves on each side were a collection of ornate plates with gold rims, two copper peacocks, a watercolour of an overfilled cottage garden, a set of tiny pillboxes, and two small candelabra. On the wall opposite her was a print of a child with saucer-like eyes, clutching a cat.

Suddenly, Rhys put his head round the door. She could hear the sound of water running.

'Just checking,' he said. 'I thought you might do a runner. You won't, will you?'

She didn't reply; instead, she asked, 'Are you married?'

'Yes,' he said.

She swung her legs down automatically, and Rhys started to laugh. 'Don't worry about invading her space,' he told her. 'She works in Africa. Burundi.'

'Burundi! Doing what?'

'She's a nurse,' he said. He turned to a cabinet and took down a photograph that she had not yet noticed. He handed it to her.

His wife was a woman with short dark hair, a very round face, and a broad smile. She was squinting against strong sunlight, and wore a T-shirt emblazoned, on the left shoulder, with some kind of aid-agency insignia.

'She looks nice,' Beth said, handing the photo back. 'What's her name?'

The amiable expression on Rhys's face dissolved. 'Saint somebody,' he told her as he turned to go out.

TWENTY-FIVE

*A*T MIDDAY, Angela Naylor sat in her office gazing in to space.

She was not known for her inactivity; rather, like a famous Prime Minister before her, she slept barely four hours a night, worked ten hours a day, and looked very good on it. She wasn't known for daydreaming.

Though this particular daydream was more productive than it looked. She was thinking her way round Oliver Woods. He had just called to tell her that Elizabeth March was, to cut a long story short, out of her mind.

He had come, without an appointment, at five minutes to nine that morning. The Society was not open to the public at that time, but he knocked on the door until one of the counter staff went to him, then smarmed his way over the doorstep. It had irritated Angela intensely.

'I shan't take more than a moment,' Oliver had said. Grudgingly, she had indicated a chair.

He had sat down, all ease and straight-backed authority, his voice oozing upper-class deference. She ought at least to have respected him, if not liked him. After all, he was a respected member of the community and a long-standing member of his profession. But something about him got under her skin.

She had tried to damp it down, to remain objective; she was pretty sure that half her dislike stemmed from her solid Manchester background, where deception could be smelled at six paces and men like Oliver were given damned short shrift. She had always packed her own personal shit-detector. And it came in very handy.

And, sitting with Oliver Woods across from here that morning, she had been fairly confident that she'd be able to pick out any lies before they got half-way out of his mouth.

'I'll come straight to the point, if I may,' he had said.

'Please do.'

'It's about Mrs March. Elizabeth March.'

'Oh yes?'

'Yes . . .' He had smiled.

Angela had said nothing. She had taken her eyes from his yellow-stained fingers, lingered over the pristine starched cuff, and stopped again at the slept-in expensive suit.

'I'm not a doctor, of course,' he'd continued. 'But it's obvious, even to a layman, that she is under an alarming strain. She claims that her husband was deceiving her on all kinds of levels, and that she knew nothing whatsoever about the second charge on the mortgage. There's no evidence that this—'

Angela had leaned forward. 'Do you mind,' she glanced pointedly at her watch, 'if I ask you a question?'

'Of course.'

'Did you witness her signature?'

Oliver had said nothing for a while; then, a slight blush had crept up his neck. 'That is why I have come to see you,' he said. 'I feel sure that Elizabeth must have told you of her misgivings. And I want to put the facts before you. I did *not* witness her signature.'

Angela had leaned back, watching him. 'I see.'

He had spread his hands. 'I don't know if you will wish to take this further. Of course, whatever course of action you choose is entirely your prerogative—'

'It is indeed.'

'Quite.' He had swept an invisible thread from his sleeve. 'David March approached me to increase the mortgage. It was arranged absolutely as normal, except that, on the day fixed for the appointment to sign, David arrived without Elizabeth. He told me that she was ill; that she had flu, and was in bed.' Oliver had smiled slowly. 'He showed me the form with her signature already on it, and said that she had signed that morning, and sent her apologies.' He looked Angela straight in the eye. 'I had no reason to doubt him. As far as I knew—as far as we *all* knew then—David was an upright, respectable, honest man.'

Angela had not moved for a moment, then she took up a pen and began drawing small, interlocking circles on a piece of scrap paper next to her telephone. 'I spoke to Mrs March yesterday,' she'd said. 'She told me that you knew that David had said the extension to the house was to be a surprise. He said as much to his builder—swore him to secrecy.' She'd stopped drawing and looked up. 'How could he have done that if Mrs March had already signed the form? She already *knew*, if your story holds water.'

Oliver's bleak smile had not left his face. He had held up one finger, as if to stop her thoughts going any further along that track. 'Correction,' he said. 'David told his builder that. And my secretary—who is Alan Pritchard's wife—was told the same thing by her husband. But David never said that to *me*. And I don't think that was the case for a moment. David told *me* that Elizabeth knew. That is why I witnessed the form, in all good faith that Elizabeth March was a willing participant in the application.'

'Which she was not.'

Oliver had sighed. The sound sent the hairs on the back of Angela Naylor's neck bristling—it was the kind of weary note that she recognised in older men speaking to what they considered to be pushy young women. The sigh of authority. She gritted her teeth.

'That is what she says,' he had agreed. 'But I am not sure how far I can accept it.'

'You've just told me that David admitted deception to his builder.'

'That is what the *builder* says.'

'Ahhh . . . so the builder has got the story wrong? At best he misunderstood David March. At worse, he lied. Why would he?'

'I'm not saying at all that Mr Pritchard has lied. Possibly David said that the *exact nature* of the work was to be surprise; perhaps David had told Elizabeth that the work was for something mundane like new plumbing or sewerage . . . and all the time it was a surprise for her. The workshop, the conservatory.'

Angela was shaking her head. 'Mrs March claims to have known nothing. She's very convincing on that.'

'I couldn't agree more,' Oliver had said smoothly. 'She is adamant that she knew nothing. And I admit to you freely that my witnessing of the document has not helped at all. But—' and he placed his fingertip on the edge of the desk top, tapping it lightly with each word for emphasis—'she is in shock. She is in the centre of the most distressing set of events imaginable. She is behaving irrationally, and I am quite confident in saying that she will, eventually, withdraw this claim of fraud. I believe that she *did* sign the form. No forgery is *that* good; it's definitely her handwriting.'

'Oh?'

'Yes. It distresses me to say it, of course. She's a most valued client, and—you'll appreciate this—this conversation must be in confidence . . .'

'Naturally.'

'I believe that she authorised the application, and the fact that David appears to have been leaving the country has, naturally, appalled her. She doesn't want to admit—even to herself—that she was fooled by her own husband, fooled into thinking the money was for the house, when in fact it was for David himself. She didn't know that he was planning to go. And take the money with him.'

'So—can I be clear on this?—you think that Mrs March, now, is lying?'

He had raised both hands in a gesture of rapid denial. 'No, no, no. Mrs March is not lying to us, Mrs Naylor. Mrs March is a distressed woman. She is disorientated and grieving. It doesn't give me any pleasure to have to discuss her in this way. She is a most admirable person, and she has my utmost sympathy. No . . . I think that Elizabeth is suffering from, shall we say, selective memory at the moment. It's not her fault. I think that, in a week or two, she will withdraw all she has said.'

'And so, when she claims that she knew nothing about the signature, that you in some way have deceived her—'

'She has said that?'

Angela didn't reply.

'I'm sorry to hear it,' Oliver had said. And he did look very sorry indeed. Even offended. 'In all my years of practice I have never deceived a client, nor anyone else,' he had said softly. 'I hope I shall never be tempted to do so.' There had followed a moment or two of complete silence.

Angela Naylor had stood up. It was ten minutes past nine. The day was beginning badly. She had held out her hand and shaken Oliver Woods' cold, dry fingers. 'Thank you for coming to see me,' she had said. 'I appreciate your explanation and shall consider it, of course. I agree with you that Mrs March is possibly unreliable at the moment, though she didn't strike me as such.' She had let this sink in as Oliver turned for the door.

'Oh, and—Mr Woods?'

He turned. 'Yes?'

'I shall have to report your action on witnessing the mortgage application.'

His face had fallen. You'll report it to the panel?' he said.

'Yes. I'm sorry. I don't have a choice.'

'I see.'

'And . . .' She had paused, embarrassed that curiosity that had finally got the better of her. 'Tell me—you knew David March very well. *Was* he leaving Beth for another woman?'

Oliver's expression had not altered. 'No,' he had said. 'I don't believe that for a moment.'

TWENTY-SIX

LILIAN DAVIS STOOD WITH HER ARMS FOLDED, regarding her brother with an expression of malice.

'You can't do it, can you?' she asked.

He stared around himself, his gaze only momentarily resting on her, as though she were simply part of the meaningless jumble of colours in the room.

He was naked, crouched in the bath. The water had drained away twenty minutes before, and he sat with his arms wrapped around his knees.

'Get out,' Lilian said. She stepped forward. 'Go on, you bloody old fool. Get out!'

Arthur didn't move. He closed his eyes and began instead to whistle.

'Get *out!*' Lilian screamed

With no response, the shreds of her temper deserted her. She pulled down the towel that she had deliberately placed out of his reach—hoping he might grab for it, and fall—and threw it into the bath. 'Get up,' she shouted. 'I'm sick of this. Dry yourself!'

The towel landed on Arthur's knees. He showed no sign of knowing it was there.

Lilian bent down to him. 'I'm going to get you seen to,' she hissed at him. 'Are you listening to me, you old fool? I'm going to get you certified, and you're going to rot, and I'm going to get that money.'

Arthur's whistling stopped.

'Oh, you know that word all right, don't you?' she cried. 'You were always tight with it, even when I needed it, even when I begged you. You never gave me a penny!'

She grabbed the towel and flicked it savagely at his face. Arthur closed his eyes. She stood trembling with fury.

'You think you've got it all ways, don't you?' she said, her voice falling now to a dangerous whisper. 'You think you can sit there like stone all day, never saying a word, and have me wait on you hand and foot. And when the doctor comes round, you talk to *him* and smile at *him*, you old bastard!'

She locked her arms defiantly across her chest. 'Well, you won't get away with it,' she told him. 'I'm having that money. And I know how.'

Arthur smiled, his eyes clamped shut.

'Smile all you like,' she said. 'But Oliver Woods is going to say you've attacked me. Oliver Woods is going to back me up, and he knows people, he knows the doctor, and he'll make *sure* you're put away.'

She stared at him a moment longer. 'He promised me,' she said. 'D'you hear me? He promised me!' At the doorway, she delivered her *coup de grâce*, her eyes narrowed, her voice pure venom. 'People will do anything for money,' she said.

She walked away, slamming the door behind her.

In the bathroom, Arthur opened his eyes. He looked dazed for a moment; then, painfully slowly, his head shaking, he raised two fingers at the closed door.

TWENTY-SEVEN

$\mathcal{I}$T WAS HALF-WAY THROUGH THE AFTERNOON when Oliver called on Beth.

She was in the garden, kneeling at the edge of the stream, weeding with infinite care. After coming back from town, she had taken a mat out to the trees at the corner, and started there, uprooting the first signs of dandelion and thistle.

By the time Oliver appeared, she had worked backwards for almost ten feet, clearing a scrupulous neat brown patch.

'Hello, Beth,' he said.

She sat back on her heels; when she saw who it was her mouth closed in a tight line.

'May I talk to you?'

She looked at him for a second. 'No,' she replied.

'Oh . . . if you please.'

She returned to digging, her shoulders hunched. He remained where he was, looking down at her from the raised terrace above. 'Beth, I really must talk to you.'

Julia had said something similar the other night. *Funny,* Beth thought. *How all the bloody traitors want to talk to me so badly.* 'Oliver, I've got nothing to say to you,' she said.

He walked down the steps. 'I'll tell you what I've told Burleigh and Country,' he said. 'I witnessed the mortgage application without seeing you sign the form.'

She glanced up, then put the trowel down. He was not looking at her but across at the view, interwoven shades of green pierced by the road.

'I know that,' she said icily. 'But why the hell didn't you say so on Tuesday?'

'I should have done. I'm as shocked about David's death as you are.'

'And what about . . .' She threw the trowel down angrily. 'What about this shipping deal?'

'I'm sorry?'

She took a deep breath. 'Don't fuck with me over this,' she said.

He looked as though he had been slapped in the face; his mouth dropped open slightly. Probably he had never heard her swear before. Come to think of it, she considered, she never *did* swear; David had loathed it. He had always said it was a sign of mental torpidity. She could see him saying it now: *mental torpidity*, his voice picking out the consonants very precisely, his mouth twitching marginally upwards with a hint of humour.

'What deal?' Oliver asked.

She took a step towards him. 'Julia has told me all about the money you and David sunk into it.'

Oliver nodded slowly. 'Julia. I see.'

'So there's no use trying to flannel me, Oliver.'

He smiled briefly. 'And we all trust Julia, don't we?' he observed.

Beth waved her hand dismissively. 'Never mind. You haven't answered the question.'

'David wasn't involved in *any* shipping deal.'

She looked hard at him. She knew at once that he was lying. 'Oh, Oliver, for Christ's sake.'

'There was no deal with David.'

Beth's temper rose in a second. 'I wish someone would just be bloody straight with me!' she shouted. 'Just *one* of you! Where's the money?'

'Which? The trust fund, or the mortgage?'

'Both! Where has it gone, if not to prop up this deal?' Seeing his blank expression, she turned away. 'Forget it,' she said. 'I don't know why I'm speaking to you at all, you conniving bastard.'

She looked at the cleared space of ground in front of her, then glanced back at him. 'I'm hiring another solicitor,' she said. 'I want someone else to deal with David's will, too.'

He frowned. 'Beth, I really have done nothing wrong, other than the witnessing, which I admit—quite freely, quite freely. I made an error over the signature. But there was no reason to doubt David. Why should I? Did you?'

Turned away from him, Beth winced.

'David never told me he had any financial trouble at all,' Oliver continued in his smooth, unruffled tone. 'And other than these recent withdrawals his affairs have been meticulous. There are no other debts. Not even a credit card debt.'

Beth turned back to him. 'Why did you keep him on as a client, after you knew about him and Julia?'

He seemed not to understand her. 'Why should I not?'

She took a giant intake of breath in astonishment. 'Why *shouldn't* you?' she said. 'My God! My husband was fucking your wife!'

There, she thought. Done it again. Sorry, David. But you were, weren't you? Tidy, careful David. You were, you were . . .

'No,' Oliver said.

'What?'

'No, I doubt it.'

'Julia told me on the evening of the funeral. Don't you talk to your wife? You *know* . . . don't—' She put a hand to her head, made a pinching movement at her temple. 'Don't tell me you don't know that. I *know* that you *do*.'

He glanced at the ground, the stream, the garden. Finally, at her. 'Did David say so?' he asked.

'No! David told me nothing. *Nothing* at all!'

'Then . . .' He stopped. 'Then you had all this from Julia. Just Julia?' He let out a great sigh. 'Oh, Beth.'

He turned, walked back up the steps and towards the rear of the house. Here, in the shadow of the wall, he sat on the bench. He took out a pack of cigarettes and lit one, turning the tube around and around in his fingers. She watched him warily; then saw him begin to laugh. He sat back, his laughter rising and falling.

Exasperated, she went up the steps two at a time and ran across the lawn until she was standing next to him. 'What the hell's so funny?'

He leaned forward, patting at his chest as if to dislodge the smoke; it streamed out of his nostrils and mouth. 'We are,' he said.

She looked him over from head to foot; she had never seen him laugh outright like this. Oliver's style was more the sarcastic smile. She finally sat down next to him, though at the far end of the seat. 'Tell me the joke,' she said. 'Tell me.'

He sighed. 'Beth, I have been married to Julia for ten years,' he began slowly. 'I married her when she was my secretary in London. When she was—or seemed to be—a very impressionable young girl of twenty . . .' He drew on the cigarette, considered its glowing tip. '. . . and I, God help me, was a very impressionable old man of forty-six.'

'I know all that,' Beth said.

He shrugged. 'No doubt. No doubt Julia painted a great number of lurid pictures of the time.'

'She's told me nothing.'

Oliver looked across at Beth. 'Julia has a great talent for fiction. Have you never noticed?'

'No.'

'She also has a great need. Let us say, a bottomless pit of need.'

'For what?'

He inclined his head to one side. 'Not love. Neither mine nor David's. But . . . to be the centre, to command attention.'

'I've heard enough.' Beth stood up.

Oliver, however, was not to be deflected now he had begun. He stayed where he was. 'I wonder how Julia would describe those early days, in London.'

'I'm really not interested, Oliver.'

'Julia was a very good secretary indeed. I had suffered from one or two dreadful predecessors, and I was very grateful. We progressed from lunch to dinner . . . and the rest, naturally. I was the quarry—though that had not occurred to me; Julia, after all, was even more fragile-seeming than she is now. The contrast between the efficient working girl and the helpless, childlike dependant at the end of the day was terribly alluring.'

Beth sat slowly down.

'I suppose it began after three months or so of our relationship. Perhaps less,' he slowly continued. 'Julia came to me with a complaint that she needed a larger office. She shared one with the Senior Partner's secretary, and claimed the other woman disliked her. Naturally, I tried to get a move for her. It caused some conflict with the man concerned—his secretary was by far the senior—but, eventually, Julia was moved to a small room that had once been a storeroom. She asked for it to be decorated, and I arranged it. She chose the most advanced word-processors and the most expensive fittings, and claimed my authority. It caused an argument at the next partners meeting; an embarrassment I could ill afford, because I had only been taken on as a partner the year before. The older man—' he smiled rather grimly at the memory—'the older man said that I ought to marry the girl and get her out from under their feet. Julia did not bother to cultivate friendships in the firm.'

Beth laid her head on her hand, propped on the armrest of the seat. Oliver's words flowed over her like a slow, down-pulling current.

'Julia and I were married after six months. The honeymoon was in Antigua—Julia had booked this without reference to me. I could not persuade her that I couldn't pay for it. It was the best for her . . . only the best, always the best.'

He stretched his legs, looking down at his shoes. 'Things came to a head in the firm. Julia managed to antagonise every member of staff. It was suggested that I leave; leave a post for which I had worked hard. It was made pretty clear that no other firm would be interested in me. And so I decided to move out of London altogether, and set up in practice . . .' He paused. '. . . well, here, as it happens.'

'Why here?'

He raised his eyebrows. 'Julia saw the Lodge advertised by a London estate agent.'

'But how could you afford it, if what you're telling me is true?'

'My father conveniently died.' There was silence for a second. 'Would you like to know why so much pressure was put on me to leave London?'

'You've just told me.'

'I've told you half the story.'

'And the rest?'

'We were forced to leave because Julia had an affair with the Senior Partner. His wife agreed not to divorce him; the proviso being that I left the firm.'

Beth stared at him. She was trying to fit the picture that Oliver painted of Julia to the woman she actually knew.

'He was better, you see. A richer man, and more respected. He had a manor house in Sussex and a flat in London and property in Ireland. He drove a better car; he dressed more expensively. He was sixty-three, of course, to Julia's twenty-one, and not exactly a desirable physical specimen . . . but that wasn't the point. Julia craved attention; to be the centre, that was her need. The centre of every unfolding drama.' He shook his head sadly. 'Of course, in this case, she reckoned without the wife, who was the nearest to her equal that I have ever met.' He took out another cigarette and tapped it on the pack.

'Why didn't you leave her?'

'Because I was as much a fool as he. Because I still am, God help me, that bloody fool. I loved her.' He gazed at his hands. 'Julia rather likes older men,' he observed tonelessly. 'That is why David wouldn't hold much allure.' He pointed the unlit cigarette at Beth. 'That is why she would not have continued an affair with him. One night, perhaps. That's possible. But not an affair. David had nothing to give—nothing more than she had already.'

Beth took a long, deep breath. 'Independence,' she murmured.

'I beg your pardon?'

She looked hard at him. 'Independence,' she repeated. 'Money buys a good deal of independence.'

Oliver laughed shortly. 'Julia doesn't want independence,' he said. 'Even if David got her the money, she wouldn't use it. She would just want the drama of *demanding* it. Once the money arrived, what use would it be to her? She wouldn't go anywhere *alone*. How could she? No audience.'

'But—'

'Julia has to have an audience, and she must . . .' He raised his hands, meshing his fingers together. 'Cling,' he said. 'Cling and weep.'

Beth shrank from him, shaking her head.

'Beth, I think Julia has an illness . . .'

'I don't want to hear this. I just want you to go.'

'And leave you here? Believing Julia, believing the lies she's told you? Believing that I've somehow made off with all David's money . . . that's what she's said, I take it?'

Beth looked away. 'Julia was leaving with David,' she said. '*Without any money at all. That's what she's told me.*'

There was a long silence. When Beth looked up, Oliver was gazing at her, expressionless. 'We will never know,' he said slowly. 'Because the only person who could have told us is dead.'

At last, he got to his feet.

She did so too, taking the opportunity to step back from him, leaving the seat, turning again for the patch of ground below the terrace.

'Beth.'

'Yes?' She looked back at him over her shoulder.

Unexpectedly, he walked quickly towards her, took her left hand, and held it tightly between his own. 'I know things are terribly difficult for you now, Beth,' he said. 'And I am so very sorry if I've been a part of that distress. We all make mistakes, and I . . .'

She tried to take her hand away, but he held it tighter.

'We make mistakes, that is human,' he told her.

Beth closed her eyes, tears threatening. She squeezed them tight in an effort to stop them falling. Oliver lowered his voice to a kindly, slower tone.

'We are just the same,' he said softly. 'Both betrayed by our partners . . .'

He lifted her hand and pressed it to his lips. She looked at him coldly; after raising his head, however, instead of letting her go, he pulled her arm behind his waist and stepped forward, as if he was going to take her in his arms. She stiffened, trying to extricate her arm. 'My dear girl . . .' he said.

'Oliver . . .'

He was standing a couple of inches from her, his arm around her shoulder. 'If you and I were to . . . become a team . . .'

She almost laughed. 'A *team*!'

He waved his hand. 'Well, let us say a partnership. Of our own . . .' He smiled. 'I am very fond of you, Beth.'

She managed, at last, to free her arm and pull away from him. The touch of his arm, heavy on her shoulder, had repulsed her. She shot him a look of loathing. 'It's for the money, isn't it?' she said. 'So that I shan't pursue this whole thing! So that I shan't find out exactly what you've done!'

'No, no—'

'I *will* find out,' she said. 'And you won't stop me. Tell all the stories you like. You've lost my vote.'

He hesitated for one last moment. 'I have not betrayed your trust,' he said. 'I am the only person, out of the three of us, who has not.'

Beth turned away, her hands briefly to her face. She walked down the garden, taking the steps two at a time, and fled to the shade of the border of trees.

Oliver watched for a moment from the higher sanctuary of the lawn, his hands momentarily hovering, useless and empty, in front of him.

Then, abruptly, he too turned away.

TWENTY-EIGHT

*T*HE PHONE RANG AT TEN O'CLOCK.

Beth had just finished having a shower. She picked up the phone from where it lay on the window sill of the landing.

'Hello?'

'Hello. It's Rhys Owen.'

'Oh, Rhys . . .'

'How are you?'

'Fine,' she said, automatically. She sat down on the top stair, folding the towelling robe tightly over her knees.

'I just wondered how it went with the building society.'

'Well, I told them I was going to change solicitors . . .'

'Good.'

'He came round here this afternoon.'

'Who?'

'Oliver Woods.'

There was a momentary silence. 'What for?'

She shook her head. She was looking down into the dimly lit hall, at the door where David had stood five days before. 'He admitted to witnessing the application; he says that David came in with it already signed. He says he is completely innocent.' She sighed. 'And Julia phoned me an hour ago.'

On the other end of the line, Rhys frowned. To say what?'

Beth smiled. 'Crazy. Crazy conversation. All about Rosie being ill. The kind of conversation you'd have . . . if nothing had happened.'

'Ill with what?'

'It sounded like flu.'

'Why didn't she just call the doctor?'

'Oh, she had. She was just ringing to let me know.' And Beth forced out a semblance of a laugh.

'This is very peculiar.'

'I know. But it's nice to hear someone else say so.'

'Isn't there someone in the village you can talk to?'

Beth ran her free hand down the struts of the banister, wiping away dust that had stuck between the bars. 'I don't know anyone particularly well,' she said. 'I've always worked, so I never made those daytime friends . . .'

'Just don't answer the door to them. Oliver and Julia.'

'No.' Her gaze settled on the floor of the hall below. She saw that there was something lying by the front door. She got up, walking downstairs, still holding the phone. 'Something's been delivered,' she told Rhys. 'Hold on a second.'

At the bottom she stepped forward, bare-footed. She switched on the hall light and saw, to her surprise, that it was a small leather collar. She picked it up.

'It's my cat's collar,' she said.

'Had the cat lost it?'

'No.' And then, to herself, turning it over in her hands, completely mystified, 'How would he get out of it?'

'Is he missing?' Rhys asked.

She thought, trying to remember when she had last seen him. 'He was here this morning, I think . . .'

'Have you seen him tonight?'

'No. But that's not unusual.' She sighed, putting the collar down on the hall table. 'Strange.'

'Well, I won't keep you . . .'

'Yes. Of course.'

'But you're all right? That's why I rang.'

She bit her lip, looking self-consciously away from the phone, as if he could actually see her. 'Yes, thank you.'

'Good-night, then.'

'Good-night, Rhys. And—'

'Yes?'

'Nothing. Just thanks.'

He hung up; she switched off the phone and put it down.

Beth walked into the kitchen, opened the fridge, and looked at the contents wearily. She hadn't eaten since that morning, at Rhys's house, and she knew that she had to. It seemed like a complex mathematical task, one which mentally defeated her. She forced herself to take cheese and salad from the shelves, and cut herself two slices of bread, all the time holding herself rigid, willing herself to pay attention.

Her mind kept free-falling away to the least important memories. David tying his tie with that methodical slowness that could enrage her. David's repeated phrases . . . he would say, 'Just a little', if she asked him if he wanted anything. Anything: a sandwich, cream on his fruit, sugar in his coffee, whether he was spending any time working that evening, or sitting in the garden, or whether he was going to . . . anything, anything. It was always *just a little*. It ought to have been his middle name. Mister Justalittle. She laughed breathily and stopped abruptly, gripping the edge of the work surface, an expression close to desperation on her face.

It was just . . . so . . .

Unlike him. All this. *Unlike* him.

'Oh God,' she breathed. She willed herself to cut the sandwich in two and put it on a plate. As she took the scraps to the bin to throw them away, she caught sight of Chaos's feed tray, still full from that morning.

She looked at it steadfastly. Chaos never went without food; he was too greedy, too lazy for that. His world revolved around the time she opened the tin and put the tray on the floor.

She retraced her steps to the hall to get the collar.

And it was only then that she noticed that the door to the utility room was open. It was a narrow room, only eight by five. It had once been a scullery, when the house was first built. When she and David had moved in, it had been a storeroom, with a stone sink and a mountain of old packing cases. They had cleared it, put in a loo, and a stacked washing machine and drier, and the smallest triangular sink they could find. Then they, too, accumulated life's backwash in it. So much of it that she always kept the door closed on the mess.

Always . . .

She pushed the door wider and switched on the light. The washing machine was directly opposite, the loo and sink behind the door. She looked around, coming into the room, frowning.

It felt as if something was out of place: something difficult to put a name to. Her eyes ranged over the room. Nothing appeared to have been moved or taken. She picked up a cloth lying on the window sill and began, absently, to wipe the dust from the sill and the shelves. On the floor next to the toilet, the pile of seed catalogues and magazines had fallen over. She bent down, righted them, and wiped the closed lid of the toilet. She realised that she hadn't cleaned the house for almost a fortnight.

She depressed the handle on the cistern, and wiped the dusty sink. She turned to go, and then stopped in the doorway.

The toilet was flushing, but the water was not going down. She could hear it swilling about, filling the pan.

She walked back to it and lifted the lid. At first, she thought there was a black plastic bag in the toilet; the bottom gleamed brownish-black under the water. But only for the first few seconds. She leaned forward, puzzled, and saw that it wasn't plastic, but some kind of fabric, something thick and dense. Velvet, or felt.

The water was almost up to the brim, and, just as Beth looked about for something to pick out the dark bundle with, the thing floated up, freed a little, and three thick dark strands swilled around. The water swept down, finding a sudden channel with the release of the blockage. For a moment, the thing bobbed obscenely on top of the spiralling column of water. And in that same moment, Beth realised what it was.

'No!' she cried.

144

She sprang back from the toilet, and the form in the white pan suddenly dipped as the water vanished.

'Oh God, oh God,' Beth whispered.

For a while she stood stock still, mesmerised by complete revulsion and shock. Then pity overcame her. She ran forward and plunged both hands into the toilet pan to drag out the dead cat. The strands were his legs and tail, lifeless and fluid and slack, weightless in the water. She sobbed as she pulled at his body, liquid draining off him in a flood, down the length of his body. It agonised her to see how limp and thin he was now that his fur was saturated.

As she pulled, his body rolled in her grasp; she was forced to dig her fingers into him to get any kind of purchase. At last she got him free, and lowered him to the floor. He lay on the carpet, mouth open, eyes open, teeth bared.

Beth knelt at his side, her breath coming in a series of small, hitched moans. She looked helplessly from the toilet to the floor.

Chaos would never go near water. He kept out of the bathrooms, stayed away from the sinks. He had never even sat near the river. He even loathed the lawn sprinkler, his tail always twitching in affronted fury. There was just no way, *no way* that he had come here by accident.

Beth's gaze went back to the hallway. She staggered up, gasping for breath, and went out. The collar still lay on the hall table. She picked it up. It was fastened at the usual third slot. It could not have come off over his head, even in a struggle. Someone had taken it off, and then refastened it. And then pushed it through the letterbox.

Or perhaps they had not.

If someone had . . . Christ, the thought—just the thought—that someone had come in and done this to Chaos . . . they could have brought the collar with them. Taken it off him and . . . why?

Why leave it in the hall?

Then, gazing back to the utility room, and down again at the collar in her fingertips, she understood. It was to attract her attention, to bring her to the door of the room. It was a signpost, a signal; whoever had done it knew that the room was rarely used. She might not have found him for days, a week . . .

And they wanted her to find him.

Her mind raced back to the birds.

She thought it had been him, bringing them to the house. But . . .

She pressed both hands to her head, trying to force reason, a shape, a clue into the tangled line of her thoughts.

No one, no one on earth, surely, could come into the house; no one in this village, no one she knew, could do anything like this . . . in someone's home, in *her* home . . .

And now.

Why *now*?

She sat down, abruptly, on her heels in the hallway. She was too frightened to go back into the utility room and even look at Chaos. Too frightened, too sick. To have to look again at his drawn-back lip; to pick him up.

She would have to touch him, take him out. She would have to bury him.

She crossed her arms over her knees and her face. And pictures of Oliver and Julia and Rosie came dancing straight into her head.

'Jesus Christ,' she whispered. 'Oh, sweet Jesus Christ.'

TWENTY-NINE

As Rhys opened the gate on Sunday morning, he could hear music at the back of Beth's house. All the windows were open—fluttering light curtains on the first floor touched the flint and cob walls—and the door and the small skylight windows on the sloping roof were open too, as if to let in light. Or let out that sound.

He began to smile as he stepped forwards, suddenly recognising the melody. It was Dinah Washington singing 'Come Rain Or Come Shine'. He listened for more than a minute, relishing the luxury of the voice. The contrast between the song and the sight of the house ahead of him, the sleepy village and the green view, was huge.

A line of washing, brilliant white in the morning sun, flapped on the garden line: sheets, pillowcases, towels. Below them, scarlet lines of pelargoniums filled the borders. The paths were swept, the lawn cut, the pear tree fanned rigidly against the south-facing wall. It was a quintessential English Sunday. And Dinah Washington was laying down the blues of 1954.

He walked to the side of the house and found the door to the kitchen wide open, the breeze blowing coolly through, touching his face as he glanced inside. The room smelled prickingly of lemon and soap; the surfaces were clean, except for an enormous pile of newly-washed crockery on the draining board, a mountain of overlapping plates, cups, saucers and tureens.

Beth was on the floor with her back to him, a bucket at her side and a kneeling mat underneath her, scrubbing at the linoleum with a cloth.

'Hello,' he said.

She didn't hear him. He waited another few seconds for Dinah to roll to a stop.

'Hello,' he repeated.

Beth jumped. She looked over her shoulder. The record, trembling, he saw now, on an ancient turntable under a scratched Perspex cover, crackled and began playing 'Teach me Tonight'.

Beth stood up and went to it, turning it off. 'I found it,' she said.

'One of my favourites.'

'Really?' She considered the record cover, put it down, and splayed the remainder of her collection with wet fingertips. 'I found them in the attic,' she said. 'I bought them at college. When we got married, David said they were too scratched to play on the good deck. I put them away . . .' She picked up the covers one by one, showing him. Don MacLean's *American Pie*; Menuhin and Grapelli's *Fascinating Rhythm*; Bach's *Toccata and Fugue in D minor*, Rod Stewart's *Blondes Have More Fun*.

'Quite a mixture,' Rhys said.

'Yes,' she replied. 'I liked everything then.' She tidied the covers back together, embarrassed. 'I forgot how much I liked things,' she murmured.

He nodded at the kitchen. 'Spring cleaning?'

'Something—'

'Something like that.'

'Yes.'

He looked hard at her. She wasn't better; he had hoped, hearing the music, seeing the hard work that she was doing, that she might have felt easier. But it was still early days. No . . . not even that. It was still the wasteland. She looked back at him with a brittle expression, a kind of refusal to concede.

'I've got a surprise for you,' he said.

'Oh?'

'In the car.'

She didn't move.

'What's the matter?' he asked.

'I already had one surprise,' she said. She walked from the kitchen into the hall. 'Look.'

He saw a black plastic rubbish sack folded in the corridor.

'Look inside,' she said.

He did so. It was Chaos's still-wet body.

'Oh God,' he exclaimed, stepping swiftly backwards. He looked up at her.

'I found him last night. In the toilet.'

'The *toilet*?'

She crossed her arms, leaning against the wall.

'What the hell happened?'

'You tell me.'

He looked back at the cat. 'But cats don't . . .' He saw her face, stood up, dropping the plastic back over the cat's body. 'Somebody did this? Is that it?'

'I can't think of any other explanation.'

They stared at each other for a long moment.

'Who has been in here? Who has a key?'

'I gave a key to Helen Pritchard.'

'The—'

'No, no. Not Helen.'

'Who, then?'

'It could be anyone. I often leave the doors unlocked.'

Rhys's expression was intense. He walked up to her. 'Then you must stop,' he said. 'Whoever did this is . . .' She was looking at her feet. 'Do you know who it is?' he asked.

'No, I—'

'It's not Julia?'

'Julia. Oliver. Perhaps.' Her voice was level, cold.

'*Why?*'

She pushed her hair back. 'Why anything? 'Why *anything*? David . . . the money . . . It's like the world has just turned crazy, *crazy*. I keep thinking, I must wake up soon. I must wake up.'

He held her wrist, halting her gestures. 'Have you called the police?'

'To report what? That my cat drowned? They'd think I'd gone mad!'

'To report that you've had an intruder that *killed* the cat.'

'Does it sound likely? I mean, would *you* believe me?'

'Of course I believe you!'

She gave a tenuous smile. 'There isn't any damage, nothing stolen. Who would break into a house to kill a cat? It's ludicrous.'

'But they *did* come in, to do exactly that.'

'It's just insane. I can't ring the police and tell them that. I'd be a laughing stock.'

She looked deathly pale. He took her arm and walked her into the living room, motioning her to sit.

'Beth, I don't like this at all,' he said.

She leaned back, closing her eyes briefly with an expression of weariness.

'You really think Julia or Oliver would do this?' he asked.

'I don't know what to think. I've been lying awake half the night.'

'Nothing like this has happened before, has it?'

Beth paused. 'Well, not exactly . . .'

'Not *exactly*? What do you mean?'

She sighed. 'On the morning of David's death there was a dead bird in the porch. Then, a couple of nights ago, there was a bird in the kitchen. A live bird.'

'Was the door shut?'

'Yes.'

'Jesus.'

'The thing is, I hate birds. I've hated them in the house, near the house, for a long time.'

'Who knew this?'

'I keep trying to think. I don't remember ever telling anyone except David.'

'Julia?'

'No, I don't think so. Though David might have told her.' She looked at him. 'I wonder if Oliver—'

'But *why*?

'Over the money? To drive me so crazy that I wouldn't pursue this fraud with the money?'

Rhys frowned. 'From what you say, he doesn't strike me like that. Too cold, too straight. This kind of thing . . . it's fevered, you know? Someone overstrung. Vindictive.'

Beth shook her head. 'It strikes me as just the opposite.'

Rhys looked away from her. 'It couldn't be Rosie?'

'Rosie!'

'Well, some children . . .'

'Rosie loves cats. She *loves* animals. She's a nice little girl. She wouldn't dream—'

'OK, OK,' he said, holding up his hands.

She was still staring at him, aghast. 'She couldn't hold him, could she? She's only six. He would struggle though . . .' She thought about Chaos, his laziness. His willingness to be picked up. His age. He *would* struggle, but probably not very effectively.

There was a prolonged silence. Beth leaned forward, resting her elbows on her knees and her head in her hands. Then, sighing deeply, she glanced up at him.

'Tell me about *your* surprise,' she said. 'I hope it's a decent one.'

'It's in the car.'

She walked back to the kitchen, picked up the full bucket of dirty water, took it outside and threw it down the drain.

'Shall I bring it in?' Rhys asked.

'If you like.'

She started to fill the kettle. Watching her plug it in, setting it to boil, and then picking up a tea towel and beginning to dry the plates, Rhys could see acutely that she was simply going through the motions.

She was just as calmly putting two cups, two plates on the table when he came back from the car.

'Look who it is,' he said.

She glanced up. He was carrying Aesculapius. The dog took deep umbrage at being carried at all, and was making a warning noise of outrage, like a small generator. His disgust was made worse by being wrapped in a rug, a wildly chequered affair of definite female slant, with a pink ribbon edging.

'He hates me for this,' Rhys said. 'It was all I could find in the shops yesterday afternoon. It ought to belong to a pregnant Yorkshire terrier.'

Beth came up to them, stroking the dog's head. 'You poor little bloke,' she said.

Rhys felt his heart turn sluggishly over. It was an extraordinarily unpleasant sensation—not at all the dancing anticipation supposedly associated with love or lust. It had the feeling of a piece of meat turned on a butcher's slab.

'By the way,' he said. His own voice sounded odd. 'I owe you an apology. Aesculapius *was* a Greek god. The Romans just borrowed him. Shows how much I know.'

She smiled. 'Would he like a drink?' she asked.

Rhys eased down the image, the heart under a sharp knife. His imagination surprised him; the peremptory detail of the picture. The empty valves and arteries. He concentrated on Beth's face grudgingly, as if she were responsible for the revolting illustration. It took quite an effort of will to answer her.

'Probably.'

'He's allowed to eat and drink?'

'Yes. He got over the anaesthetic quickly.'

She was pinching back the cover. 'Let me see his leg.'

It was pathetic; the dressing looked bigger than the dog. Ace rolled his eyes, begging sympathy, and Beth stroked his head.

'I'm sorry,' she said. She put back the cover and added, 'I want to pay for the vet. It was my fault.'

'No. That's OK.'

'It's not OK. I'll pay for it.' Her tone brooked no objection.

Rhys put the dog down on the floor. They brought him a bowl and Ace took a few condescending mouthfuls of water.

Beth smiled as she stood up. 'Tea or coffee?'

'Coffee.' Rhys had almost kissed her as she had come level with his shoulder, and he turned away, mutely horrified at himself. 'I wondered if you'd like to go out anywhere,' he said, looking carefully at Beth's memo board, at the notes and the milk bill and the library times.

She poured. 'Where?'

'Anywhere. A walk.'

'But Ace can't walk.'

'I can carry him. I thought maybe Attledene, or Mabberton Park . . .'

'The sea.' She was holding a cup in front of him, and, at last, there was some semblance of interest in her face, spontaneous interest. She gave him a spoon, and, seeing his inactivity, quietly stirred the sugar in for him. 'Yes. I think the sea,' she said.

Thank you, God, he thought.

They drove to Abbots Sands. A curiously undescriptive name for that part of the coast, ten miles from the house, that had hardly any sand at all, but an enormous shelving bank of pebbles that stretched for several miles.

The route to the sea took them through undulating farmland, with deeply scooped hollows and bracken-topped hills. To their right, the coastline could be seen curving around in a wide bay, green and gold above blue.

'I think this must be one of the most beautiful roads in England,' Beth said. 'I come up here on my own sometimes, just to look.'

'Without David?' Rhys asked.

'He doesn't . . . he didn't like walking much,' she murmured. 'He wasn't the outdoors type.'

They parked in the lane before the empty beach.

There were rarely any families here, only fishermen casting from the last high shelf of pebbles before the sea. The land dropped dramatically away underneath the breakers, so that any foolish swimmer was immediately in deep churning water within six feet of the shore.

The sea was blindingly blue, the air almost cold, the surf a textbook white. They walked alongside it for more than a mile, saying nothing at all. Finally, Beth sat down, gazing at the water, her eyes screwed against the glare; then she lay back on the stones, closing her eyes, spreading her arms on either side and plunging her hands deep into the small slithering stones.

Rhys sat down beside her.

There was no one else along the beach; it was still only ten o'clock. He set Ace down on the blanket and watched as the dog struggled to get up, stagger a pace, then pee determinedly at the edge of the waves.

The noise of the sea was thunderous; Rhys could feel the vibration under him.

He looked back at Beth, and saw that she was looking at him.

'How are you?' he asked.

She sat up, closing her fist at the base of her throat. 'Angry,' she said. 'I wake up angry . . . it's *stuck* here.'

He smiled, feeling sorry and helpless. She gave a shuddering sigh, and dropped her hand to her lap.

'Were you happy—before?' he asked.

He expected her to say yes, to cry perhaps, to demonstrate the locked-up fury that she claimed she carried. Instead, to his surprise, she replied, 'I don't think I was.' And, more softly still, 'And I don't think David was either. With or without Julia.'

'How long had you been married?'

'Eleven years.'

'A long time to be unhappy.'

She frowned. 'Not *consciously* unhappy.' She shook her head, as if this thought weighed too heavy. 'Tell me about your wife,' she said.

'Chris? There isn't much to tell.'

'Tell me anyway.'

'Well . . .'

'How did you meet?'

'At a hospital dance.'

'And . . . ?'

'And . . . we got married, very quickly. And bought the house. And she went abroad. Very quickly.'

'How long ago?'

'Two years.'

'Why did she go abroad?'

'She was tired of working for the NHS and didn't want to go private, and she was always . . .' Beth waited while he chose his words. '. . . altruistic. Idealistic. She wanted to help more, help where it really mattered.'

'How often does she come back?'

'She doesn't.'

Beth leaned forward, resting her arms across her knees. Rhys shifted stones from one hand to the other, staring down.

'She's never come back—in two years?'

He glanced up at her. 'Oh yes, she came back after six months. She came back to tell me that she could never see herself staying in England, saw her future working long-term in Africa. She'd met another aid worker who was very . . .'—he shrugged—'. . . effective, very charismatic . . .'

'A man?'

'Yes.'

'I see.'

Rhys began flicking the stones, one by one, towards the water; Ace watched alertly, whining as each pebble rolled to a stop. 'It's not an affair,' he said. 'I don't *think* it's an affair. Actually, he was on the TV about a month ago. There was a programme about Third World aid, and they interviewed him . . . ?'

'No,' said Beth. 'I don't remember.'

'You'd remember *him*. Tall and thin, with glasses . . . he looks your archetypal weed. I started to laugh when he came on the screen. That's what this fuss is about, I thought, when they showed him. Pasty white in a weave hat, hitching up his shorts—he kept hitching up his shorts— and I thought, well, shit. So that's Jesus Christ, the miracle worker.'

Beth was watching Rhys closely. His tone was offhand.

'Then he began to talk. He's like those fire and brimstone evangelists. An Irish gift of the gab, and a voice like Richard Burton, out of this streak of . . .' He stopped, then started to laugh. Beside him, Aesculapius wagged his tail. 'I really admired him in the end,' he said quietly. 'I was ready to despise him and, while I listened, I admired him instead. He was angry. Steaming angry, the way we all ought to be. He was getting things done. I understood, then, what it was. Why Chris was going back.'

'For him?'

'No. Not just for him. For the difference.' He stopped, his mouth set.

'She'll come back,' Beth said.

'No. She loves the place. It's not just this guy. She likes the people out there, all of them. She won't come back.'

'And what about you?'

'What *about* me?'

'What about your marriage?'

He shrugged. 'She has no interest in that.'

'Did she say so?'

'No. But it's incidental. Irrelevant.'

Beth considered a moment. 'Was it always?'

He shook his head. 'No. Not in the beginning.' He looked at the ocean, gestured towards it. 'I feel as if she's been swept away. One minute she was there, the next—by accident—she's gone. She stepped off here . . . now she's there.'

'Do you hear from her?'

'All the time. She writes every week.'

'Well, that's—'

'She writes about the villages and the weather.'

'She's keeping in contact, though. That must mean something.'

Rhys had taken to skimming the stones instead of merely pitching, and it was too much for Ace. The dog hauled himself up and tottered like a drunk to the waves, keening as each stone flew past.

'Little lies,' Rhys murmured.

'Pardon?'

He smiled half-heartedly. 'Little white lies,' he said. 'The weather, the work. How fine she is. How she hopes that *I'm* fine. Asking about the neighbours and my work. But it's got nothing to do with her. It's not in *here*.' He briefly touched his chest.

'Isn't that what we all do?' Beth asked. 'It's to oil the process. Being polite. It doesn't mean anything. It doesn't hurt. There isn't anything sinister about it.'

'No?'

'Oh, come on. Chris isn't lying to you. She's being kind, yes—but she's not lying.'

He looked almost angry. 'But that's the worst kind,' he said. 'The polite lie. The little quick one that doesn't *seem* to matter.'

'No—'

'*Yes*,' he insisted. 'If I could have a fight with her, a stand-up, knock-down fight, then at least I would know. If I could let off steam. If she would look me in the eye, or write the truth.'

Beth fell silent for a while. She was thinking of Oliver; thinking of him looking her in the eye and telling her anything *but* the truth.

She glanced back at Rhys. 'What about the house?' she asked. 'Will you keep it?'

'I don't know.'

'Why don't you sell it?' Beth was thinking of the room in which she had so recently sat, and of the furnishings that crowded out any trace of Rhys's character.

'I don't want to,' he said.

'So you think that there *is* a chance she'll come back?'

'No. I just don't want to touch her stuff. I don't know what to do with it.'

'You still love her,' Beth said.

He didn't reply.

She lay down again staring up at the sky.

'It's *because* she's so polite,' Rhys said. 'I'd like to smack her in the face, frankly. But I can't do that, can I? Never mind the thing of hitting a woman—I can't smack someone who's right. I can't hit out at someone who never loses their temper.'

'She isn't right to leave you.'

'She's right in every other way. She's dedicated and she's got courage . . . I feel like a shit asking her to come back.'

Beth was still looking up into the enormous, cloudless vault of sky above them. 'Then don't ask her again,' she said. She meant that she was guessing at Chris's feelings; the girl was in an agony of polite guilt. She had fitted into a slot that had always been waiting for her, and recognised now the blind alley that she had been in when she was trying to do the right thing and be a good wife. Now she was doing what she wanted. She had gone as far as marrying him. And now she was writing her letters.

'You don't think it's worth trying at all?' Rhys asked.

Beth rubbed her eyes, then let her hands drop back and saw that Rhys was above her. She reached out and touched the side of his face, feeling overwhelmingly sorry for him.

'And . . .'

He began to say something, stopped, and then abruptly kissed her. Whether it was meant as a swift kiss of sympathy or of affection rapidly ceased to matter; at the first sensation of his breath and skin, Beth slid both arms tightly around his neck, and he pressed down on her, the full length of his body rolling on to her. She was seized with a kind of blind need, not so much for sex, or even touch, but to be taken out of the day, out of the pit in which she was floundering. She was so tired, and so cold, and his face and hands and body were so warm . . .

As he kissed her his hands moved down, and she grasped them and guided him; in a moment, his hand was moving on her breast. She touched him, trying to find the catch to his belt; he tried to move her hand away, to help her, to do it himself, and the movement forced his head up. They stared at each other for a second, and, suddenly, he sat back from her, inching away against the stones.

'God, I am sorry,' he said.

'It's all right . . .'

'I'm really so sorry.'

'No, I—' She couldn't say it. She couldn't say that she had wanted him. It was so grotesque, so soon after David. Over Rhys's shoulder, she glimpsed someone coming along the beach; a man and a woman walking two Golden Retrievers. The dogs were soaked, their coats dark and stringy.

Rhys stood up.

'I don't want to go back,' she said, her voice almost lost in the sound of the ocean as she looked up at him.

'I think we should,' Rhys told her.

He picked up Ace carefully in his arms and started to walk back, along the narrow fringe of hard-packed sand.

She watched him, astounded and breathless at her own need—and feeling disappointedly guilty to the bottom of her heart.

They arrived back at her house at eleven o'clock.

As Rhys's Citroën pulled into Beth's drive, they both noticed Rosie at the same time. The little girl was sitting inside the stone porch.

Getting out, Beth called her name.

'Hello,' Rosie replied.

They both walked to the door. 'Are you on your own?' Beth asked.

'Yes. I want to see Chaos.'

Beth and Rhys exchanged a look. 'He's not about just now,' Beth said. 'Where is Mummy?'

'At home. Tired.'

'Is Daddy there too?'

'No.'

Beth sat on the stone ledge and reached down to stroke Rosie's shoulder. 'How are you today?' she asked.

'All right.' Rosie didn't look up. 'I thought you might be having tea,' she said. 'It's eleven time. And Chaos—'

'Oh. And you'd like a cup of tea? A drink of orange?'

'And a biscuit.'

'You're right,' Beth said, standing up, smiling. 'Eleven o'clock is time for a drink of something. And—you don't know if Daddy is at home or not?'

There was no reply.

Beth bit her lip. She had no desire at all to go over to the Lodge. She had no objection to Rosie being here with her, but the child's arrival, unannounced, and so early on a weekend morning, struck her as odd. She had never done it before.

'What is Mummy doing?' Beth asked.

'She's in bed. Lying down.'

'I see.'

Rosie grinned. 'I dressed myself. I got my breakfast by myself.'

'Well! You *are* getting grown-up. And Daddy was nowhere about?'

'I think he went out.'

'This morning?'

'In the car.'

'And . . . ?'

'She was sick.'

'Who? Mummy?'

'Sick in the toilet.'

At that very second, Julia herself appeared, walking quickly down the lane, looking anxiously from side to side. Her face was drawn and pale, her eyes weary and dark-circled. She looked exhausted. She noticed them and stopped.

'Rosie!' she shouted.

Rosie did not look up.

'Rosie—come here.'

Julia had got to the gate; she tried to open it and failed, her hand slipping. She almost overbalanced, grabbing the wall alongside. Beth took Rosie's hand. 'Come on,' she said.

They walked to the gate, and within three feet of Julia Beth could smell the drink.

'Don't you know I've been looking for you!' Julia said. 'Everywhere!'

'I want to stay here,' Rosie murmured.

Julia made a grab for her. 'You're coming straight home. Straight *home.*'

'No!' Rosie shouted.

Julia glared at Beth.

'We only just got in,' Beth said. 'She was sitting in the porch.'

Julia's gaze flickered from Beth to Rhys and back again.

Beth found herself blushing. 'This is Rhys Owen,' she said. 'Rhys, this . . .'

But Julia ignored her. She had a hold of Rosie's wrist and was tugging her. 'No,' Rosie was repeating. 'No, no, no!'

'She can stay here for a while, if you like,' Beth offered, torn between mother and child. 'She can help in the garden.'

Julia's expression froze. 'You'd like that, wouldn't you?' she said in a vicious tone.

She wrenched Rosie away from the gate and into the road. Rosie began to scream in earnest. 'Hurting! *Hurting!*'

The grip on the arm, if anything, grew tighter. Beth could see white rings forming around Julia's fingertips on Rosie's flesh.

'You wait,' Julia muttered into Rosie's upturned face. Then she straightened up, turned, and walked away, dragging the child after her.

Instead of giving any resistance, Rosie began to trot alongside her, whimpering and squealing by turns, her face turned questioningly towards her mother. She pleaded all the way to the Lodge entrance. 'Mummy, no. Mummy . . .'

Rhys came up alongside Beth. 'What should we do?' he asked.

Beth glanced at him, then crossed her arms and stared down at the path.

'I really don't know,' she said.

THIRTY

$\mathscr{H}$ELEN PRITCHARD WAS EARLY INTO WORK on Monday morning. A year ago, she had negotiated an agreement with Oliver to come in late and finish late, leaving the typist to begin the day. It suited Helen well; she would rather begin work straight away when she came in at eleven than spend an hour filling the coffee machine and sorting post.

But today was different; Christina had a family crisis and Helen was in to cover. And the moment she walked through the door from the silent eight-o'clock High Street, she knew that something was wrong.

For a second she thought the office had been burgled. The filing cabinets behind Reception were all open, and papers were spread on the desk. She put her bag down and walked round the side of the counter, frowning. As far as she could make out, the papers were from unconnected files; she looked across at the phones and saw that they were off the hook. She hesitated, wondering if she ought to go straight back out and call the police from a public box. Then Oliver Woods appeared in the corridor.

'My God, Oliver,' she said, her hand on her chest. Her heart was beating heavily. 'You frightened me to death. I thought we'd been burgled.'

He took a couple of steps.

'We haven't, have we?' she asked.

'No, no.' He walked into Reception. She thought that he looked ghastly, but the fact didn't surprise her. Oliver often looked ghastly; he was predisposed to look ghastly.

'Are you looking for something?' she asked. 'Can I help?' She reached for the papers, to pick them up and re-file them, irritated that he should have searched through her meticulously ordered records.

'Leave them, please,' Oliver said. He came around behind her and shuffled the papers together in a bundle. He smelled rank, unwashed. She stepped back from the odour of his skin. He had a half-burned cigarette in his hand, with a long grey tip of ash, and seemed to be unaware of it; she watched it hovering above the letters and memoranda. He turned and smiled. 'I'm searching for one account,' he said. 'I put it in here and misfiled it.'

'What's it about?' she asked.

He didn't answer directly. 'I shall come across it no doubt,' he said.

'If you tell me the subject, the addressee . . .'

'It doesn't matter,' he said. By now he had picked up every sheet, and was closing the cabinet doors.

She looked at him, caught between ignoring this behaviour and questioning it. For all she knew, in the last year Oliver might have made this a daily habit. Perhaps he didn't trust her, and went through the files when he got into work, checking what she had done. That would be just like him.

'I'll make some coffee,' she said, taking off her coat.

Oliver paused at the edge of the counter. He pressed the cigarette into an ashtray, and she saw that his hand was shaking.

'Are you all right?' she asked.

He didn't reply. He was leaning on his free hand, and holding the papers to his chest with the other. His broad and yellow-stained fingers were splayed on the leatherette top. She thought that he must be catching his breath, or feeling some sort of pain; then, to her dismay, she saw that his eyes were full of tears.

She experienced a second of acute embarrassment. She would have given anything not to be there, not to be within those twenty inches of him, not to be obliged to walk forward to put her own hand on his. She was terribly aware of the intimacy of the situation.

'Oliver . . .'

He lowered his head. She found her eyes fixed on the few strands of thin hair behind the ears. It was as if he had bowed his head down to be blessed; there was not a more defenceless posture in the world.

'Oliver,' she repeated. 'Is there anything I can do?'

He said nothing for a second. Then, he raised his eyes to hers. 'I've done nothing wrong, that's the irony of it,' he said vaguely. 'Unless, of course, being foolish is a crime.' He covered his eyes with his hand.

'Sorry?' Helen said. She pressed her fingers on his arm.

Immediately, he stood up, as if appalled by the tenderness of her touch.

'Nothing,' he said, turning abruptly away from her.

THIRTY-ONE

*I*T WAS PAST EIGHT when Beth woke the next morning.

She lay looking at the window, where the curtains were drawn back. For a while, she couldn't think what the difference was in the scene outside; then, sitting up, she realised that it was broad daylight, and not the half-light she had grown used to since David's death. She looked at the clock, and rubbed her hands over her face.

She had slept for almost ten hours; an extraordinary time. She remembered going to bed last night in a kind of stupor, flinging herself down naked on the bed, drawing the cover from David's side across her.

She had been dreaming. Disintegrating walls, and shifting floors. Newspaper articles that she had seen in the spring of the previous year, of houses on the south coast teetering on the edges of eroding cliffs— gardens and paths dissolving as the owners stepped on them, as they touched them—had invaded her sleep.

She had walked towards a familiar table, opened a familiar door, and it had instantly melted in her hands. Wood and tile and brick assumed impossible liquid shapes. She had stood on a single small island of solid ground while everything around her slid into the past, shrank down again into the ground, where the grass smoothed over it like thick green fondant icing, implacably smooth. She had lain on the grass and tried to plunge her hands through the colour. But it had responded like green rubber, pushing down as she pushed down, springing back when she released the pressure.

She sat forward now, resting her arms on her drawn-up legs and laying her head on her arms. In this automatic, robotic state she had come back to their bed. The last time she had woken up here, it was to watch David dressing at the window, meticulously tucking his shirt into his trousers, his hand turned palm out, smoothing the shirt tail into flat pleats under the material.

She got up and walked slowly to the shower.

After breakfast, she sat down with her order book, desk diary and the phone. Some of those that she rang had heard about David, and she listened through half a dozen sympathetic eulogies, saying, 'Thank you' at intervals.

'But you won't be working now, will you?' one woman asked.

'Yes, I'm still working. Perhaps I can come to you on Wednesday . . .' She saw the garden in her mind's eye, a very small plot, with a raised bed close to the window that the couple wanted sectioned and replaced with a ring of paving stones to provide a sun trap for the summer.

'But I couldn't ask you. My dear, I have read it all in the paper and we are quite devastated for you. One must rest, you know. Absolute rest and peace.'

'Mrs Latimer, you'll be doing me a favour.'

'You ought to go away somewhere. Have you anywhere to go to? Somewhere remote?'

Beth gritted her teeth. 'I couldn't do that,' she said. 'I would be barmy within a couple of days. I've got to work.'

'Well, if you're sure . . .'

'I'll come at nine. You'll probably get the stone delivery earlier that morning, or the previous evening.'

'You really shouldn't at all—'

'Is nine all right?'

'Yes, if you're quite, quite sure . . .'

'Good.'

'I don't know *what* people will think of me. They'll think I've demanded that you come as originally arranged. They'll think I've insisted that you come. I should so hate them to think . . .'

So that was it. Not so much about Beth, this concerned what her neighbours would say about her. 'I'm sure they know you better than that,' Beth cut in, making a conscious effort to keep her voice even.

'Well, my dear . . .' The woman's voice was full of misgiving, a kind of contained terror that she would be forced to handle Beth in some way—placate her, probably. Deal with some sort of hysterical fit. It was as if grief were contagious; as if the bereaved spilled agony wherever they went, through the look on their rigidly still faces. As if they trailed it like drops of blood, left it on seats and on the rims of cups and on cutlery, and they communicated it in the touch of their hands.

Beth shook her head as she put down the phone. She wanted to wear a sign around her neck. It would say: YOU CAN'T CATCH IT FROM ME.

In an hour, she had reorganised her diary. They were all mercifully short jobs, until next week, when she had a landscaping to do for the offices of a print firm on the outskirts of town.

There was only one other thing. She would, she decided, walk down into the village, to the oak tree that had occupied so much of her attention until last week. She would see the Parish Council chairman, a retired colonel who lived on the green. In his study, comfortably and shabbily upholstered, with its shelves of militaria and photographs of his regiment, she knew she would be offered sherry with a cup of real coffee, a slice of warm gossip laced with insults about other councillors—and no mention at all would be made of David.

Just as she was going out, the phone rang again. Sighing, she went over to it.

'Yes, hello?'

'Beth . . .' It was Julia.

'What do you want?'

There was a prolonged silence. In the background, Beth thought that she could hear weeping—whether Julia's, or perhaps Rosie's, it was hard to tell.

'Beth. I just want to say . . .' More silence; another dragged breath. Beth moved the phone away from her ear.

'Don't put the phone down! Beth—'

'Julia, I'm going out.'

'Beth, please. I just wanted to say . . . how sorry I am . . . how—'

Beth hung up. For a good five minutes she walked round the ground floor, maddened. Then she caught sight of herself in the mirror. She looked completely distracted. She stopped, putting both hands to her cheeks, smoothing down her hair. 'Don't think about it,' she told herself. 'Just don't think about it.'

She went down the village lane slowly, relishing the fresh air and the bright blue sky with white clouds scudding across it. She almost managed to forget Julia, until, as she drew level with the Lodge, she saw a car parked in the drive, and a woman on the steps of the house.

The woman turned and saw her. She waved. 'Hello!' she called. 'Can you help me?'

Beth walked a little way up the drive. The woman came towards her, a regulation officer's wife in frilly-necked blouse, navy skirt and navy court shoes. Beth had never seen her before.

'Do you know Mrs Woods at all?'

'I know her. I live across the way.'

'Have you seen her today?'

'No.'

The woman clicked her tongue against her teeth. 'I can't understand it,' she said. 'I'm in the pool to collect Rosie this week, and when I came at half past eight I was sure that I could hear Rosie's voice inside, and their car was in the drive, but no one answered the door. *Most* impolite. There *was* someone there.'

Beth looked up at the house. 'There's no car here now,' she said. 'But she must be in.'

'Oh?'

'Well, I presume she is. I—'

'Julia was to come with me to a Wives' Club at half past ten.'

Beth sighed. 'I'm sorry.'

'It's very annoying,' the woman said.

'It must be.'

'But someone answered the phone.'

'When?'

'Someone picked up the phone when I rang after dropping the children at school.'

'Well, she—'

'They picked it up,' the woman said irritatedly, 'and I thought I heard Julia's voice. But when I replied, no one said anything.'

Beth frowned. Where had Julia's call come from, if not from home? The woman got back into her car and slammed the door. She wound down her window as she put the engine into gear. 'It really is very rude,' she said. The car pulled away.

Beth watched the Volvo turn out of the drive, then looked up at the house. Although the top curtains were drawn, the windows were wide open. She chewed on her lip uncertainly; then, walking to the side of the house, she saw that the doors there too were open.

'Julia?' she called.

She went further and looked in through the study windows. It was unkempt, with dying plants on the shelves.

'Julia!'

Nothing.

'Rosie?' She thought she had heard a sound. The back door was slightly open. Pausing on the threshold of the house, she turned her head. It was hard to distinguish where the noise had come from. Very faintly, she thought she could hear the mechanical drumming of a washing machine or dishwasher.

She hesitated again, not wanting to see Julia, but worried that Rosie might be alone and Julia sick upstairs, as she had been yesterday.

'Rosie . . .'

The kitchen was empty. There was no noise here; everything was switched off. Beth's gaze ran over the unwashed dishes, the newspapers spread in a heap on the table, the unpleasant bright pink tiling.

The sound had gone now. It had been clearer in the study and hall. She re-traced her steps, pausing at the foot of the stairs.

'Rosie!' she called.

Nothing from up there. Surely Rosie, even ill, would call back to her. She stood absolutely still, holding her breath for a second. The peculiar sound was clearer now.

Frowning, Beth walked back the way she had come. On the path outside, she realised that the noise was coming from the rear of the house, but slightly to one side, near the garage. She began to trot, the first slight tingling of apprehension crawling over her. She bent down as she ran—to avoid the lilacs drooping heavily and brushing her shoulders with their green gloom—to the small black door of the stone outhouse that had been converted to a garage years before. Here, the noise was quite distinct.

A running engine.

She tried to open the door, and found it locked. 'Julia!' she called.

There was a window next to the door, covered with webs inside, the glass filthy. 'Julia. Julia!' she called, hammering on the pane.

The significance of the drumming engine now ran through her like an electric shock. She ran to the front, to the maroon-painted door, pulling on the old steel handle. It was locked too. 'Oh God, oh Christ,' she whispered.

Panic hammering in her head, she dashed back to the house, running full pelt up the hall. She picked up the telephone and dialled 999.

'Emergency. Which service please?'

'Ambulance. I don't know. Fire brigade. Someone is locked in a garage. I can hear the car's engine running . . .'

'And your name . . . ?'

'Mrs March.'

'And the address?'

'The Lodge, Girton Marshall. It's about a hundred . . . God . . . a hundred, a hundred yards from the big tree. It has two stone pillars with lions on top, holding shields. It looks across the river to the main road, the Yeovil road.'

The Yeovil road. This morning, at Stag's Fall, on the Yeovil road . . .

'Oh God,' Beth whispered again. Then, to the anonymous stranger on the other end of the line, 'I can't get in; everything's locked. Please hurry. The doors—'

'Someone will be there very soon.'

Beth dropped the phone and ran back out of the house. This time she went straight to the front of the garage; here, a set of stone steps led to the vegetable garden. At the side of the steps was a rockery. With the breath scalding her throat, Beth prised a piece of Portland stone out of the terrace, and ran back with it in her arms. It was heavy; as she ran, she wondered if it was too heavy, in fact, to lever upwards.

At the back of the building, at the little window, she hauled the stone up and threw it at the glass. It smashed through with a deafening sound, and immediately the distinct and sickly petrol smell rolled out.

'Julia!'

Beth put her hand through the broken glass, feeling around for the lock to the door. She found it easily. She turned the thick bolt, but the door didn't respond. She closed her eyes, desperately trying to visualise how the lock worked. A rectangular piece of metal, with the bolt and . . . a catch. A locking catch. A snib you pulled downwards so that the bolt didn't turn. Glass was cutting Beth's skin as she moved her hand around, the fumes swarming over her. She found the snib and slipped it downwards, turned the lock, and simultaneously squirmed her body so that she was applying pressure to the door. It came open.

She pulled back her arm and pushed inside. The Mercedes was neatly wedged in a very small space. Julia rarely if ever used the garage for the car, and consequently it was filled with the assorted dross of both garden and house: old tubs, paint pots, boxes, piles of newspaper, wood for the fires, a stack of plastic cartons that Rosie had once used as toyboxes—red, green, blue. Beth turned sideways and edged through to the driver's door, her hand over her mouth. The noise of the car in the confined space filled her head. She leaned down to the closed driver's window.

Julia was sitting with her head resting on the back of the seat and her hands on the steering wheel. Her eyes were closed. She looked as if she were calmly asleep. Cream-coloured masking tape bordered the window.

Beth's attention was caught at the same moment by a band of colour on the seat behind. She squinted, gagging and gasping for breath, further into the car. Rosie was lying on the back seat, her legs curled up to her chest, a white fur rabbit clutched to her chest, her mouth hanging slackly open, and her eyes not quite closed. She looked, Beth realised at once, quite dead.

Violent fear almost closed Beth's throat; her heart slammed in her chest. 'Oh no,' she murmured. 'No, no . . .'

She tried the front door. Locked. And the back. Locked. She inched as fast as she could around the boot, to the other side. Locked . . . locked. From the exhaust, a tube, the kind one might find on the back of a tumble drier, led upwards and into the nearside back window which was half open. Beth stood for a second, wondering why there was tape on the other windows when there was a gaping hole in this one. Beyond it, she could see Rosie's head. She tried to push her hand through, but the gap was not quite wide enough, stopping her entry at her upper forearm just before the elbow. Her fingertips danced helplessly a foot from Rosie's head, an inch from the window handle on the inside of the door.

By this time, she could feel the carbon monoxide plucking dreamily at her concentration; she leaned for a second on the lustrous, shiny metal of the door, thinking absurdly that it was a beautiful shade. A deep, oceanic blue. The blue of deep water. Her legs ached and her fingers tingled distantly, the kind of tickling sensation that you might feel as you stretched first thing in the morning. Her heart was thudding like a dead weight.

A long way off she heard a siren, then voices in the drive. She could hear herself whispering some muttered litany of her own—*God, God, God*—words that drained out of her unconsciously as she felt her way past the passenger side door and up around the bonnet. The light in the garage was filmy, grey, threaded with bars of faint light, from another world's sunshine beyond the door. Under her fingers the bonnet was hot, vibrating. She tried getting forward, around the front, and found cardboard boxes in the way.

'Please,' she begged. And she repeated Rosie's name to herself, her mind fixed on the small white fingers wrapped around the rabbit's fur.

Her legs responded like two thick stone stilts. There was a prickling sensation on her upper lip, as though spots of hot ash were landing on her face.

She was just beginning the slow-motion act of trying to climb through the boxes to the door, a puppet clumsily clambering through twisted strings, when the first fireman appeared.

THIRTY-TWO

*T*HE STAIRS TO THE WARD WERE NARROW; it was an old hospital, with sixties' additions surrounding a Victorian core.

Beth took the steps slowly, her hand cradled at her side. The cuts had needed ten stitches; she hadn't noticed them when she broke the window. A dressing had been given that made her feel as if one arm were considerably larger than the other.

She emerged on to the second floor and turned left, along a highly polished and unforgiving corridor of white painted walls. A blue sign half-way down pointed the way to Intensive Care.

As she drew close to the nurse's station, she saw that Julia was there, dressed in the same clothes she had worn in the car, a creased skirt and blouse. She was standing stock still, looking into the ward.

Beth stopped. She had come to find Rosie, not her mother. As far as she had known, Julia had been admitted to another ward. She felt nothing when she looked at her, except perhaps a flash of surprise that she had fought so hard to get her out of the car. It had been pure instinct.

She had saved a woman who had lied to her, stolen her life from her. Watching the last of the bandage being taped across her arm, Beth had allowed herself the most tenuous of ironic smiles.

She came level now with Julia. A noise to her left distracted her, and she followed Julia's gaze into the side ward.

Rosie lay in a bed, perfectly still; there were two nurses and a doctor with her. An oxygen mask was clamped to the child's face, obscuring almost every feature but the shock of light hair spread on the pillow.

At Beth's side, Julia began to cry; sobs that shook her body. Instead of putting her hands to her face, she stood with them at her side, while her whole body trembled and the fingers limply moved, picking at the material of her skirt.

Beth looked at her coldly. 'How could you do it?' she whispered.

Julia didn't bother to wipe the tears away; she seemed drugged, spaced-out, and held her head at an odd angle, very like the way she had been leaning it on the head rest of the car seat, pitched backward a little.

'I never wanted this,' Julia said.

'You *didn't* want it?' Beth demanded. 'Surely this is exactly what you wanted.'

Julia turned to stare at her. 'Oh, Beth,' she murmured. 'You don't know, you don't know . . .'

Beth walked away from her. She went to the door of the ward. The patients lay wired to a battery of machines. Rosie was sharing the space with a very elderly man, and a woman perhaps in her twenties. The silence from the living was profoundly eerie.

Beth took a step backwards, afraid of being in the way.

'Stay with me,' Julia said.

Beth grimaced at her touch.

'Please . . .' A muscle twitched in the side of Julia's face; Beth's gaze fell on it and fixed itself, avoiding Julia's eyes. 'He threatened to take Rosie,' Julia said.

'What?'

'To take her. That was why—'

'Who did?'

'Oliver.'

Beth shook her head in disbelief. 'Take her where?'

'Take her away from me. He said he'd have me committed. I couldn't . . . you see that, don't you? I couldn't allow it!'

'Oliver said *that*? Why?'

Julia nodded. Then she clutched Beth's wrist and looked up at her pitifully. 'Rosie is all I've got left,' she said. 'You do understand? You . . . *you* understand . . .'

Beth tried to break free. 'No,' she cried. Their voices were rising to screaming pitch in the echoing corridor.

'I don't know what to do,' Julia said. 'Nobody believes me; they believe him.' She began to laugh. It was a truly dreadful sound. 'Not Oliver Woods, they all think, it's not him, it's his wife, she's unstable, he tells them that, he tells them lies about me, when all the time it's him, he's the one.' Julia began to wail like an animal. '*He's* the sick one, *he's* the sick one . . .'

People further up the corridor, thirty yards away, turned to look at them.

'Keep your voice down, for God's sake,' Beth said.

Julia took no notice. 'He's not going to take her away.' She looked directly into Beth's eyes. For a second Beth saw something infinitely out of control in that glance.

Julia's clutching fingers fluttered and plucked at Beth's sleeves and her shoulders. 'I don't know what to do,' she said. Her tone cracked; she stammered over the letters of the next word. 'He says that I'm not a fit mother.'

Beth grasped Julia's arms and pushed her to the wall, where a plastic chair, its shape a rigid and unforgiving shell, was the only place of rest to be seen. She forced Julia to sit. A nurse had come to the door of the side ward, frowning, and she made a move to come out to see to Julia, but her attention was called back inside. She gave Beth a warning look, as if it were Beth's business alone to calm Julia down.

'For Christ's sake shut up,' Beth hissed. Julia's sobs diminished to a faint trail of a single note, infinitely worse to hear than screaming. 'Shut *up*. If things are so bad with Oliver, then why don't you bloody well leave him? You've got a sister, haven't you? Somewhere in Scotland? Why don't you go and stay with her?'

'I can't, I can't . . .'

'Why can't you? If life's so desperate?'

Julia wasn't listening. She plunged her head into her hands and began rocking backwards and forwards in the chair. 'I don't know what to do,' she moaned.

Beth stood up and walked away, seven or eight paces. As she passed the door to the ward, her eye caught the pathetic little figure on the bed and she stopped.

At that moment the fire door along the corridor opened, and Beth glanced back to see Rhys. He started to jog when he caught sight of her. She shook her head; not because she did not want to see him, but because she was lost in this situation, and had no idea of what she ought to do or say next, or whether she could actually speak. Anger continually washed over her. It was as if, in the last few days, every single minor irritation of her life had congealed into one massive resentment.

She began to walk quickly to meet him.

'What's this?' he asked, touching her arm.

'It's just a cut.'

'We heard the sirens up on the site,' he explained. 'We heard them come into the village.'

Beth glanced at Julia. She couldn't bring herself to say what had happened, and was relieved when Rhys added, 'Alan Pritchard came up to the Rise. His wife . . .'

He stopped, staring at Julia.

'I don't know why they've let her up here,' Beth said.

'Where's the little girl?'

'In the ward.'

'How is she?'

'I don't know . . . unconscious.'

Rhys frowned. 'You're as white as a sheet,' he said. 'Sit down. Let me get you something.'

Beth held his sleeve to stop him walking past her. 'No,' she said. 'I'm fine. I think I ought to do something about Julia. Talk to someone. She's going on about Oliver, and—'

'What about him?'

'She says he drove her to it.'

Rhys raised his eyebrows. 'You think he did?'

They both looked at Julia. She was standing a few inches from the door of the ward, trembling from head to foot, staring down at the floor.

'God knows,' Beth said. 'Why would he?'

'Over this thing with David?'

Beth closed her eyes momentarily.

'I'm sorry,' Rhys said.

'It doesn't matter.'

'Do you want to go home?'

She smiled slightly. 'I wanted to see how Rosie was. But I don't know about Julia . . .'

'She isn't your responsibility,' he said. 'I'm surprised you give a toss. For God's sake, don't pity her.' To Rhys, Beth looked in no condition to be standing, let alone hanging around in a hospital. He would have liked to take her arm and walk her out of there, but he didn't want her to think he was bullying her.

He tore his glance from Beth; Julia was coming towards them.

'Helen is trying to find Oliver for you,' Beth said.

Julia froze. 'Is he coming here?' she asked.

'Helen said that—'

'He's coming here,' Julia said. She looked past them, along the corridor.

'He's out. They're trying to find him,' Beth told her.

Julia took hold of Beth's wrist. 'He'll take Rosie,' she said. 'Don't let him come here.'

'No one is going to take Rosie,' Beth said. And, for the first time that day, she pitied the distracted woman in front of her. Julia seemed to read her thoughts. She made a visible, protracted effort to straighten up, to control herself. Fresh tears flooded her eyes, and she put a hand up to them, this time wiping them quickly away. A ghost of an expression that was not quite a smile drifted over her face.

'Beth,' she said. 'I know you think I'm a bad person. But I don't know who to ask. You see? I want to ask for help, and I don't know who . . .'

Rhys looked away in embarrassment.

The doctor came out of the ward. The Sister followed him, glanced for a second at Beth and Julia and Rhys, then rested her set of notes on the station counter and began writing at speed.

The doctor came over. 'Mrs Woods,' he said. 'You ought not to be here. I have explained to you—'

'I want to see Rosie,' she said.

'Mr Reynolds is coming up to see you.'

'I don't want any bloody consultant,' Julia said. The fragility had vanished from her voice. She tried pushing past. 'I want to see my baby,' she said.

'Your daughter is very ill.'

The Sister came over. She held Julia's arm.

'Couldn't she just look in for a moment?' Beth asked. 'I'll come with her.'

The doctor hesitated; he glanced at the Sister. 'For a minute, no more,' he said.

Beth took Julia on one side; the nurse on the other. They walked into the ward and to the side of the bed. Rhys stayed back at the door.

Rosie's skin had a healthy pink, even reddish tinge. She looked untouched, carved from rosy glass. Surprisingly, Julia seemed to be quite calm now. Her tread was almost sprightly between the door and the bed. She leaned forward over her daughter, her lips parted, almost as though admiring a work of art.

'How long was it?' she asked Beth.

'What?'

'Before you found us.'

'I don't know. When did you go in?'

'About nine.' Her voice was steady, even animated.

'Ten minutes, then.'

'Fifteen minutes would have killed you both,' the Sister said.

Julia didn't look at her. 'I had to tape the . . . tube . . . the windows . . .'

Beth had been gazing at Rosie. 'She didn't object? She didn't say anything?'

'No,' Julia answered. She looked across at the nurse and Beth. Suddenly, her body sagged until she was almost level with the bed.

For a second, Beth thought that she was going to fall on the child. The Sister evidently thought the same thing; she jerked on Julia's arm to haul her backwards. Julia flopped in their grasp, her knees sagging.

'I didn't mean it,' she said. 'I'm so sorry. Rosie, Rosie!' There was a moment—just the merest fraction of a moment—when the voice arched theatrically. A show; a mimicry of feeling. But the tears that fell were real.

'Get her out,' the Sister said.

Beth couldn't grip Julia's arm with her dressed hand, so she cast a pleading look in Rhys's direction. He came forward immediately, catching Julia under the arms, trying to help her stand.

Julia's head rolled. 'Don't let Oliver take her from me,' she whispered.

THIRTY-THREE

*R*OSIE WAS DRIFTING.

She was a bird with wings outstretched, looking down into an empty sea. Sun baked her back. A hundred feet below, she could see the current of the water as clearly as contour lines on a map.

At first, she thought there was silence; then, very gradually, she heard the shifting tones of the wind. She flexed her wings experimentally, delighted at the newfound power. She liked birds; liked the touch of their feathers. Liked the silky threads of feather and fur. If she couldn't have the things she liked, she had to take them in secret. Hold them against her, tight.

Even altering her height changed the sounds. Air rushed past her in white bands as she fell downwards; it crushed inwards into bright blue as she soared back up. In between, the space between the ocean and the sky whispered and waved.

She looked at the tips of her fingers and saw her wings. She was very black, an oily iridescent black. She flew on with her throat stretched forward and her body dragging behind. She had no sensation of her feet any longer, or anything beyond her waist. She had become a curved shape, all breast and wing and long throat. She felt she could fly for miles. For ever. For ever, in this wind-coloured space, with its small light voices and the wrinkled water far below.

And then, her wings began to fail.

It was nothing at all at first; just a lessening of the warm thermal that supported her. She pressed downwards with her wingtip fingers, feeling the muscles in her back arch. She turned her head upwards and opened her mouth.

But the chasm of colder air grew. It was shadow now, slipping under her, blanking out the sea for seconds at a time. Looking ahead, she saw a whirlwind growing in the trackless sky, and her heart shrank and began to flutter inside her. She knew that, sooner or later, she would come to the edge of the spiral.

She struggled to change her course, thrashing weakly, trying to turn her head away from the shadows.

But it was no good; the whirlpool was bigger and much stronger than she was. It was making a noise. Not the comforting faint voice of the warm air, but an echoing, booming sound. It was angry. It was icy.

It was dark.

Panicking now, she tried to find the lower half of herself, to use her body for purchase in the melting and revolving sky. But nothing helped. She was being sucked down, out of the blue and into the dark.

She tried to squirm from side to side.

When she tried to breathe, the air wouldn't come; the darkness had taken it all away. She opened her mouth as wide as she could, desperately trying to pluck a mouthful of oxygen out of the suffocating cloud.

But the darkness swarmed in, pressing down on her tongue, filling her throat and lungs. Her chest burned. She felt her body rapidly changing, the freedom of the wings, retreating back into the helplessness of flesh and blood.

She was very heavy, crashing to earth. And she could hear the water now, caught in the storm, roaring and swirling underneath her. She was going to fall straight into the open chasm that the whirlwind had carved in the sea. She was going to fall straight down into the mile-deep canyon that the ocean usually concealed. She would fall down through the tube of water, and, when she got to the sea bed and couldn't fall any further, then the whirlpool would close over her.

'Rosie,' said a voice.

It was no one she knew.

'She was moving,' said another.

She lay back, and the air suddenly, blessedly, rushed through her. She started to tremble, but she kept her eyes closed.

Someone had sealed off the sea and closed down the wind. She could breathe again, and she was very small.

But she was not awake yet.

She lay on her back and let herself be carried, and the voices that had been so clear a few seconds ago retreated, and abandoned her to sleep.

THIRTY-FOUR

*I*T WAS NINE O'CLOCK IN THE EVENING.

Beth sat on the patio, staring out on to the shadowy fields. She had been here for some time, motionless, with the letter still grasped in one hand.

She had read it several times; she probably knew it by heart. Now, she looked down at it again, folded it carefully, and put it back in the pocket of her towelling dressing gown. Her feet, bare from her shower an hour ago, were cold. She stood up, sighing. At the same moment, she heard someone open the front gate.

She listened to the sound of feet approaching the front door, heard the ring of the bell, followed by an insistent knocking.

'Beth!' Oliver called.

She did nothing for a second; then she turned back into the house, swiftly closing and locking the patio doors. But she wasn't quick enough for him. He came round the back of the house and, just as she came in the kitchen, he was at the door and opening it.

He took in her bare feet and the bathrobe. He glanced at his own hand on the door handle, paused, then stepped fully inside, closing the door behind him. Beth stepped behind a chair.

'Rosie is conscious,' he said.

'I'm glad.'

He stared at her. 'Can you believe that she has done this?' he asked. 'That Julia could *do* this?' He passed a hand over his face. Beth didn't reply.

'May I sit down?'

'I'm going to bed. I'd rather you left.'

He sat down anyway. His usual air of weary sarcasm was more pronounced than ever; he spread both hands on the bare table top, then, after a second, balled both to a slack fist. After a moment, he took out a pack of cigarettes.

'Don't smoke in here,' Beth said. He looked at her acutely, frowned, and replaced the pack in his jacket. She turned away; in her pocket, the paper of the letter rustled. She looked down and put the flat of her palm against it.

'I always told myself that I would never divorce Julia,' Oliver was saying at her back. 'But this illness is something I cannot fight.'

Beth turned back, looking pointedly at the door through which he had come.

'I wanted to warn you,' he continued, ploughing on in his grating, upper-class monotone. 'I've applied for care of Rosie.' Beth was within a foot of him now, and he touched her arm.

She sprang back as if he'd stung her. Her gaze fixed on him, and she stepped past him, opening the door again. She stood to one side. 'I want you to go.'

He stood up. 'But surely you see why I've got to do it?' he said. 'You surely don't think I have any choice? Any choice at all?'

'I don't care what choice you've got,' she told him.

'You don't see what I'm saying,' he said. 'This is to protect Rosie,' he told her. 'You see? To protect Rosie.'

Beth's expression hadn't altered at all. 'You don't give a shit about Rosie,' she said. 'And don't look at me like that. Whatever you do is for yourself. I have never once known you take Rosie anywhere; you've never gone to any school event; you barely know the date of her birthday. You know none of her friends. You're a stranger to her.'

'That is not true!'

'Isn't it?'

He stared at the floor for a moment, his eyes ranging over the pattern of the floorcovering as if trying to orientate himself. Then he looked up and met Beth's unfazed glare. 'I love Rosie very much,' he said.

'Like you love Julia? You were only telling me *that* a day or so ago. Now you're divorcing her.'

'That was before this . . .'

'Anyway, you'll need more than that,' she said.

'More? More than *what*?'

Beth's voice rose. 'You'll need more than your bloody petitions to get Rosie,' she said. 'When Rosie recovers, how do you know she'll want to be with *you*?'

Oliver was dumbstruck. 'Her mother tried to kill her!'

'She doesn't know that,' Beth replied. 'Is that what you're going to tell her? Is that going to help her, to know that? All she'll know is that she got into the car with Mummy and then she went to sleep.'

'She'll have to know the truth.'

'Why? Why will she *have* to? Is that going to help her in any way?'

Oliver was within a few inches of Beth. She could smell him clearly, smell the starch on his shirt, tainted with the day's sweat. He looked very old; old and unmoved, even now.

'The hearing is tomorrow,' he said. Beth was waving her hands to get him out. He snatched hold of her arm. 'I'm only trying to prepare you,' he insisted. 'She'll come here. The Social Services have seen her. A solicitor has been given to her. She'll be barred from the house.'

'Why!'

'I want you to be prepared, Beth, because—'

'All right. Let her.'

'What!' He dropped her arm in amazement.

'Let her. Let her.'

One moment Oliver was upright, that stone face of his uncomfortably close to hers. Then, in the next second, he was bent over at the waist, crossing his arms over himself. It looked exactly as if he had been punched, suddenly, in the stomach. Beth stepped back, expecting him to fall; then, seeing that he wasn't, she gritted her teeth and took hold of his arm.

'Get out,' she said.

He was weeping.

She took in a long, long breath. 'I don't give a flying fuck about you,' she said quietly. 'I don't want to listen to you, and I don't want to know anything else about what you think about Julia. I don't give a damn if she shows her face here again, or if she disappears off the face of the bloody earth.'

Oliver didn't respond. Beth's face contorted suddenly with the effect of a lightning decision. She had found, in that instant, a way to repay him.

'In fact, if Julia comes here and asks for my help against you, Oliver, I'll give it.'

He wiped his hand across his face, his fingers, as he straightened up slightly, pulling at the loose skin around his eyes. 'You'd support Julia . . . against me? After *today*?'

'That's what I said.'

'You can't be serious. I haven't told you the worst of it,' he said.

'I don't want to hear.'

'She just wants to bring attention on herself. That's what this is all about!' They were within an inch of each other now. He stared into her eyes. 'I can't risk her being near Rosie again,' he told her. 'It's as serious as that. You understand? It's what the proceedings are about.'

Beth closed her eyes briefly. 'She's sick,' she murmured. 'It's quite obvious that she's sick. And you drove her there.'

'Where?'

'To her *state of mind*!'

He glared at her unblinkingly. 'That's exactly what I'm saying,' he cried. 'Exactly what I'm trying to tell you. You mustn't let her persuade you that she's innocent in all this. She will say that it's my fault. But it *isn't my fault . . .*'

Beth started to laugh. 'You think that Julia tried to commit suicide just to get attention? She tried to kill Rosie, to *get attention*!' She shook her head. 'You're as crazy as she is. You're as crazy as each other! You actually think that anyone would do that to her own daughter?'

She backed away from him. 'You just don't rate what misery you cause,' she said. 'It's not a matter of not *seeing* it. You don't rate it.'

'But I've never caused Julia any misery!' he objected. 'If anything, it's the other way round!'

Beth made a face of disgust. 'Oh, *God*.'

'This is precisely what I'm talking about. She's persuaded you that she's the victim, whereas—'

Beth put up her hand to stop him. 'Julia hasn't persuaded me at all,' she said. '*You* have persuaded me.'

He stared at her, totally baffled. 'I don't understand,' he said.

'No . . . you wouldn't. You don't have a very high opinion of anyone, do you, Oliver? You think the rest of the human race crawls on its belly, while you're the only bloody primate walking upright.'

'Beth!'

She took the letter from the robe pocket, tore it from the envelope, and waved it in his face.

'Do you know who this is from?'

'How could I?' he said. 'What is it?'

'It's from Burleigh and Country.'

His eyes flickered to it, then back to her.

'I asked to see David's accounts. His private ones—the ones in his name only. It just took a fee.'

'They wouldn't allow it.'

'Oh yes, they would. I'm his next of kin.' She stared accusingly at him, waiting for a response. 'You promised you would look into David's finances for me, didn't you?' she said.

'Yes, but—'

'Did you or didn't you?'

'Yes, I promised.'

'And *have* you?'

Oliver flinched. 'No.'

She nodded rapidly. 'No, of course you haven't,' she said. 'Because you don't need to, do you? Why bother to find out what you already know? And, more to the point, Oliver, why bother to get evidence of something that'll condemn *you*?'

He tried to reach for the letter; she stepped back, out of his grasp.

'You didn't really think that I'd never find out, did you?' she demanded. She couldn't keep the tears of rage out of her voice. 'You can't *bear* it, can you, when a woman has a mind of her own? You'd do anything to keep us weak, keep us under your thumb!' And an image of Chaos, slack and helpless, rolled into her mind.

'Beth. This is plain hysteria,' he said.

'I've every cause to be hysterical,' she shouted. 'You're lucky I don't kill you on the spot!'

She looked at him with utter contempt, then held the letter out between them. 'David had a private account,' she said slowly. 'And he received £11,223 from the sale of his shares. A month ago, the same day that he wrote the letter instructing you to remove the shares from his will—the letter you showed me, Oliver—*on the same day*, he paid £11,223 into *your* account.'

There was profound silence in the room. Neither Oliver nor Beth moved for a moment. Then Oliver opened his mouth to speak. Beth snatched back the letter and shook her head.

'David owed me that money,' Oliver said.

She didn't appear to have heard him; if she did, she dismissed the remark straight away. She was already pointing to another entry on the bank statement.

'You see this?' she said. 'This is our mortgage advance. The money that you forged my signature to get.'

'*I* didn't forge it! David—'

'It's here in black and white! All your bloody lies this week!'

'He never paid *me* the second charge.' Oliver's face suddenly crumpled with despair. 'Look, about the eleven thousand,' he muttered. 'All right. I haven't been honest with you. David gave me that money freely; he believed he could double it. So did I. We had a scheme, but it failed. As for your other money, I know *nothing* about *that*! David brought me the signed application, but he wouldn't say what it was for.'

Beth curled her lip in disbelieving disgust. 'It was paid into an offshore account. Just a number. No name.'

'That proves it . . .'

'It proves *nothing*! Except that you've got some sodding offshore account!'

'I have nothing,' Oliver said. 'I'm completely innocent, I swear to you.'

She brushed past him, kicked the already ajar door back on its hinges, and stood on the threshold. 'Get out,' she said.

Oliver stood in the centre of the floor; she could see that he was shaking. She gripped the door handle behind her back.

'Let me at least see the statement,' he said.

'Get out.'

'I won't take it. I do assure you, if I could see the offshore number, I might recognise it . . .'

'Out!'

He walked forward, his head bowed in an attitude of defeat. He drew level with her, and just as she was preparing to slam the door behind him, he lunged at the hand holding the letter.

She stumbled away, pushing the letter behind her back. 'Oh no,' she said.

She lost her grip on the door, and staggered until she came in contact with the work surface near the sink. Oliver came after her, still fumbling for the letter whispering, 'Please, Beth, please . . .'

'No,' she said. Her face wore an undisguised expression of disgust.

Oliver's resolve faltered. He stared into her eyes. 'If only you knew how much I care for you,' he said.

Then, as if from a great distance away, the telephone began to ring in the living room.

It seemed to break a spell. Oliver straightened and stepped back.

Then he opened the kitchen door and looked out at the garden. She watched him as he took a cigarette from the pack, and lit it calmly. The light in the garden was almost gone; further down the lane there were lights in other houses.

Someone down in the centre of the village had lit a bonfire, and she could see sparks, bright points of amber, rushing upwards into the pressing darkness of the sky.

'I will see you tomorrow,' Oliver said.

He glanced back. 'It was David who betrayed you, not me,' he told her as he stepped out of the house.

THIRTY-FIVE

'$\mathscr{B}$ETH—BETH!'

It was Tuesday morning, market day. Stourminster's High Street was already crowded by nine o'clock, and Helen Pritchard had only caught a glimpse of Beth through the crowds.

'Beth!'

Ahead of her, the slight figure stopped and turned. As Helen approached her, she saw to her dismay that Beth March had now noticeably lost weight: probably more than half a stone, she calculated. She hugged her, as pedestrians pushed past them both.

'I'm glad I've seen you. How are you?'

Beth smiled. 'Working.'

'Here somewhere?'

'In Richmond Avenue.'

'Look . . .'

'Helen, I'm not being represented by Oliver any more. So—'

'Would you know where he is?'

'Should I?'

Helen gave her a perplexed look. 'He's not been in the office since last week. And the accountant has been in, absolutely giving me the third degree.' She tossed her head, and twitched an agitated hand at the belt of her jacket and the handle of her bag.

Beth gave her a narrow look. 'I don't want to be rude, Helen. But I can't talk to you about anything to do with Oliver. It's not only me. It's Julia, too.'

'Precisely.' Helen looked around her. 'Ten minutes. You have ten minutes?'

'Well . . .'

'Let me buy you some coffee.'

She took a peremptory hold on Beth's arm and led her down the street. They went into a store with a tiny café on the second floor, isolated in a sea of hats and racks of expensive clothes. Without asking Beth's preference, Helen ordered four scones, butter, a small mountain of jam, and two large very milky coffees, and carried the tray to the farthest corner table.

'I'm not going to beat around the bush,' she said as they sat down. 'Does Oliver owe you money?'

Beth stirred her coffee slowly. 'Yes.'

'Is it much?'

Beth looked up. 'Yes.'

Helen seemed genuinely shocked. She picked up her knife to split a scone, then dropped it back to the plate. 'When did you find out?'

'Helen . . .'

'I'm not spying on his behalf, Beth. I simply want to know where I stand.'

Beth took a sip of coffee. 'You must know what he's been doing?'

'But I don't!' Helen reached and took hold of Beth's hand. 'Dear, I knew nothing at all about your money.'

'You're his secretary.'

'His *part-time* secretary,' she corrected. 'That's exactly the point. He tells neither me nor Christina any detail.'

Beth sighed and looked at her plate. 'If you don't have any loyalty to him, I suggest you leave. And quickly.'

'It's as bad as that?'

'I should think so.'

Helen sat back in her chair. She was wearing a pale blue tie-neck blouse, and the bow trembled in indignation as she breathed. She looked outraged. 'Well, I must say, I've been taken for a fool, it seems,' she said.

'Join the club.'

'I thought, if nothing else, he was a gentleman.'

Beth gave a cynical laugh. She buttered her scone and began to eat; this took the place of breakfast, which she had not been able to face two hours ago.

'Julia was in yesterday,' Helen said.

Beth said nothing.

'Do you think . . .' Helen paused. 'I really don't know if I should be saying this,' she admitted, 'but do you think you ought to get involved?'

'Yes.'

Helen watched Beth's face carefully. 'Is that wise?'

It was Beth's turn to put down her knife; she stared almost belligerently back at Helen. 'You know that he's applied for custody?'

'No, I don't . . .'

'Oh, really, Helen!'

'I *don't*. Oliver would never confide anything of a personal nature, even when things were normal. You mean he wants custody of Rosie?'

'They don't call it that now. It's "residence and contact".' Beth grimaced.

Helen looked down at her coffee. 'She came in yesterday after lunch, wanting to see him. What could I do? She went to his office and began throwing books about; she was absolutely hysterical. Rosie has been taken out of the hospital . . .'

Beth stared at her for a second; then carried on buttering a scone, her mouth set.

'Where has Rosie gone, do you know?' Helen asked.

'No one does but Oliver, I should think.'

'This is truly awful,' Helen said. 'How very cruel of him.' She sat, deep in thought, for another moment. 'But I still can't help thinking that Julia herself . . . well, that Julia should be in some kind of care.'

'She's been assigned a social worker.'

'I don't mean that. I mean residential care.'

'A psychiatric unit?'

'Yes. Something of that order. Surely you agree?'

Beth shook her head. 'No, actually I don't.'

'But—!'

'Julia isn't insane, Helen.'

'But Rosie. You can't think that Rosie should be given back to her? That Julia would look after her properly?'

Beth frowned distractedly. 'No. Probably not. I happen to think that Rosie *would* be best cared for by someone else for the time being. Grandparents, for instance. It's a pity that neither set of grandparents happens to be alive.'

'If Oliver and Julia could come to some sort of agreement, perhaps a nurse in the house—'

Beth laughed. 'That's hardly likely! Oliver never wants Julia to see Rosie again.'

'But how do you know?'

'There's a hearing this morning.'

'My God . . .'

Beth leaned forward. 'It's one thing to say that Julia is temporarily incapable. That might be true,' she said. 'Look—I know very well that she's hardly the Brain of Britain. She never *was* very clever.' She made a face. 'All this fussing about what she would do, especially over Rosie, would try anyone's patience. But . . .' She stabbed the tablecloth with her index finger. 'You can't penalise her for that. You can't penalise her for being a weak personality, battered down by a man like Oliver. It's *Oliver*, not Julia, at the centre of this. *Oliver* who has driven her to it; *Oliver* who drove her into the affair with David. And now that she's gone to the edge, it's *Oliver* taking Rosie away. Leaving Julia aside, do you think that's right for Rosie—never to see her mother again?'

'Well . . . no.'

'That's what he wants.' She sat back, slightly out of breath from her tirade. 'Bloody damned Oliver! He thinks he's the only person that matters. The only person of any worth, any priority.' She put both hands to her eyes momentarily, then drained the last of her coffee.

Helen sat regarding her for some time. It was more than a minute before she spoke. 'You must be very careful,' she said.

Beth raised her eyebrows.

'You must be very careful, because you are very vulnerable yourself.'

'I'm all right.'

'No.' Helen's tone was low. 'No, you are recently bereaved. You might think you are behaving quite rationally, when in fact—'

'You think *my* behaviour is irrational?' And she began to laugh. 'My God, Helen—'

'Hear me out. All I'm saying is that you can't possibly be expected to be dealing yet with David's death, let alone the rest of this. You won't be making rational judgements. You ought not to become involved in this thing between Oliver and Julia. Especially Julia!'

Beth considered her for a moment. Then she got up, brushing down her clothes. 'Thank you for the coffee,' she said.

'Beth. I'm only trying to help.'

'I know.'

Helen took her arm gently. 'Leave them to it,' she said. 'Get out from between them. That's what I shall do, resign! This is *their* dispute, not yours.'

They had reached the stairs. Beth looked down for a moment at the shoppers walking through the aisles, at the glimpse of the street outside.

She took the first step down, looking up at Helen above her. 'Julia is drowning,' she told her.

'And you want to drown with her?'

'I won't.'

'That's the danger. That's what I'm trying to impress upon you, the danger . . .'

Beth turned away. 'The only danger is Oliver Woods,' she muttered. She began walking. 'And he's not getting away with anything else.'

THIRTY-SIX

$\mathcal{T}$HE COURT BUILDING WAS GEORGIAN, set in a quiet square to the south of the town centre.

Julia arrived early; she got out of the taxi and stood for more than a minute, staring at the elegant façade with its white columned portico. She was dressed in a navy blue suit, and her face was ashen.

The solicitor, John Merrit, arrived on foot; his offices were five minutes' walk away, at the opposite end of the High Street to Oliver's. She raised a hand, and he walked over to her.

He had been assigned to her from the Child Panel, but they were not quite strangers. They had met twice before yesterday, at official gatherings, and she remembered him clearly, remembered his fair colouring and his pale blue eyes. She remembered him telling a joke across a wide dinner table, though the punchline, the gist, had escaped her yesterday just as it did today.

He held out his hand. 'How are you?'

'What's the time?' she asked.

He looked at his watch. 'A quarter to.' He gave her a professional, soothing smile. 'Did you find a room at the Queens?'

'Yes,' she said.

'And you slept?'

'Yes,' she said.

'Good,' he replied.

She looked away, at the ground.

'Shall we go in?' he asked.

She glanced up, passing the strap of her handbag back and forth through her fingers, but did not move. After a moment, Merrit gently took her arm, and gave a little pull forward.

She obeyed.

The building was as beautiful inside as it was out: they walked into a large circular foyer, with a highly polished dark floor. Directly ahead, a broad staircase with a deep red carpet branched out, to right and left, at first-floor height. Below, two corridors led away, past luxuriantly wide seats upholstered in the same scarlet hue. It looked like an opulent, discreet hotel. They might have been lovers, meeting in secret.

'It's upstairs,' he murmured.

Lovers climbing to bed, climbing through blood. Her shoes pressed on the pile like fingers pressing a wound. She held his arm tightly, fearing the moment when she reached the top.

'Room Four,' he said.

She stopped. 'Isn't it a court?'

'Well, Court Four. But very informal. No wigs or gowns.'

She wished he had told her that yesterday; it was not so worrying. She relaxed a little, gave herself time to see her reflection in a long mirror, time to think that she looked right. She looked careful and calm. She had taken the sedative, as John Merrit had advised, and the world was soft-edged with a shining clear centre, like a cinema lens. Faces that passed rolled forwards in fish-eye fashion.

At the door she closed her eyes to dispel this illusion.

Oliver was sitting in court already, with his back to her. Alongside him sat his own solicitor; behind them, the woman from Social Services that Julia remembered from the hospital. As Julia came in, the woman turned, and a man that Julia had never seen before, at the woman's side, placed a hand on her arm. She looked to the front.

They walked to the opposite table and sat down. Merrit began taking papers from his case. His movements were relaxed, even jaunty. He had smiled at the court usher and raised his eyebrows, a mild expression of acknowledgement, at the group on the other side of court. A signet ring flashed on his smallest finger as his hands moved over the files he was taking out. Now, he bent his head to whisper to Julia. 'You know that this is a District Judge,' he said.

He continued going through what would happen, as he had done yesterday. She bowed her head next to his, and the feeling reinforced itself—that they were conspirators bent on deception. She watched the blood beat softly in his throat, above the collar, a starched white collar with a garish tie of pink and blue. There was a very small slit where he had cut himself shaving, there, just above the collar line. She felt that she knew him intimately, secretly. She glanced up, past him, at Oliver's face.

Her husband was looking at her.

She opened her mouth; he looked away.

She looked past the two Court Officials, and thought of him ten years before. And at Rosie's birth. She thought of him on holiday with a khaki hat pulled over his eyes. She thought of his desk and their bedroom.

The door to the corridor was closed at their backs.

The Judge came in.

It was a woman; about fifty; dark hair with strands of grey, pulled back in a chignon. Julia's gaze rested on her gratefully. Here was another woman. Perhaps a mother. Here was the port in the storm.

Oliver's solicitor began. 'Madam, we are applying . . .'

Ease suddenly flowed through Julia; its warmth invaded her knotted stomach, flowed down her arms. She leaned forward and rested her head on her hand, propping it on the table in an attitude of relief. She was sure, now that the time had come, that there could not possibly be any argument that could keep her from Rosie. The certainty seemed to hum in her head. She smiled and ran her hand over her brow.

'Is this an agreed order?'

'No,' said John Merrit.

'What is the position with Social Services?'

'We have been unable to investigate sufficiently; the attempt was yesterday morning. We have considered an Emergency Protection Order to protect the child . . .'

'There's no need to protect her,' Julia said.

Merrit caught her hand. 'Don't speak just now,' he told her.

'There's no need to protect my child,' she said, louder.

Oliver murmured something to the man at his side. Julia half rose out of her seat. 'There's no need to protect my daughter,' she said. 'I'm a good mother, I—'

'Sit down,' said her solicitor.

'Mrs Woods, sit down,' said the Judge.

Julia looked hard at her, rebuffed. The request had been loud, even harsh. She sank back down to her seat.

'I am going to adjourn this to Circuit,' the woman said.

The Court Clerk stood up.

'What did she say?' Julia asked, turning to John Merrit.

'Just a minute,' he murmured.

'What did she say?'

'I have just explained to you, when we came in.'

'You said—'

The Social Services woman was looking hard at them.

'Please wait a moment,' Merrit insisted.

Julia stared back at Oliver. She thought of getting up and going to him, taking his arm. But he was sitting back in his chair with his hands crossed over his stomach, his head tipped slightly backwards and his eyes closed, as if he might be asleep. In command. In repose.

'Oh my God,' she murmured, the carelessness of his position and the horror of the situation striking her afresh. 'I can't be here,' she whispered.

John Merrit was talking. 'We have to come back this afternoon,' he said.

She swung her head round. 'What?'

'This afternoon. We are adjourned to Circuit; we have to go to the Municipal Court building at three thirty.' People were getting up; as the Social Services representative passed her, Julia deliberately avoided her gaze.

There was another case coming up; as they moved back, others were coming forward. Julia found herself behind Oliver, pinched at the elbow by John Merrit, guided out.

'Three thirty?' she asked, bewildered. 'But why?'

'This afternoon,' he said.

They got to the door which they had passed through barely five minutes before. Julia stopped dead, frowning, her hand at her throat. Confusion filled her, suffocated her.

'Three thirty today?' she asked.

At lunchtime, Beth was driving back towards the village. On the crest of the hill she had to wait at a wider point in the road for another car. While she did so, her eyes ranged over the landscape in front of her and paused on the excavation site, a quarter of a mile away on the other side of the hill. She put the car into gear.

She didn't see Rhys for a moment when she turned into the site. The now-familiar white Ford van was parked across the entrance. She got out, and saw that a group of people at the far fence were in the process of breaking up a meeting. Alan Pritchard was among them, and he strode across to Beth, red in the face.

'We might be able to start next week,' he said. 'Miracles do happen.'

'Good . . .'

'Get the bank off my back.' He smiled at her. 'How are you?'

'I'm OK.'

'Helen was saying—'

She held up her hand. 'I know what Helen's saying. She caught me in town this morning.' Out of the corner of her eye she was watching Rhys, who was looking out over the field that bordered the site with his back to her.

'You'll look after yourself?' Alan said.

She squeezed his arm. 'Yes. Thanks.'

'Watch where you're treading, now. They go ballistic if you breathe in the wrong place.'

She did as she was told. Rhys glanced back as she negotiated the last of the excavated pits.

'Are you finished?' she asked.

'You mean today, or here?'

'Today.'

'No. Just stopping for lunch.' He smiled at her, turning fully now to look at her. 'How is that little girl?'

'I don't know.' She looked at her feet, then back at him. 'There's a hearing today. Oliver is trying to get custody of Rosie and keep Julia out of the house. I can't imagine she even grasps what's going on.'

Rhys made a low whistling sound.

Beth came level with him and leaned on the fence, gazing out at the long sweep of green crop ahead of them. It was barley, its long fronds turning a little yellow, moving almost hypnotically in the breeze, a half-mile of luxuriant, billowing hair.

'I keep thinking of David,' she murmured.

'Well, that's natural . . .'

She cut him short. 'I wonder what he would do about Julia.'

'Why do anything?'

She looked at him acutely. 'Because he loved her, enough to leave everything behind and go away with her.'

'Well . . .'

'And he wouldn't . . .' She paused, picking at a splinter on the top rail of the fence. 'He wouldn't like to see her suffering,' she said.

Rhys didn't reply. When she looked up at him, he was staring at her in disbelief. 'Now I've heard everything,' he said.

She waited a second, then said, 'Oliver came to see me last night, trying to warn me not to help Julia.'

'*Warn* you?'

'The old heavy hand.'

'He didn't threaten you?' Rhys asked, concerned now.

'No—not quite. Although I did tell him that, if push came to shove, I'd support Julia over him.'

'Why?'

She smiled thinly. 'I got a letter from the building society yesterday. I found out where some of David's money went.'

'And?'

'Oliver. Oliver's account.'

'Jesus!'

'So you see—'

'Can you get it back?'

'I'll do my damnedest. But that's not all. The rest was paid into an offshore account.'

'Oliver's?'

'Taking bets?'

He shook his head. 'No. Jesus *Christ*.' He took a moment to consider. 'But why?'

'Why what?'

'Pay Oliver all that?'

'He claims David gave it to him,' Beth said. 'But who knows what the truth might be? Oliver had probably threatened to implicate David in his own fraud, because he checked the accounts. Or maybe it was to stop Oliver telling me about his affair with Julia.'

'You think David would have been that frightened of you finding out about the affair?'

She paused. 'I think that David was caught between them, and they crushed him.'

'Julia too?'

'Julia just because she's so bloody helpless. I can imagine David responding to that.'

'But *all* that money?'

She sighed. 'I think Oliver drove him to his wits' end, until leaving with Julia was the only way out. Until he wasn't acting rationally at all. That's what I think.'

Beth turned back towards the site. She whispered Oliver's name, once, like a curse.

She stared down at an area of ground that had been excavated close to the fence, a section of deeper topsoil than the rest, where the gradient of the hill began to fall away. She took a deep breath, trying to rid herself of the thought of Oliver, at the anger that had begun to burn a slow hole in her gut. 'I've reported him to the Law Society,' she whispered. 'So we will see.' She straightened, focusing on the trench ahead, taking a lungful of clean air.

'What's this?' she asked, pointing to the disturbed soil.

Damping his curiosity, Rhys drew his glance, with some hesitation, from her, and back to the site. 'We did a little experiment today,' he told her, 'which was fruitless, I might add.'

'For what?'

'Any sign of occupation.'

'A house, you mean?'

'Yes.' He shoved his hands into his pockets. 'Clutching at straws, actually. But I can't get permission to go into the field, so—'

'Why do you want to get into the field?'

'We had some evidence of a settlement,' he replied. 'Some old boy came up to the site. He used to work on the farm. He told us he'd seen lines in the soil.'

'When?'

He grimaced. 'Well, after the last war. About fifty years ago, when he was clearing a copse here and ploughing over. He says he saw bits of pottery and animal bones.'

'Is that good?'

'It is if you stop the plough. Do you know how rare Anglo-Saxon pottery is? It disintegrates in ploughsoil. They didn't fire it at high temperatures, so when you—'

'Out in *this* field?'

'He didn't think it mattered. He never told anyone.'

'What a shame,' she said.

Rhys pursed his lips by way of comment.

'Where are your bodies now? The graves are empty.'

'With us and the museum. This is when the real work starts.'

'How many were there in the end?' They had started to walk back towards the cars.

'Seven.' He kicked a small stone ahead of him. 'How many houses is Alan putting here?'

'Eight.'

He made a noise somewhere between disgust and resignation.

'You don't like the twentieth century much, do you?' Beth asked.

'Oh, I don't know. But we won't leave such impressive bones behind.'

'Why not?'

'What will they find when they dig *you* up?'

'Me?'

'I'll tell you. Less than nothing, because we don't believe we're going anywhere. Maybe they'll find your fillings, the amalgam. Some plastic joints, maybe? A host of degenerative diseases, and—if there's any stomach contents to find—a thick layer of fat and sugar.'

'Oh . . .'

'And when the houses decay, a priceless treasure trove of UPVC window frames, just the same as a million other UPVC window frames from the Shetlands to the Scillies.'

'Don't forget the hundred billion supermarket carrier bags.'

'Them too. And, in a thousand years from now, the lovely clean water in Wookey Hole will be bubbling up pure nitrate.'

He rubbed his hands on his trousers, extracted his keys from his pocket, and shook them free of the same whitish soil that clung to them.

Beth cocked her head back towards the first grave. 'But it wasn't all hunky dory, was it?' she asked. 'This noble Saxon heritage. What about the man with the axe?'

Rhys nodded agreement. 'That's what's so interesting about this site,' he said. 'Most violent deaths found to date are at battle sites. Layers of ash and a lot of males dead. To find a single isolated sudden death . . .'

'I wonder what the woman died of.'

'We might find out. Never know your luck.' He was leaning on the car, smiling at her. 'I've been fantasising about fish and chips for the last hour,' he said. 'Fish and chips and a pickled egg.'

'Oh no!'

'Pickled egg in a pint of bitter. You ever do that?'

'Why should I? Why should *anyone*?'

'Pickled egg, fish, chips, couple of gherkins, and to follow . . . three pineapple fritters.'

Beth pulled a *no-more* face.

'Anyway,' Rhys added suddenly, 'weren't you working today? You're skiving off.'

'Mrs Latimer decided, when I was just about to lay the first pavers, that she'd like it all a different shape and wanted to discuss it with her husband.' She spread her hands. 'So I came home.' She started to smile. 'For salad.'

'What about chips?'

'Potato. Maybe.'

'Not cold?'

'Stone cold.'

'Ergh.'

'It's very healthy.'

'It's bloody deadly. How much salad?'

She mimed a large, laden plate. He wrinkled his nose.

'Look,' she said. 'Do you want feeding or not?'

He grinned, opening the door of his car.

'I'll follow you down,' he told her.

When they got to the house, the phone was ringing.

'Mrs Latimer has changed her mind again,' Beth said, going to the hallway and indicating that Rhys should put the kettle on. She picked up the receiver. 'Hello?'

There wasn't any reply for a moment. Then she heard a woman's voice.

'Beth. It's Julia.'

Beth leaned on the wall, her back to it, the mouthpiece of the phone resting just beneath her neck, closing her eyes.

'He's taken Rosie.'

Still, Beth said nothing.

'I'm at the hospital. I came to see her! He never said what he'd done, even though he was at the court!'

Beth had bitten her lip, but still didn't respond.

'We have to go back this afternoon; I don't understand, I . . .' Julia's voice cracked. 'I came here an hour ago, and I went to the ward, and they said she had recovered, but—they didn't keep her here. They discharged her!'

Beth's eyes were open now. Rhys came to the doorway and made a *who-is-it?* mime.

'Do you know where she is?' Beth asked. 'Did the hospital say?'

Julia's voice rose to a cry. 'I don't know; is she there?'

'What, here?'

'In the village? In the house?'

'*My* house?'

'No. Mine!'

'I really don't know. Why would I know? Why don't you come and see?'

'Because he's trying to keep me out of the house. My solicitor says it's best for me not to go to the house. Oh God . . .' Beth could hear her crying.

For a second, Beth took the phone away from her ear, to clear her mind, to step back from the hysteria swarming down the line.

'Listen, I'm sure—'

'Will you go and see?'

'Sorry?'

'Oh Beth, please, I beg you, please . . . would you go and see, in the house? Will you go and see if she's there? I must know where she is.'

'But—'

'Could you just knock on the door and ask? Could you see if Oliver's there?'

'I don't particularly want to see Oliver, Julia.'

'I know.' Laboured, helpless breathing. 'Beth . . . I'll never ask anything of you again. I'll never speak to you, if that's what you'd like. I'll do whatever you like, but please, just today, only this one time, *please* . . .'

'All right, all right.'

Rhys was at her shoulder now, trying to listen to what was being said, frowning deeply. Beth put her hand over the mouthpiece. 'What can I do?'

He shrugged.

She put the phone back to her ear. 'All right. I'll go.'

'Oh, thank you. Oh, thank you so much—'

'I'll ring you back. Where are you?'

'It's a public call box, in the hospital . . .' She gave the number.

'I'll be ten minutes.'

'All right. Thank you, thank you, Beth . . .'

'Wait there.'

She put the phone down and grimaced at Rhys. 'Well, what *could* I do? You heard her.'

'Do you want me to come with you?'

'Would you?'

He took her elbow. 'Let's get it over with.'

They walked down to the Lodge.

The moment they turned in at the gate, they could see that there was no one about. They went to the front door and knocked, and, after a moment, Rhys looked through a downstairs window.

Beth went to the side, fighting down the memories of the previous day with some difficulty. She knocked again at the side door. No reply. And no sound at all inside.

As she returned to the front, Rhys said, 'No car in the drive or the garage.'

She stood with her hands on her hips.

'He really took his daughter out of hospital, and they let him?' Rhys asked.

She shrugged slowly. 'He must have persuaded them that Rosie was much safer out of Julia's reach.'

'Perhaps she is.'

Beth cocked her head. 'Safer with Oliver?' She ran her hands through her hair exasperatedly. 'My God, I've got to ring Julia back. I've got to tell her that Rosie's not here.' She gave a slight groan. 'She'll be absolutely frantic,' she sighed. 'She sounds bad enough already.'

'It's not your problem.'

'No, I know . . .'

'It really is *not.*'

They turned away from the silent house.

'They certainly must think Oliver's reliable,' Rhys said.

Beth blew a gust of air, a breath of contempt.

'I mean, as far as Rosie goes,' he continued, 'safe to be with her. The hospital, the police, the child welfare people . . . Don't you think so?'

She looked at the ground, not venturing a reply.

Rosie's face was haunting her.

THIRTY-SEVEN

$\mathcal{O}$NE OF THE MAIN PROBLEMS, the police observed afterwards, was that they couldn't get Lilian Davis to sit still.

Put in a chair, she would spring from it only a moment later; not trembling, or agitated, as anyone might have expected. But full of energy. It was as if her brother's death had filled her with life.

She wore a smile of absolute satisfaction. She paraded around the shabby living room, lifting and replacing things: the ornaments, the cushions, the magazines. In one corner, Arthur's glasses lay open, one metal prong twisted, one lens shattered. Beside the frame were two small, neat spots of blood.

Lilian liked the youngest of the police officers: the detective constable who barely said a word. She gripped his arm, pulling him around with her, resisting his attempts to stop, to sit.

'I shall sell it,' she was telling him when the doctor arrived. 'How much d'you think I'll make?'

'Where is he?' the doctor asked at the door.

Those in the hallway and the sitting room indicated the kitchen. Lilian hardly paused in her excited monologue. 'It would be eighty. Maybe ninety,' she said. 'I don't want much. Whoever has it can do it up.' She grinned. 'I don't want a place like this,' she told her unwilling listener. 'It was him, his Doreen years ago. I was the skivvy, the nurse, you see? It's not my choice. My style . . .' She smoothed down her dress, grotesquely patterned now, red against the green nylon. '. . . is more to a cottage, you know? I always wanted a cottage.'

'Jesus wept,' said the doctor, his voice threading along the corridor.

Lilian gripped the young man harder. 'I couldn't have done it without help,' she said.

'Help?' Momentary silence in the room.

'Oliver. My solicitor.' She sighed as though mentioning a lover's name. 'He's helped me all along with Arthur's affairs. He wanted what was right for me.' She looked around her. 'He knew it wasn't right. The only one who could *see*,' she said.

She looked down at herself then, her gaze resting on her hands, as though intrigued with the livid pattern on them.

'Oh yes,' she murmured appreciatively. 'He encouraged me, you know. Helped me with *all* of this . . .'

The two men in the hall, leaning wearily against the door, exchanged glances.

'Is he real?' asked one. 'This Oliver?'

'Phone through and find out,' the other replied.

THIRTY-EIGHT

*T*HE THREE THIRTY HEARING was in a very different building. The municipal complex had been built on the town's outskirts; it was a sixties box, a jungle of Government and Local Authority departments. The title of the courts might have been easily missed in the list of offices on the road sign.

The atmosphere in the courtroom was different, too. Julia could sense the tension, almost a physical barrier, as she sat waiting in a high white room, where the sound of the traffic outside was barely muted.

She glanced at Oliver's solicitor as he stood to speak, loathing him, loathing his upper-class accent. On the other side of the chasm, Oliver's group gave off an air of muted superiority, a kind of colonial mentality of old schools and fair play. She felt she had lost before they even began; lost because she was not of the right caste.

Oliver's solicitor was explaining the events of the day before.

This time the Judge was male: a large man of about sixty, with beetling black eyebrows and dark hair. He wore half-moon glasses, but he was not looking at the counsel as the man spoke; he stared down.

'Both mother and child were admitted to hospital at nine forty; Mrs Woods recovered consciousness while in the Emergency Room, and her daughter Rosie was taken, after initial examination, to Intensive Care. The child has since recovered consciousness.'

Just for a moment, the Judge's eyes flickered upwards and rested on Julia. She began to smile, then hesitated, flushed, and dropped her own eyes to the desk in front of her.

'We wish an interim residence order in respect of the child, and ask the Court to order that Mrs Woods should not have contact, and that she should leave the marital home.'

'Is this order agreed?'

'No,' said John Merrit.

Julia fought down an instinct to scream.

The Social Services were beginning. They had their own solicitor, who talked at a leaping, hard-to-follow rate.

'. . . after consulting with the medical staff, the mother and the father in this case . . .'

Julia began to shake. She couldn't help it. Her hand trembled on the desk top. She balled her fist. John Merrit briefly rested his own hand on hers.

'. . . some indication that a sedative . . .'

She raised her head.

'. . . cast doubt on the mother's ability to care for the child at this stage, bearing in mind the mother's state of mental health. Failing an agreement being reached, we would apply for the child to be placed under an Emergency Protection Order . . .'

Julia grabbed Merrit's arm. 'What are they saying?'

'Emergency Protection. Foster parents, care. If you can't agree with Oliver today.'

'Oh God,' she breathed.

The Judge leaned back, at last raising his eyes. 'It isn't possible to hear this case in full today,' he said slowly. 'The Social Services need to make further investigations.' He looked over the half-moon glasses at the Social Services solicitor. 'I take it you can make a report within seven days and return for a further hearing?'

They agreed.

The Judge looked back at Julia, seemingly through her. 'You have heard what the Social Services have to say . . .' he began.

'I don't want her in care,' Julia said. 'You haven't any right. She's only little. She can't manage without her mother.'

There was a dead silence.

'I don't agree to her being in care,' Julia repeated, louder this time.

The Judge sighed. 'Mrs Woods, you have representation,' he said. 'I suggest you make use of it.'

'Isn't anybody listening to me?' she cried.

'We are sorry, your honour,' John Merrit said. Julia turned a furious look on him. 'Wait,' he whispered.

'Either Mrs Woods agrees to a review of the case at seven days, or I shall approve the Protection Order,' the Judge said.

'What?' Julia asked, whispering feverishly, tugging at Merrit's arm.

'You have to agree not to see Rosie for seven days, not to go to the house, while they make their report—'

Julia sprang to her feet. 'No!' she cried.

'Mrs Woods—'

'No! No!'

'Julia,' said Merrit.

She tore free of his grasp and ran forwards, until she was directly before the Judge. 'You don't understand,' she said. 'He's taken her. Did he tell you that? Do you know that?' She gestured wildly behind her, encompassing the Social Services representatives. 'Do *they* know? They don't know! He took her from the hospital, hell never let me see her again, and . . .' She swung round and pointed at Oliver, who, to her disbelief, wore a small embarrassed smile, the most supercilious expression of triumph. 'It's not my fault, it's *him* that forced me to it!'

She turned again to the Judge. 'You understand!' she said. 'He forced me, and now you're letting *him*—you're letting *him* look after her!'

John Merrit had got up, and was now at her side. 'Julia, please,' he murmured.

'I must see her,' she said, beginning to weep. 'I must see her. It's my right. She's my baby. I must see her . . . I'm her mother. *Her mother!*'

Merrit put his arm around her; she resisted its force for a second, then slumped, feeling for the desk, for her seat.

'If your honour would grant just a minute or so . . .'

'Take your client out, Mr Merrit.'

'Thank you, your honour.'

In the corridor outside, Julia began to weep loudly.

'You must get yourself under control,' Merrit said.

'Under *control*?' she said. 'You want me to shut up and sit quietly when all this is designed to take her away from me?' She raised her head and almost shouted, so that people sitting on the benches in the long corridors turned to look at her. 'They're taking my daughter away!' she cried.

Merrit grabbed her arm and propelled her to one side; she slipped, almost losing her footing on the slippery stone floor. 'Listen to me,' he said. 'If you don't shut up, you *will* lose her.'

Julia stopped crying and stared at him.

'I mean it,' he said.

'She's poorly. She's always been poorly, she needs me . . .'

'I know.'

'She'll be so frightened without me. She just couldn't cope. You don't know what she's like when she can't see me. She's very sensitive, *very* sensitive, like me. Just like me! You didn't see her on the first day at school, clinging to me, you'd have thought her little heart would break. I'm all that matters to her . . .'

'All right,' he said, cutting her off. 'So there's all the more reason to get her back to you as quickly as possible. Which you won't achieve by getting hysterical in court.' He lowered his voice, meeting her gaze unblinkingly. 'You've got to go along with this thing, roll with it. You've got to let the Social Services do their review, you've got to be as calm as you can—now, and when they come to see you. You've *got to get yourself under control.*'

She stood gasping. There was nothing in her face to show that she had any understanding of what he was saying.

'Have you got your tablets?' he asked.

'I took . . . one this morning . . .'

'Take another.'

'I don't want . . .' She gulped hard. 'I don't want to be fuzzy like this morning. I felt asleep; I don't want to be asleep . . .'

'Take it.'

He had walked her to the door to the toilets. She looked at it, looked at him. He nodded.

'And wash your face,' he said.

She went inside.

In the mirror she saw a stranger. A woman approaching middle age, with definite drawn-down lines on her face. In the harsh fluorescence of the overhead light, and taken by surprise at coming upon her own reflection so suddenly, she recognised the disappointment in her expression, the cheated look.

She leaned on the wash basin and brought her face close to the glass. Soon, her breath began to mist over the image, and it was possible to see the younger face, the smooth, unbetraying neck, mouth, forehead.

She could have convinced anyone once.

Now it was slipping with the unseductive advance of time. The older she got, the harder it became to keep the image. That flawless image of face. The image of cajoling care. She was losing it . . . perhaps had already lost it. Perhaps when people spoke to her they no longer saw the persuasive child in her. They only saw the woman with the disappointed lines at the side of her mouth, the horizontal fold lines on her throat. There must come a moment when it no longer works.

Maybe the moment was now.

'Maybe nothing,' she whispered.

She opened her bag and tipped the contents out, scrabbling for the tissues, wetting a bundle of them, and scrubbing at her face. When she had taken off the foundation and lipstick she appeared, briefly, as the confused girl she had once been. She took out the tube of make-up and began applying it thickly to her skin, dusted her cheeks with blusher, outlined her lips in the original shade of helpless, baby pink. She took a comb to her hair and pulled at it unmercifully.

When she was finished, she looked at herself. 'Try them again,' she whispered.

Merrit looked hard at her when she came out. He had been pacing the corridor.

'All right?'

'Yes.'

'Taken the tranquillizer?'

'Yes,' she lied.

'Good.'

They walked to the door of the court.

'We've been six minutes,' Merrit said softly. 'Apologise to the Judge.'

They walked into the courtroom and Julia did as she was told.

'Is your client recovered, Mr Merrit?'

'Yes indeed, your honour.'

'Then let us get on.'

Julia sat down. She was aware of the eyes upon her, but she didn't look up. She folded her hands in her lap and stared resolutely at them, biting the corner of her mouth.

'Your honour,' John Merrit began, 'my client agrees to the seven-day period.'

The Social Services solicitor rose. 'In this case, we are not opposed to the mother seeing the child for supervised contact in the next week,' he began. 'However, we should inform you at this point that, due to under-manning, any visit would have to be next week on a weekday.'

There was a pause. Oliver glanced round. The man continued. 'We have noted Mrs Woods' condition at this time, and the child's welfare is of overriding importance.'

Oliver's solicitor rose.

Julia, at last, looked at him.

Your honour, Mr Woods should like it to be known that he is very concerned for his daughter's physical and emotional safety. He feels that the best interests of the child would be served by his removing her from the marital home to a place of privacy, to protect her against any unwanted attentions by the press, by local gossip, and so on, until the matter is resolved next week. He does not wish Mrs Woods to see the child until Mrs Woods is . . . recovered . . .'

'There is nothing wrong with me,' Julia whispered. 'And he's already done it!'

John Merrit talked over her. 'My client wishes to see her daughter in a supervised visit, your honour,' he said.

Julia's head rolled slightly, as if she had been struck.

'I am accepting the view of Mr Woods,' the Judge said. 'I appoint a guardian *ad litem*. The Social Services will file a Section Thirty-seven report, and a preliminary report is to be available before the next hearing, which we will set as . . .'

'What guardian?' Julia asked Merrit.

'It's a panel of people,' he whispered. 'They represent the child's interests . . .'

'But what about me?'

'It's only seven days,' he said.

The Judge was still talking; he glanced irritatedly at them.

'But when do I see her? Today? Tomorrow?'

'There's no visit until after next week.' He held his hand up, palm towards her, to stop her saying anything else. 'I'll explain everything when we get outside,' he told her.

'But I've a right to *see* her!'

'No. Listen—'

Julia stood up. 'Aren't you letting me see it?' she asked, almost conversationally.

No one took any notice.

'Listen,' she said, 'she's very sick, and I have to see her—I *have* to see her!'

Oliver's calm seemed suddenly to snap. He, too, got to his feet. 'She's perfectly well without you,' he told her. 'Better, in fact.'

Julia's mouth dropped open. She stood, shaking visibly, her hands clenched at her sides. When she spoke, her voice was barely audible.

'It's a very sick girl,' she whispered.

'But not as sick as you,' he said. 'I know what you've been doing. By God, I do.'

She ran at him, her fists raised now, a thready cry escaping her, as agonising as a violin bow grinding on a low string. Oliver's solicitor, caught off guard, was pushed backwards, and stumbled over his chair.

She reached Oliver himself; he did not move at all, except to raise both arms across his face to protect himself. It looked like a practised response. She beat at his arms and then, to the onlookers' astonishment, began tearing at her own skin, as though she were trying to wrench the flesh off her own throat.

Merrit ran up behind her and grasped her hands, pushing her arms down with the pressure of his own grip, until they were pinned to her sides from behind.

'Give her back to me,' she moaned.

'Sit down,' Merrit said.

'This is what I have to put up with,' Oliver remarked, lowering his arms.

'Julia,' Merrit said, 'sit down.'

She swung her head from side to side, encompassing the whole room. Then, she turned and began to run.

She wrenched open the courtroom doors and went out into the corridor, flew down the hallway and down the wide stairs. The window in the stairwell gave a view, floor to ceiling, out into the street; Julia almost plunged straight through the glass at the bend in the steps.

At the bottom she was still running, the noise she was making—a sobbing deep in her throat—dragging behind her like a bloody trail.

In the street, she stopped abruptly on the pavement, and a hand grabbed her arm.

'Julia!' said Beth March. 'Julia . . . what is it?'

THIRTY-NINE

*B*ETH DROVE JULIA BACK TO HER HOTEL.

It was a quiet place on the outskirts of town, set back from the road. Julia got out of the car like an automaton; her hysteria had vanished and had been replaced by an unnerving calm. She walked alongside Beth, followed her up the steps, and through the doors.

'Which room are you?' Beth asked.

Julia shook her head. 'No room—not the room.'

'You're not booked in here?'

'Yes, but . . . don't put me in the room. It's so small.'

Beth shot her a questioning, confused look. 'Shall we sit somewhere down here?'

'Yes, yes.'

There was someone already sitting in the lounge, so Beth guided Julia to the deserted bar, a dark, wood-panelled room. 'Is this all right?'

'Yes.'

Beth went in search of tea, ordered it, and returned.

'Beth,' Julia said as she came back in the room. 'I can't bear it, you know.'

'Well . . . the court—'

'Yes, but I *can't.*' She gripped Beth's wrist.

'OK. Could we see Oliver, do you think? Shall I ring him? Would he come here?'

'I know where he is.'

'Fine. Well, if I rang—'

'Where he's taken Rosie.'

Beth frowned. 'You do? Where?'

The tea was brought in; they sat in silence while it was served and the waitress went out. Neither of them touched the cups.

Julia leaned forward. 'I thought of it just now. A hotel we stayed in before we first moved here. He's always liked it; he says it's the most peaceful place in the world.'

'He wouldn't put her in a hotel, though.'

'Why not?'

'How could he leave her there, on her own?'

'He must have hired someone. A nurse. A nanny.'

'Julia, I don't think—'

'Don't you see it? Rosie would remember it as somewhere nice; we've taken her there for cream teas. It's on a bay, it has a beach. It's a private hotel, like a country house, on a private road. It's secluded, it's perfect . . .'

'And you think he's put her there, when she's been so ill?'

'But they recover quickly, once they come round.'

Beth couldn't follow her. 'Who do?'

'People. People who've had carbon monoxide. They recover.'

Beth stared at her. 'How do you know that?'

Julia waved her hand, as if this was of no consequence. 'Could we go?'

'Just a minute. People don't recover, Julia. They die. Rosie almost died.'

Julia looked away from her. She picked up a serviette and began pleating it. 'They said at the hospital that she was just sensitive to that particular thing. She just slept. It was just a sleep.'

Beth looked hard at Julia's averted face. She was making no sense at all, she realised. It was almost as if she wanted to believe that nothing really serious had happened to Rosie. Perhaps it was a defence mechanism; a way of wiping her own weakness away. Of pretending it had not happened. A fantasy that Rosie was perfectly well.

'She just needs me,' Julia said. 'That's all she needs.'

'Yes, I know,' Beth said. To pacify her.

Julia looked up immediately. 'You think that, too?'

Beth hesitated, aware of treading on eggshells. The last thing Rhys had said to her before he left after lunch was, 'Don't go near that court.' She had smiled, but, as the afternoon wore on, she had been unable to get Julia's panic-stricken voice out of her mind. Sitting at the kitchen table, nursing a cold cup of untouched coffee, she had thought of her own feelings multiplied. Not just to lose a husband, as she had, but a lover, and a child, in one week, like Julia. To be barred from your own home, the only point of reference.

She had plunged her head into her hands, resting her elbows on the table top. She ought not to feel for Julia, but she did. David had gone, she knew, long before last Monday. Senseless, misguided, stupid she might be in some things . . . but Julia was right about *that*. David was absent in soul, barely there in body. Their marriage hadn't died in a blaze of fury, but by slow suffocation.

She had heard that people sometimes canonised their dead partners. Their irritating, selfish husbands and their faithless wives became, overnight, idols who could not possibly have done wrong. They were spotless plaster saints, eulogised and wept over, their faults dropping miraculously from them as they were raised on to their pedestals.

But she was not like that. There was one thing more important than everything else—more important even than finding out about the betrayals over the money, the betrayal with Julia—and that was not to lose David any further by making him something different to the man he was. She wanted to look her loss in the face. David had been an average husband. Theirs had been an average marriage. No more, no less.

She had curled her fingers and pressed her knuckles into her eyes. *Beloved husband.* In time, she would have to think of the words to put on David's stone. *Beloved husband.* It wasn't true. She had not loved David enough even to feel the deadness between them. She had ignored it, looked past it. They didn't fight. They doggedly pursued their parallel lives. It could have been worse, so much worse, and they had each mimed contentment. Contentment took no effort. Contentment was blissfully blindfold. But as for *beloved* . . .

She was not beloved.

Not loved, not worried over, not sacrificed for, not battled for . . . no fight, no sweetness, no loss, no pain in the centre of their marriage. She was not loved. And neither was David . . . except, perhaps, by Julia.

Beth had dropped her hands and looked around at her own things: the familiar plates, furniture, colours, contours. All the routines that tried to reinforce normality. In the last week, she had found comfort in putting her hand on the fabric of a favourite chair, touching the ridged handle of an old knife. They were familiar, reliable things. While the world fluxed and changed, they didn't change at all. And to be forcibly taken away from them would have been desperately hard.

Julia was not allowed back into the Lodge, she had told Beth. She was too unstable even to see her own child. Driving the car, listening to Julia's account, Beth's hopelessly indefinable feeling for Julia had finally polarised into pity.

And she could imagine Oliver, manipulating smugly to the last. 'He just doesn't see me,' Julia had said in a dead voice as they had pulled into the hotel. 'He doesn't think that my feelings are worth anything. He thinks I ought to do as he says . . . and I can't. I *won't*. Not any more.'

Beth could understand that.

My God, I can! she thought.

This began with Oliver.

All this.

Julia was staring at her, waiting for her response. Beth tried to sidestep it, glancing away, lifting the pot and pouring two cups of tea. She tried to hand Julia a cup, but the other woman seemed not to see it. She was still waiting for an answer.

'Look,' Beth said, trying to make her voice lighter. 'Is there anyone I could call for you? Family? A friend? You ought to have someone with you, you know.'

Julia continued to stare. 'I haven't anybody,' she murmured.

'There must be *someone* . . .'

'There isn't.' Julia took the cup, but put it down straight away without drinking from it. 'My parents are dead; I haven't spoken to my sister in years . . .'

'Someone in the village?'

'Who?'

'Well, I don't know . . . You must know people from your clubs and coffee mornings . . .'

'My *clubs*?' Julia laughed faintly. 'From my Wives Club, or the WI?'

'Yes. Should I call—'

'Oh—I should just call them up and ask them how the last meeting went?' she asked. 'And who is doing the—whatever—the cakes for the fête stall or something, and I should just mention, by the way of course, that my husband is trying to . . .' Her voice broke and her hand fell, so that the cup rattled in the saucer, spilling liquid that pooled on the polished table and dripped to the floor. 'No one would believe me,' she said. 'No one . . . except you.'

Beth closed her eyes momentarily. When she opened them Julia was within six inches of her, and her flowery perfume rolled over Beth like a wave.

'We are just the same,' she whispered. 'Help me.'

The drive to the Aubyn Hotel took almost an hour.

The country slipped from Dorset downland to a landscape of small valleys, river estuaries, and woods. The sign for the village was almost hidden by trees, and Beth might have missed it entirely had not Julia pointed it out.

Narrow, high-hedged lanes gave way, abruptly, to a steep road; at a wider point, the view unrolled to a green valley and a wide-mouthed, pebbled estuary.

'You can't see it from here,' Julia said. 'You have to get down into the village, then take a left. I'll tell you when.'

Beth had to stop the car on the corner of the gradient. A cottage on the bend was being re-thatched, and the thatcher's van was reversing into the small garden. Straw littered the road; a radio played loudly above their heads, surreal in the harsh woven yellow of the roof.

One of the men directing the van came alongside the car, grinning. 'You ladies not in any hurry . . . ?'

'No,' said Beth. 'It's OK.'

'Bugger, this corner.'

'Yes, it must be.'

He patted the roof of the car. 'I'll wave you when we're there.'

'Thanks.'

They waited another minute while, out of sight around the bend, the same man argued good-naturedly with traffic waiting on the other side.

'We ought to have rung, to check that Oliver was there,' Beth said.

'And warn him?'

'He wouldn't run away.'

'Wouldn't he?' said Julia.

Beth turned to look at her. 'Julia,' she asked, 'why did you marry him?'

'I was lonely,' she said. 'Nobody but Oliver took notice.'

'You didn't love him?'

'He took notice,' she repeated.

'Is that all?'

Julia crossed her arms and turned her face away to look out of the side window. 'He was rich,' she murmured.

The man was calling them on. Beth put the car into gear.

It was another mile before they took the left into a lane almost totally arched over with trees; it skirted the hillside, then dropped the last hundred feet into an arc of level pasture that gave way to lawns. The large Victorian hotel stood with its back to the hillside, facing the sea.

'What a location,' Beth said, peering at it from behind the wheel. 'It must be incredibly expensive.'

'It is,' Julia said. 'Drive up.'

Beth raised an eyebrow at the order, but said nothing. The car tyres scrunched on the thick gravel. They got out, their roles reversed from two hours before—Julia now leading, Beth bringing up the rear.

As they went through the entrance, Beth whispered, 'My God,' at the stone lions guarding the elaborate black boot-scrapers. Someone had painted their tongues and claws red, their eyes brown.

Inside, there was no Reception; just a squarish space at the foot of the stairs with an open door leading to a dining room. The tables were set in batches of two. The chairs were high-backed and heavily upholstered in dark blue and gold. There were candles and silverware and arrangements of early roses on each table. At the side, a *chaise-longue* in gold brocade was shaded by a huge display of dried hydrangeas and artificial fruit—pears and apples sprayed green and silver, peacock feathers, ostrich plumes.

'Can I help you?' asked a voice.

It was small, dark-haired man. He seemed to have appeared from nowhere, until Beth glimpsed an open door under the stairs.

'We are looking for Mr Woods,' Julia said.

'Mr . . . ?'

'Woods,' Beth repeated. 'Oliver Woods. He's a guest here.'

The man frowned. 'Just a moment,' he told them. He pushed the low door, and they heard his footsteps echoing back along a stone corridor.

'What a place,' Beth said. 'It looks like a brothel.'

Julia's expression did not alter. She was staring at the half-closed door through which the man had gone. 'They call it theatrical in their brochure. I think they used to be designers of some kind.'

Beth smiled. 'With a taste for the grotesque. God, would you bring a child here?'

The man returned. He smiled. 'I thought I would double-check,' he said. 'Just to make sure my memory wasn't failing me again.'

'Where is he?' Julia asked.

'I'm afraid we don't have a Mr Woods registered,' the man replied.

'Yes you do,' Julia retorted. 'A tall man, of about sixty, with a little girl . . .'

The man folded his hands in front of him. 'That wouldn't be possible,' he said. 'You see, we don't take children here.'

Julia took a step forward. 'You remember me, don't you?' she asked. 'We came here on our honeymoon; we've come since . . .'

'I'm sorry. We have so many guests.'

'But . . .' Julia stopped. 'I see. All right,' she replied. 'I'm sorry; I must have made a mistake.'

'That's perfectly all right.'

Julia turned to Beth. 'Come on,' she said.

Beth followed her out. The man watched them from the steps, then closed the oak door behind them. Beth opened the door of the van, her heart sinking. It had been a stupid exercise. She was half expecting Julia to name another hotel—somewhere that had also featured in her and Oliver's past. She was ready to refuse.

They got in.

'Drive round the back,' Julia said.

'What?'

'Drive round the back; look, down the drive again, then up that little path . . .'

'Julia!'

The other woman gripped her hands in hers. 'He's here.'

'But the man just said—'

'*Please*, Beth.'

Grudgingly, Beth reversed. Almost at the entrance, she turned right into a grassy alley.

'It's for deliveries,' Julia said.

'How do you know?'

'I remember. Come *on*, Beth.'

Sure enough, the track led to the rear of the hotel, to a stable block and outhouses shaded from the main building by trees.

Julia got out, beckoning Beth to follow her. They walked around the rear of the stables, along the side of a hillocky lawn that tipped away, past wind-bleached shrubs, to a beach that was half grass and half pebbles. In one corner of the lawn was a tennis court, and, further still, under the trees, a row of seats. All were empty.

'This way,' Julia said.

They were at the very edge of the house, circling round to the front. The sea was incredibly calm, the sound of waves two hundred yards away barely audible. Julia caught Beth's arm and pointed.

There was a conservatory here; an original part of the house, it seemed, with a grey metal roof and brick-built piers. The roof must have been at least thirty feet high, and the interior was shaded by palms.

'It looks like Kew Gardens,' Beth murmured.

But Julia wasn't listening. Her gaze was fixed on the far door; here, at a table, a man sat staring out to sea. It was Oliver, and, at his side, was Rosie.

'I knew it,' Julia said. She started to run.

'Julia!' Beth took after her.

Oliver turned his head, saw his wife, and rose to his feet. Rosie leapt up. They saw Oliver trying to restrain her as she hung on the handle of the door.

'Rosie!' Julia shouted.

The door opened. Rosie shot out, almost catapulting herself into Julia's arms. 'Mummy!' she cried. 'Mummy. Mummy!'

Julia knelt on the grass, crushing her daughter to her. The child wriggled slightly, so that she could look in her mother's face, her hands clasped around Julia's neck. 'Did you fly?' she asked.

'Sorry, darling?'

'Did you fly, on a plane?'

Julia was weeping. 'No, darling. A plane? Why should I be on a plane?'

Oliver had come to the doorway.

'Daddy said you were on holiday, miles and miles,' Rosie told her.

Julia looked up accusingly into Oliver's face, then back at her child. 'Yes, I flew back,' she said. 'All the way. To see you.' She stood up, wiping her face, and taking Rosie's hand. 'What a very grand place,' she said.

'This is our holiday,' Rosie replied. 'In a big hotel.'

'It's lovely.'

Mother and father were staring at each other over their daughter's head.

Oliver glanced at Beth, then back at Julia.

'We are having tea,' he said.

Beth reached out to touch Rosie's arm. 'What about showing me round the garden?' she asked. 'So that Mummy and Daddy can talk for a while?'

'No,' Oliver said.

Beth stared at him. 'I thought—'

'No.'

Beth realised what he meant. He thought she had struck some bargain with Julia to take Rosie away while he was distracted. Furious, she blushed to the roots of her hair.

'There are peacocks,' Rosie was saying, oblivious to the fraught atmosphere around her. 'There are white ones, and they go up into the trees.'

'Rosie,' said Oliver. 'Come and sit down.'

'But I want to show Beth the peacocks.'

'Come and sit down.'

Rosie looked from one adult to the other, her eyes finally resting on Beth.

'Go on,' Beth told her.

Oliver had stepped back. He picked up a small bell from the table and rang it.

'No,' said Julia.

He continued ringing, a look of utter contempt cast back at his wife.

A woman appeared, carrying an empty tray in one hand. She stared from Beth to Julia, then at Oliver. 'Oh, Mr Woods,' she said. 'I'm so sorry.'

'You *see*,' Julia whispered savagely to Beth. 'You *see* what he does?'

'We thought they had gone,' the woman was continuing.

'It doesn't matter,' Oliver said. Roughly, he took hold of Rosie's arm. 'Rosie, I want you to go with Mrs Spencer.'

'No!' cried Julia.

Oliver almost hauled his daughter off her feet. 'With Mrs Spencer, Rosie.'

'But I don't want to,' Rosie said.

'Come on, darling,' the woman replied, pulling at the child's free arm.

'Do as you're told,' Oliver said.

Julia rushed forward. 'Don't order her!' she cried. She slapped at the stranger's hands. 'Get *off* her, get *off* her.'

The woman responded by promptly picking Rosie up and gripping her tightly round the waist.

'Mummy!' Rosie screamed.

Julia tried prising the woman's fingers loose.

'Please, Mrs Woods,' the woman gasped.

Julia turned to Oliver. 'How can you?' she said.

'All right, Mrs Spencer,' Oliver said. He nodded in the direction of the door.

'*Noooo*,' wailed Rosie.

The woman turned; Rosie was reaching over her shoulder, both hands extended helplessly to her mother.

Beth grabbed at Oliver's sleeve. 'Just let them be together for a moment,' she said.

Oliver looked down at her. 'Do you realise,' he asked her coldly, 'that I could call the police over this? I have a court order,' he said.

The scene behind them was developing into a struggle. Rosie holding Julia's hands; the woman from the hotel vainly trying to drag her burden towards the door. Oliver cursed under his breath. He walked rapidly forward, tore Julia's hands away, and pushed her to one side.

'Hurry up,' he hissed.

Mrs Spencer obeyed. She had been looking wildly at Julia, evidently very frightened of her. Beth wondered what stories Oliver had been telling her. Her relief at Oliver's intervention was palpable. She ran to the door, Rosie's small body still thrashing in her arms.

'Mummy!' Rosie called. 'Oh Mummy, *please* . . .'

The door slammed shut after them.

Oliver turned to Julia. She was leaning against a table, rubbing one wrist with her hand.

'Get out,' he said.

'Oliver!' Beth said.

'Both of you. Out.'

'How can you be so bloody unfeeling?' Julia muttered.

Oliver turned to Beth. 'I'm surprised at your part in this,' he said. 'Surprised . . . and, frankly, disappointed.'

Beth bridled. 'She just wants to see that Rosie's all right,' she retorted. 'I don't see what's so terrible about that.'

'What is so *terrible*,' Oliver replied, mimicking her, 'is that Rosie needs complete peace. This was all discussed and agreed in court.'

'Discussed!' Julia broke in. 'You all decide between you, and then you *tell* me, you all *order* me,' she said. 'That's a bloody discussion, if you like!'

'Julia,' Oliver said with a disgusted expression, 'you are hysterical.'

Beth began to laugh. 'Are you surprised?' she asked.

Oliver took no notice of her. He was still staring at his wife. 'You have caused Rosie distress. You can see that,' he said.

'Distress!' Julia said. 'What about *my* distress!'

Oliver made an exasperated gesture. 'This isn't about you. You cannot understand, can you?' he said. 'That is exactly what the hearing was about. To protect Rosie. She need never have seen this. Never have known.'

'She doesn't need protecting from me,' Julia said.

Oliver's whole face darkened. He stepped forward, towering over Julia, the flesh at his neck mottled with fury. As he spoke, the underside of his lip showed, wetly red; an old man's mouth. Beth turned her head so that she would not have to look at it.

'Yes she does,' he told Julia. 'And you know that very well.'

'I don't. I don't . . .' She began to cry noisily.

'Oh, for God's sake,' Oliver snapped. He raised his hand; Beth, looking at a point on the floor between them, thought that he was about to hit Julia. But the fist stopped short.

'We had the lab reports from the hospital,' he said.

'What reports?'

Oliver laughed shortly; a totally cold sound. 'You really are a most stupid woman,' he said.

He turned back to Beth. 'You think she's such a victim,' he said. 'But let me tell you who is the victim here.' He walked back to the outside door, as if to get his breath, or to control his rising temper. 'The reports have shown Temazepam,' he said.

'Temazepam?' asked Beth. 'What's that?'

'It's a sedative.'

'Sedative?' Beth looked at Julia, then back at Oliver. 'In Rosie's blood, you mean?'

'Quite.'

'But how did it get there?'

Oliver gestured at his wife. 'Ask her.'

Julia coloured, her skin flushing deep red. 'I don't know what the hell you're talking about,' she said.

'Don't you?' Oliver retorted.

'Just a minute,' Beth said. 'You mean that Julia gave Rosie a sedative? That's what you think?'

'Exactly.'

'But why?'

'I did not,' Julia interrupted.

'She gave her a sedative to get her to sleep, so that she could put her into the car.'

'I did not!' Julia shouted.

'She gave her a sedative to control her.'

'No, no . . .'

'Oliver,' Beth said. 'Do you know how ridiculous this sounds? Perhaps they gave her a sedative in hospital.'

Oliver made a brushing-away movement of denial. 'They were trying to get her round in hospital,' he said.

'It was the car fumes,' Julia cried.

'No,' he said. 'They thought that at first. Then I told them to look for Temazepam.'

There was a short silence.

'*You* did?' asked Beth. 'Why?'

'It's not true,' Julia said.

'Because of Rosie's constant ill health.'

Julia let out a kind of scream, a tortured, animal sound.

The back door opened. The man who appeared was the same one who had told them that Oliver was not staying at the hotel.

'Mr Woods?' he asked.

Oliver held up his hand. 'It's all right, Michael.'

'Should I . . .?' His gaze fell on the distraught Julia. 'Should I call anyone?'

'No, no,' Oliver said.

Beth turned to Julia, looked at her wonderingly for a second, and then handed her a crumpled tissue from her own pocket.

'I'm sorry, Michael,' Oliver said.

'It's just that other guests have returned for tea . . .'

'We'll go outside,' Oliver told him. He held open the door.
One by one, they went out into the light of the fading afternoon.

FORTY

IT WAS ALMOST FIVE IN THE AFTERNOON when Helen Pritchard noticed the car pull up outside the offices in the High Street.

She was wiping the shelf in the small kitchen, where, earlier that day, she and Christina had been celebrating Christina's birthday.

'Pity the old devil couldn't show his face,' Christina had said, demolishing the last eclair with an expression of luxurious delight. 'Last year he gave me fifty pounds! Couldn't believe it.'

Helen had smiled. 'Generous when you least expect it,' she had agreed.

'Where d'you think he is?'

Helen shrugged. 'He didn't tell me anything. But you've heard about the court case?'

Christina had not. Helen had only learned the details through the roundabout route of Rhys and Alan. The two women had talked at some length about Julia and the daughter caught between the two warring adults.

'He must have driven her to it,' Christina had said. 'You can imagine it, can't you? Imagine him coming home and sending his wife right up the wall.'

Helen was not so sure. 'I know what he's like with us, at work,' she agreed thoughtfully. 'But I know that he idolises that child.'

Christina had pulled a face. 'All the same,' she'd said, smirking a little now. 'Think of that horrible old cadaver getting into bed next to you. Ugh!' And she'd broken out in a peal of laughter.

Helen had merely smiled. She was twenty years older than Christina. Christina's *cadaver* was her *mature*. 'Still . . . I'll be surprised if we see him at all between now and next week,' she murmured.

Christina had sighed deeply. 'Which leaves us two to run the show.'

'It looks that way.'

'Charming,' the girl had commented. 'That's what he is. Absolutely bloody charming.'

Helen stepped back now from the kitchen, and frowned at the parked car visible through the front windows. It was a double yellow line there. She saw two men get out, speak for a second, and then push open the door into Reception.

'Is Mr Woods in?' the first man asked. His voice was cultivated, low, and pleasant.

'No,' she replied. 'Can I help?'

The two looked at each other. 'And you are . . . ?'

'Mrs Pritchard, Mr Woods' secretary.'

'Do you have the key to the files, and so on? The safes?'

Helen's heartbeat picked up a pace. 'Look, who are you?' she asked.

The first man smiled, reaching into the inner pocket of his jacket. 'I do apologise,' he murmured. And he showed her a card. 'My name is Matthew Keller, of Keller, Wright and Porteous.'

She looked at the card, then at the diary open on the desk in front of her. 'I'm afraid there's no record of an appointment,' she told him. 'And I don't expect Mr Woods to be in today—possibly not for a few days.'

The man's smile was nothing if not charming. 'And would he have told you where he was going?' he asked.

'No . . . he didn't tell me. I think there are one or two problems at home at the moment,' Helen said.

'Yes,' he answered. 'One or two problems.' He raised an eyebrow at the man with him. 'Quite.' He put his case on the ground, leaned on the counter, and asked, 'I see you are ready to go home. Might I ask you to stay on for a while?'

'Why . . . what for?'

'We would need to search through the files, and put a seal on any further transactions. To begin with.'

'I don't understand,' Helen said.

The man's partner spoke up for the first time.

'We have been appointed by the Law Society, Mrs Pritchard,' he said. 'We have authority to investigate various irregularities in Mr Woods' business.'

FORTY-ONE

$\mathcal{A}$s they walked from the hotel, across the lawn towards the sea, Oliver stopped abruptly and took Beth's hand.

Beth, bringing up the rear of the small group, glanced from his fingers to Julia, who continued to walk ahead, her arms crossed, her head bowed.

'Beth,' he said.

She held up her hand. 'You had better get this straight,' she told him. 'I've only come because Julia begged me. Go ahead and talk to her. Sort something out. Then let us go home.'

'Yes,' he said vaguely. Then, 'Beth, I have a confession to make.'

'Another?' she said sourly, watching Julia, who had reached the fine pebbles and stopped, staring out at the water.

'I am almost bankrupt.'

She said nothing.

'I have spent the last few days trying to find a way out of this, trying not to involve you; I thought I could put it right, and you would never need to know. I even thought I may be able to repay the money David gave to me, the trust fund.' His voice trailed away as he gazed after Julia. Then, he looked back at Beth. She saw how tired he was; small bruised haemorrhages marked the white of one eye. As he spoke, his head nodded slightly, exhaustion emphasising every word.

'Two months ago, I told David about an investment deal. I had already put a lot of money into it. It was supposed to be ironclad, a fifty per cent return within twelve months, provided the amount that you invested was large enough. I expected David to tell me that I was being foolish, going out on too weak a limb . . . but he didn't. He suggested putting more money in. He gave me his £11,000. I sank everything I owned into it. The company was well known, respected . . .' A ghost of a smile flickered. 'Well, as you know,' he murmured. 'I have been rather disappointed.' His expression told her of the enormity of this understatement. 'Ironclad companies fail too, it appears.'

'And take the greedy with them,' she observed.

He saw her contempt, and glanced back to his wife. Julia had begun walking again, albeit extremely slowly, along the beach ahead of them.

'Of course, then there was the mortgage,' Beth said sarcastically. 'Don't forget that.'

Oliver straightened, turning back to her. 'I swear to you now, Beth, on my honour—'

She laughed. He spoke through her.

'On my honour,' he repeated, 'I know nothing about that. I witnessed your signature because David asked me to. He seemed so anxious for it to go through quickly. I have no idea where the money went or what he wanted it for. You *must* believe me.'

Beth met his gaze levelly. 'I've reported you to the Law Society,' she said. 'They'll soon tell me if you've been telling me the truth, no doubt.'

Oliver didn't seem to be angry; rather, he gave her a smile that was almost gallant. She sensed his utter resignation. 'That's all right. They'll find nothing,' he said. 'Because there is nothing to find.'

He paused, his eyes ranging sadly over her face.

'There's something else more important,' he added.

'Christ, I hope not,' she told him.

'It's Julia.'

'Oliver, don't drag me any further in.'

'Beth, I must ask you to listen to me. I am trying . . . that is, we are trying, to get Julia into hospital.'

'Hospital? What hospital?'

'Psychiatric care.'

'For . . . not for this week . . .'

'*Not* because of this week. Not *just* because of this week.' Oliver put his hands on Beth's shoulders. 'Beth, you must listen to what I am going to tell you,' he said. 'The hospital think that Julia has an illness. They have consulted with our own doctor, and with the Social Services, and we think she has something called . . .' He paused, watching Beth's face carefully. 'It's called Münchausen's syndrome,' he said. 'Münchausen's by proxy.'

Beth stepped free of his hands; they felt like dead weights. 'I've never heard of it,' she said.

'No . . . it's a disorder . . .'

'What *kind* of disorder?'

'They don't know why it develops. The person draws attention to themselves by a series of imagined illnesses . . .'

'You mean hypochondria?'

'More severe than that.'

'But Julia's never complained of being ill!'

'Münchausen's *by proxy*,' Oliver corrected her. He paused, as if to weigh his following words with significance. 'Julia doesn't make herself ill,' he said. 'Julia makes *Rosie* ill.'

Beth stepped back, appalled. 'You're joking,' she said.

'That's why she didn't come round in hospital. It wasn't the carbon monoxide, it was the sedative. Julia was prescribed Temazepam after Rebecca's death. She's been giving it to Rosie for some time. Or so they think.'

'But the GP would have known.'

'No. Münchausen's sufferers are very convincing. It is only when a series of things come together and you are able to go back over time and see the link—'

'No,' Beth said. She turned away. 'No, that's not possible. How can you say that! Julia *loves* Rosie. She adores her.' She gestured towards the hotel, now hidden from them by the trees of the garden. 'You *saw* how they love each other,' she said. She whirled back towards Oliver. 'How can you say that about your own wife?'

'Because it's true,' he told her. 'People with this illness often go undetected because they *seem* so very loving towards the children they are slowly destroying . . .'

They stayed, locked in the same place, staring at each other. 'Please try to understand,' he said. 'Not for my sake. But for Rosie's. I have to protect her, and now . . .' He put his hand to his head. 'I may not be able to be with her all the time.' He looked at her. 'And Rosie knows you, Beth. She needs someone to take care of her when I can't . . .'

Beth stared at him for just a moment longer, then brushed past him and began to run.

'Beth!' Oliver called.

She ran until she reached Julia. She was standing at the top of a short pebble incline; behind her, the beach shelved to a dip, where the grass and chalk dunes met the shoreline. Ahead, the beach smoothed down to a narrow strip of sand.

'Julia,' Beth said, grabbing her arm. 'Come with me. Let's go.'

Julia hardly responded. She stood with her arms resolutely crossed, tight in to her body. She didn't meet Beth's eyes. 'He's going to win,' she murmured. 'There's no use being here, is there?'

Beth glanced at Oliver, who was struggling to catch up with them. 'Come on,' she said. 'You've nothing to gain here. You need to see a doctor.'

Julia looked at her.

Beth was still trying to drag her by the arm. 'Oliver's got some sort of wild medical theory,' she told her. 'Unless you get another opinion, and damned quick, you're going to lose this case.'

'What medical theory?'

Oliver had reached them.

Julia turned. 'What have you been saying?' she asked softly.

Oliver glanced at Beth.

'What have you been saying?' Julia demanded.

He tried to take hold of her. Beth dropped her own grip. Julia raised her hand; to ward him off, Beth thought. But Julia brought her hand down, clenched, tipped backwards slightly, and struck Oliver in the side of the face.

The blow connected with the temple. Beth saw Oliver's eyes widen for a moment; then his head rolled back, his jaw slackened, and he tipped backwards without even bringing up an arm to defend himself.

For a terrible second, Beth saw him suspended against the backdrop of sky, staring upwards, his mouth open. Then, he toppled over completely, hitting the slithering bank of shingle. His knees buckled and twisted. He lay on the ground with his head snapped back on his shoulders, arms half extended, and the lower half of his body crumpled. The slope and the heavy torso bore down on his lower half, until, compressed in terrible slow motion, he lay curled on his side, his legs doubled under him.

Stones pattered down the slope for a second. It was the only sound.

Beth stared in total incomprehension. Her first thought was that he must have had a seizure of some kind. An attack at the very second that Julia hit him. She looked at him for another quick moment, then across at Julia.

It was only then that she saw the stone in Julia's hand. It was a rock about five inches across, and had been concealed in Julia's rigidly folded hands.

'My God,' Beth said. 'What have you done?'

Julia said nothing. She stood above Oliver with a totally expressionless face.

Beth kneeled down. Her fingers hesitated above Oliver's face, then she pressed them to the side of his neck. 'I can't feel anything,' she whispered.

She put her head on his chest.

Still nothing.

On his face, the mark of the blow was obvious; a thick bloody scar on his temple. His eyes were still open.

Beth tried his wrist. She had never taken any kind of first-aid course, and she had no idea of what she ought to do. She could trace nothing, no beat or movement, on his arm. She held her hand, palm downwards, over his mouth, trying to see if she could feel air, the merest sign of breath.

Nothing.

'Julia . . .' she said.

Julia was holding the stone flat in her hand. She looked at it for a moment with silent interest; then, as casually as a boy skimming stones, she threw it overarm at the waves, where it disappeared in the first ten feet of gently churning water.

Beth got to her feet. 'Julia,' she repeated.

The other woman looked at her. 'We ought to cover him up,' she said.

'What?'

'We ought to cover him up so that no one will find him.'

Beth's gaze flickered from Julia to Oliver's body, and back again. 'Do you know what you've done?' she said again. 'Julia!'

'No one will find him,' Julia replied. And she grabbed at the inert body.

'No, no . . .' Beth cried.

Oliver's dead weight slumped. The shingle bank took him down as Julia pulled at his arm, sliding him sideways. Julia let go of the arm, and started pulling at his feet. She took off his shoes and threw them down the slope behind her. Her hands fastened around his ankles. 'Pull him,' she said.

'No, I—'

'Pull him!'

Beth stared at Julia; she had a look of brisk, almost careless pleasure. Fear trickled along Beth's spine; she glanced back along the empty beach, afraid to run. Afraid of the insanity at her back. She did as she was told. She caught Oliver under each arm, and they staggered up the last few inches of slope. At the top, however, what she was doing struck Beth like a thunderbolt; she dropped her burden with a cry of disgust.

Julia let him go too. She stood with her head on one side, as if calculating something; then, getting behind him, she shoved the body in the small of the back.

Oliver's body rolled forward, down the slope, pebbles falling after him in a slow avalanche. When he reached the bottom, he lay face down in the mixture of sand, stone and grass. The trickle of a stream dammed up behind him for a while, rapidly soaking his clothes. The absorption crept downwards, darkening his jacket. One leg was cramped underneath, turned at a terrible angle. One arm lay bunched at the shoulder, the fingers curled upwards.

Julia suddenly slid down the pebbles and, picking them up in handfuls, started throwing them over him.

'Help me,' she said.

Beth stood shaking on the top of the slope. 'No,' she whispered. 'Oh, no.'

Julia continued shovelling. It was hopeless. She clambered half way back up and began pushing with her feet, forcing a ridge of pebbles, wet under the surface, downwards.

'They will find him,' Beth said, in a faraway voice that she hardly recognised as her own.

'They won't,' Julia said.

The darkness of his clothes disappeared; only the grotesque outline of his head and hands and uncovered feet remained. Julia worked faster, guttural notes of effort escaping her. Beth could not take her eyes from Oliver's head, the hand half-clenched at his neck. The few frail wisps of his hair moved in the breath of wind. Eventually, they too were covered.

It took perhaps three or four minutes.

Julia looked up at Beth.

'The water will uncover him,' Beth murmured.

Without taking her eyes from Beth, Julia climbed the slope on all fours, her feet sliding back a step with every two. It was as if the dead man below was clawing her back.

Emerging at the top at last, she stood up.

Beth thought of the burial cairns, piled with whitened stones on the ridges of hills; the barrows that marked the skylines along this coast. She thought of Rhys. Getting to Rhys.

Julia took hold of her hand. 'Come with me,' she said. 'Beth! Are you listening? Come with me.'

FORTY-TWO

*J*ULIA RAN BACK THROUGH THE CONSERVATORY of the hotel, calling Rosie's name.

There was a party of four guests sitting in the shaded dining room, with a tea of Edwardian proportions laid on the table. A woman of about sixty had been pouring tea, and sat now with the teapot suspended mid-air. All four heads were turned.

Julia stopped at the door. 'Have you seen my daughter?' she asked.

'I'm sorry . . . ?'

'My daughter. My daughter.' Julia walked forward impatiently. 'She's about so high . . .' she said, holding her hand at her waist. 'Fair hair.'

The guests looked at each other, surprise mingling with distrust at Julia's dishevelled appearance. One of the men looked her over from head to foot, his gaze lingering on her scuffed shoes.

'No . . .'

Julia clenched her fists. 'I must find her,' she said.

One of the other women spoke up. 'Wasn't there a little girl on the stairs just now?' she asked.

Julia ran out to the hallway. She looked wildly from left to right.

The stairs stretched in a long curve, dividing at the very top. The hotel had at least twenty rooms. Rosie could be anywhere.

She threw back her head, and screamed.

'Rosie! Rosie!'

The two women came out from the dining room.

'*Rosie!*' Julia repeated.

'Oh dear,' said the guest. 'Is she lost?'

Julia began to cry. 'She's only six,' she wept. 'Only six . . .'

'Do you have a room? Will she be in there?'

'Rosie!'

The elder woman walked forward and put her hand on Julia's arm. 'You mustn't panic,' she said. 'She'll be here somewhere. She can't have gone far, surely?'

'Why don't you go and look in your room? I'm sure she was on the stairs.'

'Oh God,' Julia wept.

There was a patter of footsteps on the landing above them. All three looked up. Rosie's face, wreathed in smiles, appeared over the wooden banister.

'Mummy!'

Julia ran, two treads at a time, up the stairs, catching her daughter in her arms and sweeping her off her feet.

'There now,' said the woman below. 'You see? Not far.'

Mrs Spencer had run along the landing after Rosie. She appeared now, a look of near terror on her face, and saw Julia running down with Rosie still clutched in her arms, the child's face turned upwards, a pale disc receding into the gloom of the hall.

'Mrs Woods,' the owner called. 'Please . . .'

Julia had reached the bottom. 'Don't you come near us!' she shouted.

Mrs Spencer was negotiating the long stairway as quickly as she could, one hand held outwards. Julia switched Rosie to her left side, where the child laid her head almost casually on her shoulder, watching with wide eyes.

'Is Mr Woods here?' the owner asked.

'I ought to have you arrested,' Julia said.

'I beg your pardon!'

'Do you know what you've done?' Julia demanded. She looked back at the women guests. 'Conspired with my husband to take my child away from me,' she said. 'Only that! From *me*!'

The protests stuck in Mrs Spencer's throat. She had time only to see Julia's fist swing in her direction; she stepped backwards, stumbling on the stairs, and felt the blow whisper past her face. Julia staggered.

'Oh, really. Oh dear,' the woman behind said, as if nothing more serious than an inappropriate word had been uttered.

Rosie had closed her eyes and was clinging to Julia's neck, hiding her face.

'Don't ever interfere in my life again,' Julia said.

She turned, ran to the outside door, and wrenched it open.

FORTY-THREE

$\mathcal{O}$UTSIDE, BETH HAD RUN TO THE VAN.

She got in, distantly aware that she was shaking, but nothing more. Shock had deadened her. She put the key into the ignition only with the greatest difficulty, like an invalid trying to grasp, to balance. She wanted to get away; that was all. That was everything. To get away as quickly as possible. To drive to the police. No other thought was in her mind.

She put her foot on the clutch and jammed the gearstick into reverse. There was an arc of clear driveway behind. The accelerator roared.

'Come on,' she whispered. 'Damn you bloody thing, come *on*.'

The van leapt backwards, spraying gravel against the underside. Her fingers slicked on the wheel. As she tried to negotiate the turning, there was a grinding sound. She banged her palm against the gearstick, lodged intractably in reverse.

Out of the corner of her eye, she saw Julia coming out of the front door of the hotel. To her amazement, Rosie was in her mother's arms. Up until that moment, Beth was determined to drive off; she would have risked running Julia down to avoid her getting back into the van.

But the sight of Rosie, hands fastened around Julia's neck, her face pinched and pale, more like that of a sick old woman than a healthy child, wrung her heart.

She paused, torn, the van still juddering. Her foot slipped from the accelerator; she watched them coming, running over the drive towards her.

Julia opened the door.

Rosie came in first, pushed headlong by her mother.

Beth held out her arms. 'Hello, sweetheart,' she said. Her own voice belonged to a stranger: high-pitched and flat.

Rosie wriggled into the seat.

'Drive off,' Julia said.

'I can't. The gears . . .'

Julia fastened her hand over the gearstick. 'Put your foot down.'

Beth stared at her. 'I can't, Julia.'

For a second, Julia returned the look with absolute calm. Then she leaned forward and neatly took the keys from the ignition. 'Get out, then.'

'No, I . . .' Beth looked down at Rosie. The child had reverted to her old solace, the thumb lodged in her mouth, her eyes travelling between Julia and Beth. Looking over her head, Beth gazed at Julia: the pale blue eyes, pale skin, pale hair. A face of ethereal calm. As Beth watched, a smile crossed Julia's expression: light chasing dark. It was chilling to see.

Beth's hand instinctively strayed to Rosie's shoulder. 'This isn't right,' she said. 'We must call . . .' She didn't want to say *the police* in front of the child.

Julia talked over her. 'Either you drive, or I do.'

'Where's Daddy?' Rosie asked.

Beth gave Julia a pleading look. 'You can't run away,' she said. Julia stared back glassily, the smile tweaking her mouth into a parody of humour, the keys swinging between thumb and forefinger.

'I'm not getting out,' Beth added.

'Then drive.'

Beth had a vision of Rosie, in the seat next to Julia, pleading in that terrified tone that she had used the other day, when Julia dragged her home along the lane. Slowly, Beth took the keys, started the engine.

'Going home now,' Rosie said, patting both knees in excited anticipation.

'Going on a trip,' Julia told her.

The van at last accepted first gear. Beth drove forward, out of the drive, along the lane and past the thatcher's cottage. At the junction, Julia waved her hand to the left.

The traffic was steady along the main road. After a mile or so, Beth glanced over at Julia.

'Where are you going?' she asked.

'I'm thinking.'

'You—'

'I'm *thinking.*'

Rosie reached forward to run a finger along the windscreen; Julia slapped her hand down.

'Julia,' Beth said. 'We must turn in at Wynfirth Newley.' Newley was the County Police Headquarters, a detour of some five miles after the next roundabout.

'We're going to Poole.'

'Julia, for God's sake!'

'Where is Daddy?' Rosie asked. 'Is he coming with us?'

'Julia,' Beth persisted. 'It was a spur of the moment thing. If you talked to them now . . .' Her voice fell. 'They're going to find him. You could say—the stress of the situation . . .'

'Will you bloody well fuck off!' Julia said.

Rosie sat up. 'You don't say that word.'

'I'm turning to Wynfirth,' Beth said.

Julia grabbed the wheel.

Beth fought to disengage her fingers. The van swayed towards the other lane. 'For Christ's sake!' she shouted. Rosie screamed.

There was a milk tanker coming the other way. Beth glimpsed its white and blue colouring, the picture of the jolly milkman on the front, advancing on them at sixty miles an hour. Its lights flashed. She pulled the wheel to the left at the last moment and it swept past, horn blaring. In her rear-view mirror, she saw the driver of the car behind them make a *crazy* sign, finger screwed against temple.

'Oh, God,' Beth whispered. Her heart was hammering hollowly in her chest. 'Oh, God.'

Julia was looking at the road. 'Go to the house,' she said. 'I need my passport.'

Ahead of them, the traffic was slowing. A hill was coming up. Four cars in front, a caravan was being towed.

'Play *I went to the shops*,' Rosie said.

'Not now,' Julia said.

But Rosie was not to be dissuaded from this memory game, where progressively more elaborate items were added to an imaginary shopping list. 'I went to the shops and I bought a . . . a . . .'

The hill was steepening. Beth changed down to third.

'. . . a dog.'

Julia didn't reply.

'Mummy, I said a dog. Your turn.'

'I'll play,' Beth said. 'I went to the shops, and I bought a nice dog . . .'

'It's a corgi dog.'

'A . . .' Beth's mind froze as she watched the white line in the centre of the road. Panic swept through her. Unadulterated panic and fear, quick and nameless.

'A little corgi dog.'

'A . . . corgi dog, and . . .' Beth's words were strained thin, as desperate as a prayer. 'A tin . . . a big tin of sliced peaches.'

Rosie sat forward smiling. 'I went to the shops and I bought a corgi dog . . .' She held up her fingers, ticking the remembered items off. '. . . and a big tin of *sliced* peaches, and a big big *blanket*.'

'I counted on you,' Julia said. Beth glanced at her. 'Police. Do you think I'm bloody stupid?' Julia continued, as though thinking aloud. 'The same, the same. More of the same.'

The traffic dropped to twenty miles an hour; Beth engaged second gear. The hill swung to the left here, a gradient of one in eight. The caravan in front was in trouble.

'A *blanket*,' Rosie prompted.

'A blanket,' Beth said. She spoke to Julia. 'I don't understand.'

'You forgot! You forgot!' Rosie cried, laughing. 'It's the corgi dog first!'

'You all turn against me,' Julia murmured.

Beth tore her eyes from the road for a second. 'What?'

'All of you. Him and Oliver, and now you.'

'Who?'

'Ignore me, all of you. Ignore me.' Julia put her hand to her face. She pinched the flesh together over her forehead, making a vicious vertical crease, her nails digging deep, the skin pulled white at the hairline. 'You *and* him.'

'David? *David?*'

Just in time, Beth looked back at the road. The traffic had stopped. She slammed on the brake, stopping within an inch of the blue Escort in front. Behind her, she heard other brakes screech, and then a sudden impact, metal on metal. 'Oh shit,' she whispered.

'Love her, love her, love her,' Julia chanted in a low monotone. 'Love her, love her.'

'Julia . . .'

'Can't do that. *Love her too much. She's my wife.*' She was imitating David's voice. The slightest burr of a Dorset accent, the clipped tone.

Up ahead, the engine of the towing car roared. Abruptly, and as neatly as a flipped card, the caravan jack-knifed at right angles to the car, pitched upwards on the hill. Hazard lights began to flash. The oak trees on the corner hung down over them all, waving above their heads as if in an effort to caress the chain of vehicles below.

The driver of the Escort got out. They could hear him shouting. At the same time, Beth heard doors behind them slamming.

'Try again. Try another one,' Rosie said, tugging at Beth's arm.

'You told me he was leaving me,' she said.

Julia grimaced. '*You* told me. *You* made that up. You decided that at the funeral.'

'Made it up? For Christ's sake, you told me you had an affair!' Beth cried.

'It would have been,' Julia said.

'*Would* have?

'Sooner or later,' she said.

'But . . . !' Beth was rigid with disbelief. 'What about going to Spain?'

Julia looked down at her lap. 'I told him,' she said. 'It would have happened. Sooner or later. You can't ignore me for always.'

'But—' Beth took a breath in gasps. 'You told me you had slept with him—slept with him, the last time, only ten days ago . . .'

Julia looked out of the window, away from Beth, so that her face could only be seen in barest profile. 'I *told* him I'd follow him,' she muttered. 'You can't do that to a person once, and let it drop. You can't neglect them after that.'

Beth stared at her. Outside, someone was hammering on the driver's window. A man, yelling. She barely registered him. 'Oliver told me the truth,' she said. 'You and David . . . it was only once. Only once, a long time ago.' The blood thundered in her head. 'You never had an affair at all,' she whispered. 'He wasn't leaving me at all.'

Julia's head snapped back. 'Oh, he was leaving all right,' she retorted. 'Leaving both of us! I went to the harbour and waited for him that day. I'd have stopped him,' she added, in a tone of satisfaction. 'But he chose to kill himself first.'

'Kill himself!'

'What else?'

'They said it was an accident.'

'Running straight into a lorry?'

Beth stared at her. 'You think that?' she said. 'You think he committed suicide?'

Julia shrugged. 'Probably.'

'But why?'

'Because of the money! This money with Oliver.'

'The money?'

Julia waved her hand, dismissively. 'Oh, his reputation,' she mimicked. Through Julia's mouth, David's voice came rolling. 'The *shame*, the *reputation*, never hold his head up again, never look you in the eye again . . .'

Rosie, between them, had begun to tremble, tears threatening, glistening on her lashes as she stared at the man at the driver's window. 'Stop him,' she was saying. 'Stop, stop the man . . .'

Beth opened her door.

'Don't get out,' Julia warned.

'Are you bloody crazy, or what!' the man yelled.

He was half in the car as soon as the door was open. He must have been about fifty, and was red-faced, dressed in a lurid pink striped shirt, his stomach hanging down over the waistband of his trousers. He pushed his face close to Beth's. 'You wasn't looking at the road, you silly bitch!' he shouted. He waved his arm behind him. 'Look what you done!'

Beth looked. Behind her, three cars were concertinaed, bumper to bumper. The second driver back had cannoned into the man's nearside wing.

'I'm sorry,' Beth replied.

'Get back in!' Julia said.

'Give me y'bloody name and address. This is down to you,' the man said.

Beth glanced back at the car.

Julia was leaning across. 'Get back in,' she repeated.

The man snorted. 'You keep out of this.'

Beth looked from one to the other. Then she saw Rosie sidle into the driver's seat. The little girl gripped the wheel happily, her legs kicking above the pedals.

The passenger door opened. Julia got out.

The man glared at her as she walked round to their side.

'Beth,' she said softly, 'we must be getting on now.'

The driver laughed. 'Oh, we must, must we?' he retorted. 'You women! Give me a break.'

Watching Julia, Beth turned to him. 'This is an emergency,' she said. 'Do you understand?'

'I understand all right.'

'He doesn't understand anything,' Julia said.

The man pointed a finger at her. 'Right. I'm calling the police,' he said.

'You're not,' Julia replied.

Rosie swung herself out of the driver's seat. She stood up in the road, smiling unsurely.

'Come here, Rosie,' Beth murmured, holding out her hand.

The man had grabbed a mobile phone from his own dashboard. 'We'll see,' he warned them both.

'Ring Wynfirth,' Beth said, catching hold of Rosie's small, sticky fingers and swiftly fastening her hand around the little girl's wrist.

The man raised an eyebrow.

'Quickly!' Beth said.

At their side, there was a strangled sound. Beth looked up to see Julia staring back at her, the betrayal registering. In a flash Julia squatted down and lifted Rosie from the ground, an arm snaking around her daughter's waist.

Beth's grip on Rosie's wrist increased. There was no way she was going to let Rosie go now.

'Give her to me,' Julia said.

Beth slipped her free arm behind Rosie's back, between her and her mother. With her fist balled, she hit backwards, catching Julia just below the ribs. Julia cried out—a small, suffocated protest—and took a step back. By now, Beth had insinuated herself between mother and child, forcing her shoulder and body forward, her back to Julia, her arms encircling Rosie. Julia let go, pounding Beth on the back.

'Give her to me!' she screamed.

Beth ran forward, Rosie wriggling and shouting in her embrace.

The man had dropped the phone from his ear. Beth ran behind him, towards the other cars, shouting over her shoulder. 'For God's sake, call the police!'

'What *is* this?' he said.

'No!' Rosie shouted. 'Want Daddy! Daddy!'

A woman who had just got out of the third car, dressed in an expensive suit, the very manifestation of corporate chic, stepped directly into Beth's path.

'What exactly are you doing?' she asked. She might have been enquiring about the time.

Beth stopped, gasping for breath.

There was a scream of brakes behind them.

The van was turning in the road, Julia behind the wheel. The driver in the pink shirt was prancing about in front of it, in an effort to block its progress. 'Hey,' he was saying. 'Hey now . . .' Like a father cajoling an awkward boy. 'You can't do that,' he shouted.

He shuffled backwards as the van corrected and came forward. For a moment, the pink shirt performed a little ritual jig. Only at the very last second did the man jump to one side, banging his fist on the van's bonnet as it narrowly missed him.

'You bloody idiot!'

The van accelerated.

'Mummy!' Rosie shouted. She kicked Beth hard, scratching her hands, twisting and turning.

'Rosie—don't—don't . . .'

But Rosie was down, feet connecting with the road, throwing herself towards the van, arms outspread.

It was only ten or fifteen feet away.

'Rosie!' Beth screamed.

'Look out!' gasped the woman at Beth's side.

Julia's face could be glimpsed for an instant through the glass. She fixed on her daughter, on the light hair streaming against the jumbled colour.

Through the oncoming windscreen, Beth saw Julia's eyes register, empty, and close. Her mouth was pushed forward, the lips pursed. She had switched to some inner landscape, and her expression was one of abstraction, her head slightly turned, her chin lifted. She might have been posing for a photograph, altering her gaze for the camera, smiling at images only she could make. Beth ran out. 'No, no,' she was whispering. A feeble little chain of words flung in the child's direction.

She ran with hands extended, palms uppermost. She could reach Rosie before Julia, she thought; she could fly in this confined space. This neat square of hot road, the black surface reflecting tar spirals of heat. Her hands were at Rosie's shoulders now, touching. Each fingertip rigid.

A centimetre, an inch. A mile.

It wouldn't matter, just as long as Julia missed her.

As long as she missed.

FORTY-FOUR

$\mathcal{T}$HE SMALL GROUP WAS WAITING ON THE SHORE.

The two policemen came forward slowly and carefully. They looked out of place in their dark uniforms, next to the four they approached: four men in T-shirts, light canvas trousers and shorts, with canvas rucksacks on their backs. Following the policemen was the owner of the hotel, looking uncomfortably sick.

'Mr Hinton?'

'That's me,' said the nearest man. He was holding the collar of a dog: a collie, straining to be set free, its pink tongue lolling from the corner of its mouth.

'You'd better show us, Mr Hinton.'

'It's this way.'

The incongruous party made its way back along the beach, slipping on the dry stones. It was six o'clock, and the humid afternoon pressed down on them, the ground and the ocean sealed to a low grey sky.

'When did you find it?'

The man checked his watch. 'Half an hour? But it wasn't me. It was Rufus here.' The dog leapt and barked, pleased at the game, pulling on the man's grip.

'Have you looked at it?' the sergeant asked the hotel owner.

'Yes,' he said.

'And you're sure it's him?'

The owner's face went whiter, if anything. 'He only walked out of here a couple of hours ago,' he murmured. 'With his wife, and the other lady.' He wrung his hands. 'I've never had anything like this,' he said. 'Never had a death, even a natural death in the hotel. Never, in fifteen years . . .'

They had reached the slope. 'It's not good for business,' the owner murmured.

Standing on the stone bank, they looked down into the dip. The hand and the shoulder were clearly visible now.

'He went back to it,' the dog's owner said. 'Sorry. Dug and everything. Sorry.'

The police officers went down the slope, the stones giving their muted accompaniment, falling one over the other around their feet.

The sergeant leaned down and picked the stones away from the body one by one, piling them carefully at his side. Oliver Wood's face was revealed, the mouth open, the eyes open, the skin yellowish. The man felt his neck, and the pulse at the wrist.

'He's dead all right,' he said to his colleague. 'Not much doubt about that. Cold as ice.'

They stared at the obvious bruise on the temple, the brownish trickle of blood that was almost dry; and new marks where the dog had wildly burrowed and torn the skin.

The sergeant sighed heavily. 'I can confirm the identification,' he said to his colleague. 'I've seen Woods around court occasionally. Decent chap.'

The constable lowered his voice. 'This is the same man they're looking for on the Davis murder?'

The older man nodded. 'Yes . . . but that's just routine. The woman was having all kinds of delusions—apparently Woods tried to get help for her last week. Spoke to the GP about care for them both. And the first word back from forensic is clear—she killed her brother alone. No help.' He looked away from the body. 'We just wanted to let him know that he had nothing to worry about.' There was a silent moment of consideration.

'It couldn't be suicide?' asked the owner.

The sergeant smiled grimly. 'Haven't met a suicide yet who covered themselves up when they were dead,' he commented. 'Let's get Scenes of Crime down before we do anything else.'

'It's the wife, then?'

'She took the daughter.'

'Or the other woman?'

The senior man shrugged, wiping down the salt and sand from the knees of his trousers. He turned away. The collie was whining, wriggling to get free, desperate to plunge down again to the delicious scent.

'Hell hath no fury . . .' the sergeant said.

FORTY-FIVE

*I*T WAS DARK when the Citroën drew into Beth's drive. The humidity of the day had not eased; the air was oppressive, damp on the skin.

For a while, Beth and Rhys sat silently in the car, looking out at the shadows of the garden. Then, they got out, Rhys coming round to Beth's side.

'Can you manage?' he asked.

'I'm fine,' she told him. 'It's just my knee where I fell.'

'Well, take it easy. Give me the keys. I'll open up for you, and get the kettle on.'

She smiled, laying her hand on his arm. 'I just want to sit in the garden for a while,' she said. 'Do you mind?'

'Of course not.'

They walked down the path and the stone steps. Across the stream, and the border of the field beyond, they could see cattle, wandering back from the water, their forelegs dark with mud, their black-and-white bodies glimmering like ghosts.

Beth and Rhys sat down. Without a word, he took her hand and kissed her. It was a quiet embrace. Beth barely closed her eyes; she glimpsed him, white against dark for a second, then he drew back from her.

'You needn't go in at all,' he said. 'You could go to a hotel.'

'It isn't the house,' she said. 'I just wanted to breathe out here for a while. It's cooler.'

He shook his head, looking down at their linked fingers. 'Is this where it stops?' he asked. 'I don't think I could stand any more. Neither could that car. I gunned it at seventy all the way to Wynfirth. Bits actually fell off at the Warmborough roundabout.'

She laughed. The sound was curious, full of distortions. But then, all the hours of the day were warped in the same way; looking back on them was like walking through a fairground house of mirrors.

The worst part had been trying to calm Rosie. Hearing Rosie's cries from another room as she tried to tell the police her side of the story. Rosie had screamed for her mother for what seemed like hours.

The Social Services had arrived by seven. A brisk, bright girl in her mid-twenties called Maggie. She was very good. Calm, unshockable.

Beth had been interviewed separately. Sitting in the furnished lounge, with its prints of wallflowers, its regulation green sofa and mint green cushions, and the box of toys on the floor, she had struggled to find the words. She kept seeing the impact of Julia's hand in Oliver's face; and the same hand trying to pull back her own fingers on the driving wheel. She had leaned forward, resting her elbows on her knees.

'Have you seen a doctor?' the woman had asked.

'I don't need one.'

'For shock.'

Beth had given her a crooked smile. 'I'm beginning to think I'm immune.'

'No one is. Remember that over the next few days and weeks. It will creep up on you.'

A bone-deep weariness had begun to wash over Beth. 'What will happen to Rosie?' she'd asked.

'We have a very nice family she's going to tonight. They have a little girl of five of their own, and two older ones.'

'Did the doctor see *her*? Did he give her anything? She was really frantic. Any sedative?'

There was a weighted pause.

'We have difficulty with that,' Maggie had said. 'She's probably dependent on them.'

'My God,' Beth had breathed. 'Oliver told me this afternoon. Just before . . .' She'd looked away, down at the Lego boxes stacked at her feet, the exclamation of blues, reds. 'He was telling me the truth, and I didn't believe him. He was innocent of everything, just as he said. And yet I thought he was trying to justify taking Rosie, by whatever impossible story he could find.'

'It *is* hard to believe.'

'And all this flu of Rosie's . . . this lethargy, these spells from school . . . ?'

'Likely to be side-effects, or even totally fabricated.'

'But the GP . . . !'

'It's notoriously hard to tell,' the woman had said. 'How do you deny that a child is in pain? The child is subdued, the mother frantic. You err on the side of caution. Maybe there isn't a shadow on the lung when X-rayed, but the mother *insists* that the child coughs all night . . .' Maggie had sighed. 'And so on, and so on, indefinitely. Münchausen's is thought to be increasing, especially among women who feel isolated. But no one really knows why.'

Beth had shaken her head. 'Julia wanted for nothing,' she murmured. 'She couldn't even say she had an unhappy childhood; there isn't that excuse. She told me once that her parents doted on her.'

Maggie had shrugged. 'Maybe that's the problem. Adoring parents die. The real world moves in. You cease to be the centre of the universe. All that devotion fills the ego like water filling a sponge. Then the water stops. But the thirst doesn't stop. Or . . .' She had paused. 'Perhaps something that happened more recently—something that was never understood, resolved . . .'

'You've researched it?'

'I've read a little.'

'How did they find out?'

'In the hospital, when Rosie didn't come round. Mr Woods said that his wife had been on Temazepam for some time . . .'

'And she'd been giving her own prescription to Rosie?'

'Yes.'

'But she *loved* her so much . . .'

'MBPs are, outwardly, perfect mothers. But actually, they don't see the child *as* a child. Just a thing, a tool. Unfortunately, many of the children die. Poisoned by chemicals in drip feeds as babies, or by smothering. They die in their sleep, or by falls . . .'

Something appalling had occurred to Beth while the woman spoke. It seemed at first so terrible that it was hard to say. 'Do you know,' she had managed to utter finally, 'that Oliver and Julia's second child—'

'Fell from her nursery window. Yes, I know.'

'Do you think that was really an accident?'

'That's one of the things that will be looked into.'

Beth remembered the funeral of that child. Remembered the small grave in the village churchyard. Rebecca Juliette. The two names on the headstone, the dates spanning barely a year. She remembered too how many people called on Julia afterwards . . .

Her stomach had seemed to lurch, and she'd clamped a hand to her mouth.

Maggie had started to rise from her seat. 'Shall I get you—'

Beth had waved her free hand. 'No, nothing. It's all right. Really.' She'd wiped her forehead, then straightened up. 'I could have done something,' she said. 'To help Rosie. But I never guessed. Never.'

'There is absolutely no need to blame yourself,' Maggie had responded briskly. 'You didn't see it, and neither did anyone else until a few days ago.'

A few days ago.

The phrase echoed in Beth's head. A few days ago the world had seemed perfectly calm and ordered. David was alive. She was working. Julia was taking Rosie to school, waving and smiling at Beth if their cars passed in the lane.

Beth had looked up at Maggie. 'Have they found her?' she'd asked.

'Not yet. But they will.'

'She was going to Poole.'

Maggie had reached forward, laid her hand on Beth's. 'The thing we have to look out for now is Rosie's well-being,' she'd said. 'We don't labour the past. We build futures. These children have been told that they're ill, almost been *rewarded* for being ill for so long. That's the danger. Rosie has to be well, to *learn* to be well, to *see* herself well.'

Maggie had begun to gather up her notes. 'Oh, and something else, of course,' she added. 'She's taken her lead from her mother, learned from her. Perhaps even wants to be like her.'

Beth had frowned. 'You mean, Rosie will have this problem herself, this . . .'

'Münchausen's.'

'She'll have the same thing? How do you know?'

'I don't.' Maggie had smiled very briefly. 'We'll have to wait and see.'

Recalling the evening now, Beth sighed.

'Are you going in?' Rhys asked.

'Yes. I'm tired.'

They walked arm-in-arm to the door, where Rhys opened the lock with the keys Beth handed him. The house felt stifling; Beth walked immediately to the windows and flung them open.

'Would you like me to stay?' Rhys asked.

She looked up at him.

'I don't mean *stay* stay. I mean sleep on the couch.'

'No . . . you're shattered too.' She smiled at him. 'Thank you for everything today.'

'You shouldn't be on your own,' he told her.

She shook her head. 'I'd prefer it,' she said. 'I feel . . . *crowded*. I just want to stop and lie still and sort it all out in my head.' She saw his doubtful expression. 'It's not you,' she said. 'I just couldn't bear . . . a fuss. I don't want to be watched. I'm sorry.'

'I'd keep my eyes averted.'

'All the same . . .'

He sighed, picked up her hand, and kissed it. 'I'll come back in the morning.'

'That's fine.'

He still paused on the doorstep. 'Lock this after me.'

She made a shooing motion. 'I'll be perfectly OK,' she said. 'If I'm just *left*.'

She watched the car reverse out of the drive; listened to the sound of the engine receding along the lane.

She did as he had said: locked the door, and hung the key on the rack by the cooker. She hadn't the strength to make herself a drink, even though she was thirsty. All she wanted was to have a bath and get into bed. The idea of cool cotton sheets—and the blissful silence of being alone—seemed fantastically alluring.

She went up the stairs painfully slowly. Her joints ached, particularly the knee. She had landed glancingly on that, then fallen on her hip, Rosie pushed ahead of her, rolling into the grass verge, screaming because she scraped against hawthorn and nettle. Poor little Rosie, Beth thought. Dear God . . . poor Rosie.

She went into the bedroom and opened the window. The air was still sticky. She stood looking out, her hand to her mouth, chewing absent-mindedly at the knuckles on her loosely closed fist.

Then she came to a decision.

She walked swiftly out on to the landing and took the smaller flight to the attic room. There, at the door, she looked down at the lock for a second. Then she opened it, and turned on the inner light.

FORTY-SIX

THE FERRY TERMINAL AT BREATON WAS DESERTED. It was just past midnight, and the small port, never crowded at the best of times, was now a ghost town. The Pavilion Theatre, peeling and weatherbeaten on the end of the harbour wall, was long shut. The front doors of the row of hotels were closed, their neon lights extinguished. The only light showing was at the end of the catamaran dock, a small yellow square of brightness.

The ferries did not go to France from here, but to Guernsey. Not every hour, but twice a day. She thought it was safer, much safer, than Poole.

The boy behind the ticket counter looked up as the doors opened. He stopped talking to the girl who kept him company. She stopped mid-sentence too, eyeing the fragile-looking woman in the expensive clothes who now came up to the counter.

'Can I buy a ticket?' the woman asked.

'It's gone for tonight. I'm just closing up.'

Her face crumpled. 'I thought you had an overnight sailing,' she said.

'We do. It left at 11.55.'

The woman looked down at her feet and whispered something. The boy's girlfriend smirked at him, raising an eyebrow.

'There's another at six,' he said.

'All right. I'll have a ticket for that.'

'You can come back and just walk straight on, you know. We're not booked up for the first one.'

'I'll pay now.'

'OK' He told her the price.

'Aw, *Derek*,' muttered the girlfriend. 'You was packing up half an hour ago.'

'It won't take a minute.'

'I'm not standing here half the bloody night.'

'Will you shut up,' he told her.

The woman seemed not to have noticed the exchange. She was taking cash from her purse, sorting notes and coins on to the counter in intractable slow-motion. 'Is that enough?'

He gave some of it back to her, opening her hand, and putting it into her palm. 'Two pounds twenty too much.'

The woman closed her fist over the money and the ticket. She went to the wooden bench and sat down.

The boy leaned forward on the counter. 'You can't wait here,' he said.

The woman did not look up.

'I said, you can't wait here,' he repeated. 'I have to lock up. There'll be someone back at five.'

The woman got up, walked to the door, and went out without a word.

'Bloody hell,' the boy's girlfriend muttered. 'What planet was *she* on?'

She looked back in time to see the boy lifting the phone. 'Oh Christ, Derek . . .'

He signalled for her to be quiet.

'Who're you ringing now?'

'The police.'

'What for?'

'Hello?' he said, turning away from her and putting his free hand over his ear. 'Can I speak to whoever it is who wants to trace this blonde woman?'

FORTY-SEVEN

THE LIGHT REVEALED DAVID.

He might have been standing in the room; such was the strength of his belongings.

Beth walked in slowly, looking around her. She had brought his things here in a fit of fury; and they lay tumbled about in the kind of mess that he would have hated. She began to tidy them. Eventually, she sat down next to the pile of his books that she had taken from the shelves downstairs. She started to arrange them in alphabetical order. Exhausted as she was, she felt she owed him something. More than this, of course. But it was still *something*.

She and David had first met at a house in Stourminster on a filthy January day. A lunch party for someone who turned out to be a friend-of-a-friend to both of them. They had both drifted to the side of the room, feeling out of place. She recalled thinking that David looked a very awkward man.

And then he had begun to talk, and he was drily funny. They had arranged to see a film in the week—a truly dreadful film, as it turned out. They had met for dinner the following weekend. All their early meetings floundered through mediocrity. They must have both been lonely, she thought.

She had been very touched by him. He had spoken with a self-depreciation that would have been almost sad, had he not lightened it with humour. He had small fixations—about time, about keeping track of money—that she had found funny. At first.

With her hands on his books, she mourned them both. Mourned their inability to thrive. He had been both severe and naive. He was the kind of man who believed salesmen; he believed the people who tried to sell him cars, stereos, washing machines, whatever. He would clutch the catalogues and listen to the usual drivel intently, while behind the salesman's back Beth invariably made frantic signals to go, knowing they were being bullied.

David had believed the written word. He would read the instructions for objects they bought—the kettle, the water filter, the iron—and would never disobey them. He never let a bill drift to the red reminder. He knew every damned relevant fact by rote: the exact frequencies of the radio stations, bank codes, expiry dates, phone numbers, and the numbers on his cheque cards and credit cards. Where he had once charmed and intrigued her, even made her laugh with his understated jokes, he started to drive her to exasperation with his precision.

The very sight of him at the kitchen table, with the lists of cheque stubs and the carefully drawn budget sheet that mapped their every move for months to come, had made her want to scream until the windows shattered.

'Oh David,' she said now, into the silence.

It must have been something monstrous to make him change. He must have been coming to that same silent screaming pitch. He must have been longing to alter. He had never asked her if she felt the same. If only he had.

They had let themselves wade far out, into a dead grey sea, and David must have felt it, lapping at the edges of the world, threatening to drown him. Perhaps he'd looked into the future. Or the mirror. Seen himself projected in ten or twenty years' time. Felt that deadly sick plunge of misgiving. He would reach sixty, reach seventy, and still be drowning in the same viscous, stultifying purgatory, his head barely above the surface, invisibly and inaudibly drowning in that same sluggish dead calm.

He had wanted this enormous shift that the money would bring, stepped out into space to take it. Stepped off his safe dark shelf straight into the blinding sun. Made the only irrational move of his life.

David had only gambled once.

But oh, what a gamble, Beth considered, her grip tightening around the spines of the books in her hands.

What a bloody tragic gamble.

She caught sight of the envelope that had been given to her by the police on the morning of his death. She picked it up, her fingers suddenly striking the small tape. She hadn't taken much notice of it before, but now she held it up. It came from a dictation machine. As far as she knew, David didn't own one. He relied absolutely on the Psion, and typed his letters from the memos on that.

Beth stopped and looked at the books. Statistics. Mercantile law. Employment Protection Acts. The thicker volume of a politician's diaries. A *Halliwell's Film Guide*, perhaps the only concession to relaxation or amusement, and still a kind of list.

She couldn't touch them any more. David seemed to be screaming up from the titles and covers, his face ringed by the encroaching dark, trying to tell her something. Something between the titles of the books, the scattered clothes, the case, the papers. It was so like the dream in which she herself had been drowning.

Overcome by guilty grief, she got to her knees, to stand up.

The suitcase was still propped by the chair, its lid open. On top of David's clothes, she had flung a small plastic bag that the undertaker had given her on the day he had called to discuss the burial. She had looked briefly inside it after he had left and seen a small brochure, apparently describing the firm: a booklet with a cross and a display of flowers on its front cover. She picked the plastic carrier up now, and turned it upside down.

The booklet fell out, opening to reveal verses and suggestions for inscriptions on headstones. A few slips of paper fell forward into Beth's lap. One was a subscription slip. Payment by standing order for your beloved's memory. She took the sheet by each corner, about to tear it in two.

Then she saw the small folder.

It was thin. Plastic. The funeral director's logo on the front. She opened it. Inside were two pieces of paper. The top one was a short hand-written note.

Mrs March.
This was in your husband's jacket.

The second piece of paper had been smoothed straight, but still bore the marks of having been screwed into a ball. On it was another hand-written sentence. It was very short.

I'll still follow you.

Beth knelt with the message in one hand and the incomprehensible tape in the other, facing the wall, staring at it, as if the answers might suddenly be projected on to it.

I'll still follow you.

That last morning. The dead bird in the porch. And, as she came downstairs, her hand to her eyes against the light, David had put something, a piece of paper, into his jacket.

The dead bird in the porch . . . and the note. Someone had killed the bird, and put it, with the note, in the porch for David to find. She thought of the bird fluttering in panic around the kitchen only a few nights ago. And of Chaos.

She opened her palm and looked at the tape.

'Where do you go?' she asked it. 'I don't know what you fit into. I don't know where you go.'

'Into my answerphone,' Julia said behind her.

FORTY-EIGHT

$\mathcal{T}$HE MOMENT THAT RHYS OWEN GOT HOME he put on the TV.

He sat in front of it for half an hour, flicking the channels for a minute, then settling with a documentary. After it had finished, he switched the set off altogether. He began, half-heartedly, to roll a cigarette, but gave it up.

The study was knee-deep in paper. Feeling wide awake, he lay face down on the couch, his head hanging over the edge, and spread the surveys on Oak Rise about with his hands. Alison Warley's draft report was a work of art, the male skull so delicately drawn, the detail extraordinary. She had listed the effects of the blow to the young male, the intrusion into the occiptal and parietal lobes. It was like poetry; soothing in tone. *The posterior fossa . . .*

He rolled over and looked up at the ceiling.

He had only had one passion when he was a teenager. It wasn't sport, or cars, or even girls. Whenever he went for a walk, it usually took in a cemetery. At school, they thought for a while that he had found something forbidden in Aylesham Road Crematorium; his mates were convinced that he had a girl down there.

And so he did. In a way. She was Charlotte, daughter of Henry

Coffett, aged twenty-four; and she had departed this life in 1822. Her stone was an angel with wingtips rounded by age, a foot missing, and the book it had once held broken away from its hands. Charlotte intrigued him. Unusually, there was no biblical text on the stone, but a single sentence. It had said, *Farewell, thou child of my right hand, and joy.*

For a long time he thought her parents must have composed it. Then, in a calligraphy competition at school, he had found Ben Jonson's *On My Son*. Rhys had been fifteen that year, and the competition was a national one. He was grudgingly pressed into writing; the same sonnet, scratched over. Even now, he saw it in thick italic script on pencil lines. Despite his previous loathing of English classes, the damned thing got into his skin, as if absorbed through the ink. He couldn't shake the words from his mind.

He had scoured the untouched anthologies in the school libraries for more, and found them. Tons of plaintive verse on children, on wives. Even on dogs. Nobody ever disturbed him as he rummaged through the books looking for elegies on annihilation. As far as his friends were concerned, he went through a funny patch. He came out even funnier, though. He emerged fixed on the idea of archaeology.

He found Robert Bridges—*go lie there in thy coffin, thy last little bed!*—and George Meredith—*thus piteously Love closed what he begat*—and the one that still stayed with him and echoed in his head whenever he worked: *Think how many royal bones, sleep within this heap of stones.*

And think how many people must have walked over them on Oak Rise. Seven sets of bones under the soil. Just four inches under the soil. Other feet, and, just four inches under someone's heel, the upturned face of the dead.

Think how many royal bones . . .

There were probably two murders on that site. The old man and the young one. One obvious injury, one crushed and hastily buried. The human frame was remarkably fragile; it took only seconds to pierce skin and flesh and interrupt the complicated system of life. Perfect repetitive functions that had carried on for decades could be stemmed by a little piece of metal. The arrowhead, the knife, the gun. It was so easy and so quick. And yet the bones remained for centuries. Hundreds, even thousands of years. The million-year jawbone of human ancestry, once a part of a breathing machine.

He wondered who, in the Oak Rise site, was there first. Did the woman come to mourn at the side of either of the men? Or did *they* bury *her*?

Think how many . . .

He crossed his arms over his head, closing his eyes. Did one of them kill her? he wondered. And was killed for the crime himself? Or perhaps one of the men's wives . . .

Suddenly, Rhys shot upright on the couch. 'Oh, holy shit,' he said.

There was David. Oliver.

Beth.

He saw Oliver on the beach as Beth had described him, the thin wisps of hair plucking at the shovelled stones, the last remnant of him before Julia succeeded in covering him. Face down. And David, in a box six feet down in the ground at the side of the church. And Beth . . .

Her image rushed in on him, crowding out everything else. Beth's face being choked by raining soil. Beth, face down in a quick cairn of salt and sand pebbles.

Within this heap of stones.

He pulled on the boots he had dragged off only half an hour before, cursing under his breath as he staggered across the room, dragging one foot behind him.

Aesculapius got up and shadowed him, whining, pulling at the last flap of leather.

'Not this mission,' Rhys said to the dog, grabbing his keys, and opening the door. 'Stay here.'

FORTY-NINE

$\mathcal{T}$HE TWO WOMEN LOOKED AT EACH OTHER across the silent room; Beth still kneeling on the floor, Julia in the doorway.

Beth was waiting, breath caught in her throat, for Julia to move— but she did not. Her face was wiped of any emotion. At last, Beth's attention strayed from those lifeless blue eyes down to Julia's hands, limp at her sides. And to the floor. Julia was barefoot.

Julia looked down, seeing the direction of Beth's gaze. She lifted one foot almost experimentally, like someone considering a new pair of shoes.

'Not since I was little . . .' she murmured.

'Since . . . ?'

Julia smiled. 'No shoes.'

She walked forward. Beth scrambled backwards, trying to stand upright. But Julia wasn't coming for her. She walked to the far side of the loft, where the smaller window looked out on to the village road.

'They're still there,' she said.

'Who?'

'Someone at the Lodge.' She picked up the hem of her skirt and wrung it, though no moisture dropped to the floor. 'I saw them,' she said. 'I turned up by the bridge and came across the field. I left my shoes on the other side of the stream.' She dropped the hem after smoothing it, glanced towards Beth. 'I'll have to go back and get them, I expect.'

Beth had stood up. She looked at the door. 'How did you get in?' she said.

'With my key.'

'*What* key?'

Julia felt in her pocket, took out a key, and held it up. 'The copy I took. Ages ago. You do leave your things lying about, Beth. You always did.'

Beth stared at her.

'Where is she?' Julia asked.

'Who?'

'Oh, Beth,' Julia shook her head disappointedly, 'you know *who*. Rosie. Is she here?'

Beth's heart began to pound hard. 'She's with the Social Services. I don't know where exactly.'

Julia merely nodded. It was hardly the reaction Beth had expected. She had anticipated the fury of the afternoon, the panic of the phone call. Now there seemed to be only this odd, glacial stillness.

Julia seemed not to be listening. She was looking around at David's things. 'He rang me up,' she said, as if thinking out loud. 'He always said I was hounding him.' She laughed, low down in her throat. 'Like a dog, you know? Following a fox? Hounding.' She seemed to find the word genuinely funny. She pointed to the tape, still in Beth's hand. 'That's what he wanted,' she continued. 'He rang on Sunday, while we were out at lunch. He wanted it back.'

She took a step nearer to Beth. 'He was always so careful,' she said. 'Why leave such a message? All that ranting, that raving. Lucky I got to it before Oliver. Why leave it at all, to be found? That wasn't my fault.'

Beth gripped the tape tighter. 'What does it say?' she asked, in a voice barely above a whisper.

Julia waved her hand dismissively. 'Oh, that I must stop ringing him, that I had all I wanted, that he had never loved me, that he couldn't stand all this with Oliver and me . . .' She shrugged. 'I gave it to him on Sunday night, but I told him then. I told him—' she pointed to the note—'just the same as that. I told him it made no difference. I'd still follow him.'

Beth looked away from her. She couldn't bear the flat expression in Julia's eyes a moment longer.

'It wasn't true, you know, what he said,' Julia carried on. 'He said he never felt anything for me. But I know he did. He did once.'

Both the note and the tape felt as though they were burning holes in Beth's hands. 'You never had an affair, and yet you blackmailed him,' she said quietly.

Julia raised her eyebrows. The colour rose a little now, growing lines of red spreading through the skin of her neck, crawling upwards like a vine. 'You don't spend a night with someone and then just— leave them. Just *drop* them.'

'One night. Just as Oliver said.'

Julia ignored her. 'Isn't that typical?' she said, as if to herself. 'To be used, and then thrown away? A person shouldn't do that to anything— to anything living. That's what you do—' she wildly mimed throwing something clinging from her hands—'when filthy things stick to you. You throw them away, get them off you, you throw them away . . .'

She stopped, her gaze fixed on the open suitcase. A smile returned, but it was wavering now. 'That happened to me before,' she said. 'I was thrown back to Oliver, like some sort of remnant. I was promised things. You're supposed to accept it and forget it . . .' She closed her eyes momentarily. 'David told me he was going where I couldn't reach him.'

Beth opened her fist and showed Julia the crumpled page.

'Yes,' Julia said. 'But I didn't need to follow him at all. He told me on Sunday that he was going to Cherbourg. There's only one sailing.'

'So you waited for him on the dock?'

'Yes,' Julia said.

'And the bird . . . ?'

Julia said nothing.

'Julia, the bird. And the note. Then the bird in the kitchen—'

Julia met her gaze unblinkingly. 'I knew you hated the things,' she said. Then, almost to herself, 'And so do I. They mean the worst. The worst thing you can imagine is coming . . .'

'But I never told you I was afraid of birds . . .'

'Yes you did.'

'When?'

Julia shrugged her shoulders. 'I don't know. Ages ago. When you first moved in here. When there was a nest in the roof or something.'

The memory came flooding back. David taking down the old nest that had been wedged under the eaves; some conversation outside, in the lane . . . She had forgotten. She had forgotten about the nest.

'Your mother,' Julia said.

'Oh God,' Beth breathed.

Julia ignored her. 'I came back here when he didn't arrive in Poole,' she said. 'After I'd taken Rosie to the doctor on the way back, of course. The Pritchard man was here, at your gate. He asked me to come in. He told me that David was dead.'

Beth closed her hand around the note and crushed it, letting it fall to the floor.

'That's what you don't understand,' Julia said.

'What?'

Suddenly, Julia did what Beth had been expecting from the start. She rushed forward, grabbing Beth by both arms. Beth staggered backwards, her body bumping against the desk. Julia's weight propelled them both towards the floor-to-ceiling window of the old grain lift.

Off balance, her back to the glass, Beth had a split second of absolute conviction: she was going to fall through the glass, either with Julia's hands on her or pushed by Julia's weight. Her feet slipped on the wood floor and she came crashing down barely an inch from the glass, Julia on top of her, the breath slammed from her.

From the front of the house came the sound of a car pulling up in the lane outside. There were raised voices, the words indistinguishable.

She tried to take Julia's hands away, tried to wriggle from under her. Julia's fair hair hung in her mouth. She turned her face.

'I loved him,' Julia said. 'That's what it was all for. That's what Oliver didn't understand. He thought it was nothing . . . but it wasn't. I loved him. And he wouldn't see . . . he wouldn't listen to me . . .'

Beth stopped struggling. She stared up at the face not six inches from her own. 'But *David* didn't love *you*,' she said.

Julia released her hold immediately. She slumped backwards.

Beth rolled away, pulling herself rapidly up into a crouching position, wedged in the corner between glass and wall. Her hand was clamped across her stomach as she tried desperately to draw in air. As if from a great distance, she heard knocking on the doors three floors below, then the sound of a man's voice, calling her name.

'What did you mean?' she asked. 'When you said . . .' The words wouldn't come out. It was so difficult to draw breath. 'If David said, on the tape, that you had all you wanted . . . what did he mean?'

Julia was no longer looking at her. She had straightened up, and walked to the long window, pressing both hands to it, staring out into the darkness of the fields.

'Only the money,' she said offhandedly.

Beth felt herself begin to shake. It was a reaction she could not control.

'What money?'

'The money,' Julia retorted impatiently. 'The *money*.'

Beth tried to stand, holding herself up against the wall. 'Julia,' she said. 'Have you got an offshore account? Did David sign a mortgage form, and get the money from it, and . . .' The room was whirling faintly, the outlines blurring. 'Did he give that money to you?'

Julia was opening the window.

'Don't do that,' Beth said.

Julia couldn't figure the catch. It was a double one: half of it operated the upper portion of the glass, so that it behaved exactly like an ordinary casement. The other half opened the whole, so that the panes swung outwards like doors. Losing her temper, Julia brought her fist down on the fastening. The doors opened, out into the darkness, out on to the ledge of the narrow balcony.

'Don't do that,' Beth repeated.

'I told him I really didn't want it,' Julia said. 'I told him that on Sunday. I told him I didn't intend vanishing, just like that. Money or no money. It was just a joke.'

Beth looked into her face, horrified at the complete distraction she saw there. 'A *joke*! This was a *joke* to you?' she whispered. 'You drove him out of his mind!'

'No,' Julia said. 'He did it to himself.'

'And on Monday . . . in the garage, in the car?'

'You wouldn't listen to me. I kept calling you. You shut me out. Nobody *listens*.'

'My God,' Beth breathed. 'It was all stage-managed.'

Julia moved further forward.

'Don't—' Beth cried.

Julia had stepped up on to the broad rail.

'Julia,' Beth said, horrified, 'Julia, think of Rosie. Rosie will want to see you, soon, tomorrow . . .'

Julia spread her arms wide on each side.

'Oh God,' Beth said. She dared not step forward now herself, for fear that Julia would move. And yet she couldn't just stand there and do nothing.

'Julia,' she whispered, trying to make her voice steady. Her heartbeat had moved into an impossible rhythm, the rhythm of the last few days: a hitched, irregular hammering. Blood seemed to fill her head, pressure building behind her eyes. 'Julia, please get down. Rosie hasn't gone for ever. She'll come back. You can get help, everyone will understand . . .'

Lies. Any lies at all.

Julia's body was swaying.

Below, in the garden, Beth could see figures gathering on the grass. At the edge of the road a car was parked, its headlights flooding into the meadow. The thistles and grass stood out in elongated and fantastic shapes, fluttering like wings as more shadows crossed them.

'Look at the birds,' Julia whispered.

Behind her, Beth reached out her hand.

Someone was banging at the back door, the kitchen door to the garden. Sounds floated up in disjointed notes, voices raised. There was an argument going on down there, an argument punctuated by repeated blows to the frame of the door. Just as Beth's fingers brushed Julia's outstretched hand, the door fell through with a crash, and the voices invaded the house below.

'Julia,' Beth whispered. 'Please, get down . . .'

Julia looked back at her.

Steps came thundering up the stairs.

'Beth!' Rhys called.

Behind him, the police were ordering him back.

Julia gripped Beth's hand tightly. She sank down, until she was squatting on the rail and Beth was at her side.

'Mrs Woods!' someone called from the darkness underneath them.

Beth could hear that Rhys had reached the second floor. She heard him crash across the landing and come racing up the narrower flight towards the loft.

'Julia, listen to me,' Beth said. Julia briefly turned her head. 'Julia, Rosie needs her mother. Think. She's lost her sister, and her father . . .'

'Rebecca,' Julia said.

'Yes. That's right. Little Rebecca. Remember. Poor Rebecca,' Beth said, aware that she was stumbling over the words. 'So many bad things have happened to you. People will understand that. Even about Oliver. It wasn't planned. You won't be away from Rosie for long, and—'

'Rebecca,' Julia said.

'Yes, I—' The words froze in Beth's mouth.

Julia was smiling blissfully, her head rolling a little from side to side, her mouth open, her eyes drifting to a point beyond Beth's face. 'I stood her up on the ledge to see the birds,' she said. 'All the swallows and swifts flying in the garden.' She stretched her free hand out, over the rail, into space, as if she could still feel her daughter's fingers around hers as she balanced on the window ledge.

'All the birds were flying close to the house,' she said. And, abruptly, she stood up.

'Julia!' Beth cried.

Behind them, Rhys was in the room. Beth glanced back, waved a desperate, helpless hand to stop him from coming any further forward. She turned back in time to see Julia raise herself up on her toes. At the same time, Julia's hand wrenched itself from Beth's grip.

'She just overbalanced. It wasn't my fault,' Julia whispered. 'We only tried to catch the bird . . .'

'Julia!' Beth screamed.

On the rail, Julia suddenly turned, pirouetting, her arms spread wide, her head thrown back.

At the very last moment before she tipped back, before the breeze clutched at the material of her clothes, before her feet left the rail and she fell, her gaze connected with Beth.

'Are you watching?' Julia whispered.

POSTSCRIPT

$\mathcal{T}$HERE'S YOUR FLIGHT CALL, Beth said.

It was the ninth of September, ten o'clock at night. Outside, the darkness pressed to the windows of the airport lounge. Rhys stood up, gathering his books and hand-luggage. On the seats opposite, Rosie was stretched full length, trying to touch another passenger's bag with her toes.

'Rosie,' Beth said. 'Stand up now. Rhys is going.' Other passengers began to mill around them, voices raised in hurried goodbyes.

Beth turned to Rhys. Now that the moment had come, there was an impossible awkwardness between them.

'You've got everything?' she asked.

'I think so.'

'The magazine?'

'I put it in the bag.'

'What time do you get to Nairobi?'

'Nine o'clock tomorrow.'

She knew. They'd been over it dozens of times. Nine o'clock arrival. Then a Kenyan Airways internal flight to Bujumbura. He would get there at five past two, in the heat of the afternoon. Then a five-hour drive to Christine.

Their silence was suddenly broken by Rosie's cries. She had somehow managed to slip from the seat and land on the floor. The jolt was slight, but she was still wailing out of all proportion to the fall.

Beth gave Rhys a look, then went to her. 'Come on, darling. Up you get.'

'But it hurts. It *hurts*.' Rosie was holding her knee.

'Let me look,' Beth said. 'Oh, just a tiny bump. You'll be fine. Upsadaisy now. Say goodbye to Rhys.'

Rosie grudgingly came forward, casting a forlorn look at the couple of people who had come forward to help.

Rhys held out his arms.

'Will you see lions?' Rosie asked.

'Tons of lions.'

'Will you bring one back?'

Rhys laughed. He kissed her cheek and set her down. Rosie held Beth's hand tightly, looking up from one to the other.

'Go on,' Beth said. 'You'll miss it.'

'I'm going,' he replied.

But not quite yet. He put down the case and took her in his arms. When he had kissed her he drew back, still holding her, looking into her eyes.

'You know why, don't you?' he asked her. 'You understand?'

'Yes, I do.'

'I have to see her, just once. Just to be sure.'

She touched his lips. 'I understand.'

He picked up the bag. 'I'll phone you from Nairobi. I don't know about Burundi. But I'll try.'

'OK.'

'Look after yourself.'

'See you next month,' she said, crossing her fingers behind her back, hoping it would be true.

He stopped, giving her a last, slow smile. Then he turned and walked down the aisle without a backward glance.

'He didn't wave,' Rosie complained.

'That's all right,' Beth said.

They walked to the observation deck. A few minutes later, they watched the plane take off into the night sky.

'Can he see us?' Rosie asked.

'Yes,' Beth said.

'Fly, fly,' Rosie whispered.

Beth turned to look at her. Just for a moment, she saw Julia in Rosie's face: that same languid, dispassionate gaze.

'Where is Chaos?' Rosie asked.

Misplaced as it seemed, Beth was used to the question.

Ever since her parents' deaths, Rosie had mentioned neither Julia nor Oliver. But whenever she was disturbed by something—a scene on the television, a child at school, an argument of any kind, or a departure like this—Rosie would always ask the same thing.

The child psychologist said it was quite normal. He even had a phrase for it. Token loss. Whenever the past threatened to surface, Chaos became its symbol. He was the guardian at the gate, shielding the other memories. If ever Rosie looked beyond Chaos, secure with the answers she got, she would be ready to see the rest. Ready to come to terms with them.

Beth bent to kiss Rosie, kneeling at her side and hugging her tightly.

'Rhys is coming back soon,' she said.

Rosie's arms tightened around her neck. 'I took it off because he scratched me,' the little girl whispered.

Beth held her away from her, looked at her. 'Who did?' she asked, not understanding. 'Rhys scratched you?'

Rosie began to smile. 'Not Rhys. Chaos.'

She put her hand on Beth's neck, her fingers curling around the lapel of the wool jacket. Coldness suddenly invaded Beth's blood, closing her heart to an icy fist.

'What did you take off, Rosie?' she asked. But she knew the answer already.

'His collar,' Rosie said. She stood up, giving a last protracted wave to the lights of the aircraft, mere specks now in the darkness.

'He was a bad cat,' the little girl said in a careless voice, 'not to catch us any more birds.'